THE HOUSE OF
UNEXPECTED SISTERS

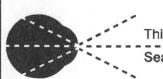

This Large Print Book carries the
Seal of Approval of N.A.V.H.

THE HOUSE OF UNEXPECTED SISTERS

ALEXANDER MCCALL SMITH

WHEELER PUBLISHING
A part of Gale, a Cengage Company

Farmington Hills, Mich • San Francisco • New York • Waterville, Maine
Meriden, Conn • Mason, Ohio • Chicago

LIBRARY OF CONGRESS CIP DATA ON FILE.
CATALOGUING IN PUBLICATION FOR THIS BOOK
IS AVAILABLE FROM THE LIBRARY OF CONGRESS.

ISBN-13: 978-1-4328-4446-2 (hardcover)
ISBN-10: 1-4328-4446-6 (hardcover)

Published in 2017 by arrangement with Pantheon Books, a division of Penguin Random House LLC

Printed in the United States of America
1 2 3 4 5 6 7 21 20 19 18 17

In memory of Gina Pollinger

CHAPTER ONE:
THE CLOTHES OF OTHERS

Mma Ramotswe, owner of the No. 1 Ladies' Detective Agency (as featured in a two-page article in the *Botswana Daily News,* under the headline "A Lady Who Definitely Knows How to Find Things Out"), had strong views on the things that she owned. Personal possessions, she thought, should be simple, well made, and not too expensive. Mma Ramotswe was generous in all those circumstances where generosity was required — but she was never keen to pay one hundred pula for something that could be obtained elsewhere for eighty pula, or to get rid of any item that, although getting on a bit, still served its purpose well enough. And that, she thought, was the most important consideration of all — whether something worked. A possession did not have to be fashionable; it did not have to be the very latest thing; what mattered was that it did what it was supposed to do, and did this in the way expected of it. In that respect, there was not much difference between things and people: what she looked for in people was the quality of doing what they were meant to do, and doing it without too much fuss, noise, or complaint. She also felt that if something was doing its job then you should hold on to it and cherish it, rather than discarding it in favour of something new. Her white van, for instance, was now rather old and inclined to rattle, but it never failed to start — except after a rain storm, which was rare enough in a dry country like Botswana — and it got her from place to place — except when she ran out of fuel, or when it broke down, which it did from time to time, but not too often.

She applied the same philosophy to her shoes and clothing. It was true that she was always trying to persuade her husband, Mr. J.L.B. Matekoni, to get rid of his old shirts and jackets, but that was because he, like all men, or certainly the majority of men, tended to hold on to his clothes for far too long. His shoes were an example of that failing: he usually extracted at least four years' service out of his oil-stained working boots, his *veldschoen*. He recognised her distaste for these shoes by removing them when he came back from the garage each evening, but he was adamant that any other footwear, including the new waterproof, oil-resistant work boots he had seen featured in a mail order catalogue, would be a pointless extravagance.

"There is no point in having fancy boots if you're a mechanic," he said. "What you need is boots that you know will always be there."

"But new boots would also always be there," she pointed out. "It's not as if they would march off by themselves."

Mr. J.L.B. Matekoni laughed. "Oh, I don't think shoes would be that disobedient," he said. "What I mean is that you want shoes that you know — that you trust. I have always liked those boots. They are the ones I've always worn. I know my way around them."

Mma Ramotswe looked puzzled. "But surely there's not much to know about shoes," she argued. "All you have to know is which way round they go. You wouldn't want to put them on back to front, nor put the left shoe on the right foot. But is there much to know beyond that?"

The conversation went nowhere, as it always did when this subject was raised, and Mma Ramotswe had come to accept that men's clothing was a lost cause. There might be a small number of men who were conscious of their apparel and did not hold on to old shoes and clothes for too long, but if there were, then she certainly was not married to one of them. Her own clothes were a quite different matter, of course. She did not spend an excessive amount on dresses, or on shoes for that matter, but she believed in quality and would never buy cheap clothes for the sake of saving a few pula. What she wanted from her clothes was the ability to stand up to the normal demands of the working day, easy laundering, and, if at all possible, light ironing qualities. If clothes had that, then it did not matter if they were not of the latest style or were of a colour that had ceased to be fashionable. If Mma Ramotswe was comfortable in them, and if they responded to the structural challenges posed by the traditionally built figure, then she embraced them enthusiastically, and they, in their way, reciprocated — particularly with those parts of her figure that needed support.

Given this attitude to the functionality of clothes, it was no surprise that she and her erstwhile assistant, now her co-director, Mma Grace Makutsi, wife of Mr. Phuti Radiphuti of the Double Comfort Furniture Store, should not see eye to eye on fashion matters. When she had first started at the agency, Mma Makutsi had not been in a position to spend much money on clothing. In fact, she could spend *no* money on clothes, for the simple reason that she had none. What savings Mma Makutsi and her family had were committed almost entirely to the fees she had to pay the Botswana Secretarial College, leaving very little for anything else. Then, when she was given the job at the No. 1 Ladies' Detective Agency, Mma Ramotswe had been unable to pay her much of a salary, as the truth of the matter was that the agency's minuscule profits did not really justify the employment of any staff.

But Mma Makutsi had talked herself into the job and had been prepared to accept the tiny salary on the grounds that in the fullness of time things would surely look up. They did, and when she found she had a bit of money in her pocket — although not all that much — she spent at least some of it on replacements for her two increasingly worn dresses. She also splashed out on some new shoes — a handsome pair of court shoes with green leather on the outside and blue lining within. She had never seen anything more beautiful than that pair of shoes, and they had imparted a spring to her step that Mma Ramotswe, and all others dealing with Mma Makutsi, had noticed, even if they did not know to attribute it to new footwear.

Following her marriage to Phuti Radiphuti, Mma Makutsi's wardrobe expanded. Phuti was well off, and although he did not believe in flaunting wealth, he was strongly of the view that the wife of a man of his standing, with his herd of over six hundred cattle, should be dressed in a way that was commensurate with her station in life.

Mma Ramotswe had helped Mma Makutsi on that first big spending spree, when they had gone to the Riverwalk shops and purchased a dozen dresses, several petticoats, a rail of blouses, and, of course, several pairs of new shoes.

"It's not that I'd buy all these things," Mma Makutsi had observed apologetically. "You know that I am not one of these people who like to wear a different outfit every day — you know that, don't you, Mma Ramotswe?"

It had seemed to Mma Ramotswe that Mma Makutsi needed reassurance, as we all do from time to time, and she gave it. "Nobody would accuse you of being that sort of lady, Mma," she said as they staggered under the weight of numerous boxes and bags to Mma Ramotswe's tiny white van. "I certainly wouldn't."

"It's Phuti, you see," explained Mma Makutsi. "He wants me to look smart."

"That's very good," said Mma Ramotswe. "It is better to have a husband who knows what you are wearing than to have one who doesn't even notice. Some men never notice, you know. They have no idea what women are wearing."

"That is a great pity for their wives and girlfriends," said Mma Makutsi. "It must be very discouraging to dress up all the time only to find that your husband doesn't even see what you have on."

The taste of the two women was similar in some respects — but different in others. Their views diverged on shoes, but they both agreed that women should dress modestly and should not wear skirts that were too short. This view was probably shared by the vast majority of women in Botswana, even if not by absolutely all of them. Some young women, they had noticed, seemed to have picked up the idea that the more leg a skirt displayed, the more fashionable it was.

"I do not understand that," said Mma Makutsi. "Men know that women have legs — that is one of the things that they learn at an early age. So why do you have to show them that you have legs when they are already well aware of that?"

Mma Ramotswe agreed. She might not have put it exactly that way herself, but she shared the general sentiment.

Mma Makutsi was warming to her theme. "Of course, I remember the first time I saw really short skirts," she went on. "It was when I came down from Bobonong and I went to enroll at the Botswana Secretarial College. I remember that day very well, Mma."

"I'm sure you do," said Mma Ramotswe. "It must have been very different for you, coming from Bobonong and then finding yourself in Gaborone."

Mma Makutsi stiffened. "Why, Mma? Why do you think that?"

Mma Ramotswe quickly corrected herself. Mma Makutsi was proud of Bobonong and she would not wish to offend her. One of the things she had learned about human nature was that people tended to be inordinately proud of the place they came from, and that any disparaging remark about that place was hurtful — even if it happened to be true. There were some towns — indeed some countries — that were, by all accounts, difficult places to live; and yet even if everything that was said about them was true, you could not say as much to people who came from such places. What they wanted to hear was that you had heard good reports of their home town or their country, and that one day you hoped you would be able to visit it. That brought smiles of satisfaction and assurances that half of what was said or written about the place in question being difficult — or downright dangerous — was exaggeration and lies.

"What I mean," Mma Ramotswe said, "is that Bobonong is not as big as Gaborone. That is all. I was thinking of how it must feel to come from a small place to a big place. There is nothing wrong with Bobonong, Mma. It is a very fine place."

Mollified by this explanation, Mma Makutsi pointed out that Mma Ramotswe had herself made a similar transition. "Of course, you came from Mochudi, Mma," she said. "That is just a village, after all."

"Well, there we are," said Mma Ramotswe, relieved at the defusing of the discussion. "We are both village girls at heart." She paused, and then added, "But coping very well in the city — both of us."

They returned to Mma Makutsi's first day at the Botswana Secretarial College and to the topic of short skirts.

"There I was," Mma Makutsi continued.

"I was, I admit it, a bit nervous about being at college. There were thirty-two girls in my year and they all seemed to be so much more confident than I was. They knew Gaborone well, and talked about places I had never even heard of — about which shop sold what, and where you could get your hair or nails done. These were things I'd never even thought about, let alone explored, and I was very much out of it, Mma. I had no idea what to say."

"We've all had that sort of experience," said Mma Ramotswe. "Every one of us, Mma. We've all had a first day at school, or a first day in a new job. We've all been unsure what to do."

Mma Makutsi gazed out of the window. "I just sat there, Mma. I sat at the back of the class with all these other girls talking to one another as if they had been friends for many years. I knew nobody, Mma — not a single soul. And then . . ."

Mma Ramotswe waited. She could picture Mma Makutsi in those early days at the Botswana Secretarial College — earnest and attentive, desperate to make a success of this great chance she had been given, trying hard not to worry about where the next pula or thebe was coming from; hungry, no doubt, because she would have had to choose between food and textbooks, and would have chosen the latter.

Mma Makutsi took off her large round spectacles and began to polish them. Mma Ramotswe had noticed that this was an action that preceded the recollection of something painful, and so she was not too surprised by what followed.

"And then," she continued, "at the end of that very first lecture — it was a lecture on the importance of high standards, Mma, and it was delivered by the principal herself — at the end of that first lecture we went outside for a short break. Because I was sitting at the back, I was the last out, and the others were all standing in groups, all chatting in the same way as they had been earlier on. I did not know where to go and so I was pleased when one of the girls called me over to join her group. She said, 'Why don't you come and talk to us?' And I said, 'Yes, I'll come.' "

Mma Makutsi replaced her spectacles. "And do you know who that was, Mma Ramotswe? That was Violet Sephotho."

"Ah," said Mma Ramotswe.

"Yes," Mma Makutsi said. "It was her."

"And was that the first time you had seen her, Mma?" asked Mma Ramotswe.

Mma Makutsi nodded. "I must have seen

her in the lecture room, but I had not really noticed her. Now I noticed her, because nobody could miss what she was wearing."

"Oh, I can imagine it," said Mma Ramotswe.

"Can you, Mma? I think it may have been even worse than what you think. A *very* short skirt, Mma."

Mma Ramotswe did not find that surprising.

"The skirt was red, Mma, and then there was a blouse that was hardly a blouse. In fact, you might even have thought that her blouse was made from that stuff they make curtains out of — you know those curtains you can sort of see out of — not proper curtains. What do they call that material, Mma?"

"Gauze?"

"That's it. Phuti's aunt has curtains like that in her bathroom. I am sure people in the street can look right through them, and so when we go to visit her I always hang a towel over the window, just in case."

"That is very wise, Mma," said Mma Ramotswe. "People have no business looking into the bathrooms of other people."

"They certainly do not, Mma. Or through any other windows for that matter."

Mma Ramotswe pursed her lips. She was

about to agree, but realised that she herself occasionally — and only very occasionally — glanced through the windows of others if she was passing by. She would never go up to the window and peer inside — that was very wrong — but if you were walking along a street and you walked past a window, then surely it was permissible to have a quick glance, just to see the sort of furniture that they liked, or the pictures on the wall, or possibly to see who was sitting in the room. If people did not want anybody to see what was going on in the room, then they should pull down a blind or something of that sort — an open window was an indication, surely, that they did not mind if passers-by looked in.

And, of course, as a private detective you had to know what was going on. If you kept your eyes fixed straight ahead of you, then you would be unable to gather the sort of everyday intelligence that was part and parcel of your job, and without that intelligence your ability to help others would be limited. So, looking through an open window was not so much an act of idle curiosity as it was an act of consideration for others . . . But this was not the time to have that debate with Mma Makutsi, and so she waited to hear more about this early encounter with Violet Sephotho.

"So, she called you over, Mma?" prompted Mma Ramotswe.

"Yes, she called me over. And then she said, in a loud voice, 'Mma, tell me: Are you going to a funeral today?' "

Mma Ramotswe drew in her breath; she thought she could tell what was coming.

"She asked me that, Mma Ramotswe," Mma Makutsi continued. "And I did not know why she should say that. So I told her that I was not going to a funeral, and why did she think I was? She did not reply immediately, but looked at the others and then said, 'Because you're dressed as if you are.' "

Mma Ramotswe expelled air through her teeth. It was the most dismissive, disapproving gesture she knew, and this was precisely the sort of situation that called for it.

"The other girls all burst out laughing," Mma Makutsi said. "And Violet was very pleased with herself. She smiled and said that she hoped I had not taken offence, but being a secretary was different from being an undertaker, and so were the clothes you should wear for the job.

"The others thought this very funny, and they all laughed. Have you noticed, Mma Ramotswe, how people love to join in when one person is laughing at another? We like to do things together, it seems, even if the thing everybody is doing is cruel or unkind."

Mma Ramotswe thought about this. Mma Makutsi was right. "Especially if the thing is cruel or unkind," she said. But then she added, "But that is only a certain sort of person we're talking about there, Mma. And I think that most people are not like that. Most people do not want others to suffer. Most people are kind enough right deep down in their hearts."

"Not Violet Sephotho," said Mma Makutsi.

"Perhaps not," said Mma Ramotswe. "Although even Violet might change one day, Mma. Nobody is so bad that there is no chance of change."

Mma Makutsi looked doubtful. "You're too kind sometimes, Mma," she said.

"Perhaps," said Mma Ramotswe. "But you'd think the college would have told her to dress more modestly."

"I think they did," said Mma Makutsi. "Not directly, of course — they gave us all a lecture on the importance of high standards in the way in which we presented ourselves. They told us that when we dressed for the office each day we should dress as if we believed that the President was going to call in and inspect us."

"And what did Violet Sephotho make of that?"

"She just smiled," said Mma Makutsi. "She smiled and then later on she said to the others that she knew what the President would like to see if he came to inspect an office. It would not be formal clothes but rather the sort of clothes that she wore — bright and optimistic clothes, she called them."

"Nonsense," said Mma Ramotswe. "The President does not want to see that sort of thing. Look at what he wears himself. He wears sober dark suits. He wears khaki when he has to go out into the country."

"That is for camouflage," said Mma Makutsi. "It is so that he cannot be seen by lions and wildebeest and such things."

Mma Ramotswe looked doubtful. "I'm not sure about that, Mma. But anyway, I don't think we shall ever get a visit from the President."

The mention of camouflage made her think. It could be unnerving if a very important visitor were to come into the office wearing camouflage. He might be there for some time before anybody noticed him, lurking by the filing cabinet, perhaps, or in a corner, watching, waiting.

"Stranger things have happened," said

Mma Makutsi. "You never know."

That, thought Mma Ramotswe, was true: you never knew.

Chapter Two:
A Lady With
a Late Husband

Every Morning, just before they went to work, Mma Ramotswe and Mr. J.L.B. Matekoni liked to spend a few minutes together, sitting on their verandah, trying to catch up with life before the day and its demands took over. With Puso and Motholeli — their two adopted children — dispatched to school, they could catch their breath, either speaking or not speaking, depending on how they felt. On that particular morning nothing much was said until Mma Ramotswe suddenly remarked, "Poor Mr. Polopetsi. You know, I feel very sorry for that man."

Mr. J.L.B. Matekoni looked surprised. "He seems all right to me. I saw him the other day when I went to the supermarket. He was pushing his shopping cart around, filling it up with biscuits, as far as I could make out. And, funnily enough, I noticed that he had bought some dog biscuits. So I said to him, 'I didn't know you had a dog, Rra.' And he said, 'No, I don't have one.' And so I said, 'But you've bought dog biscuits, I see. Perhaps they're for somebody else's dog.' "

Mma Ramotswe, who had red bush tea at her side during this conversation, took a sip from her teacup. "Speaking as a detective, Rra, I would say that there must be some explanation."

"Well, there was," said Mr. J.L.B. Matekoni. "He had made a mistake. He hadn't looked at the label closely enough. If he had looked, he would have seen that there was a picture of a dog on the packet." He paused to utter a brief chuckle. "That should be enough of a sign for most people, Mma — a picture of a dog, don't you think?"

Mma Ramotswe had started the conversation by saying that she felt sorry for Mr. Polopetsi; she was not going to laugh at him now. "It's very easily done, Rra," she pointed out. "These mistakes are very easy to make if you're not paying one hundred per cent attention. And even if you are, you can still make them."

Mr. J.L.B. Matekoni seemed abashed. "I wasn't saying that I couldn't make a mistake, Mma. I wasn't laughing at him." He paused. "But look at the mistakes people like Charlie make. Look at them."

Charlie was the apprentice at Tlokweng Road Speedy Motors. Mr. J.L.B. Matekoni had taken on two young men some years earlier, and while one of them, Fanwell, had eventually passed his mechanic's exams and had been taken on as an assistant, the other, Charlie, was stuck as an apprentice and seemed unlikely to make much progress. Charlie was strong on personal charm: he was popular with young women — and with some older ones as well — but he was feckless in so many ways, and his ministrations to cars often resulted in the car being in a worse state than when it had first come into the garage.

Mr. J.L.B. Matekoni shook his head as he recalled Charlie's latest mechanical disaster. "The other day, Mma Ramotswe, he tightened a gearbox drain plug far too much. How he did it, I'll never know. That made a tiny crack in the gearbox and it meant the oil leaked out."

Mma Ramotswe was not sure what a gearbox drain plug did — she had not imagined that cars had drains — but it was evidently not the sort of thing that a good mechanic would have done. "I know you get cross with him," she said. "I know that you don't want to, but you do."

"It's because his mistakes go on and on," said Mr. J.L.B. Matekoni. "To make a mistake once is understandable, maybe, but to make it twice, three times, sometimes even four times — then that's a different matter. Surely you can blame a person for that?"

She conceded the point. And he, as the conversation went on, conceded that it might be harsh to blame somebody for a single mistake. "I think we agree, Mma Ramotswe," he said at last. "And so . . . Mr. Polopetsi: What about him, Mma?"

Mma Ramotswe shrugged. "Nothing, really, Rra. I was just thinking about him. You know how people pop into your mind for no particular reason. You're walking along and suddenly you think about Mma Makutsi or Mma Potokwane or, in this case, poor Mr. Polopetsi. And then you think a bit more about them. You think about the things they've said to you, or you wonder what they're having for dinner, or whether they've put on weight — that sort of thing."

Mr. J.L.B. Matekoni nodded. "Mma Potokwane has put on a bit of weight, I think. She brought her car round the other day for me to check something, and I noticed that its suspension was in a bad way. That is often the case with the cars of traditionally built ladies. They go down on one side because . . ."

He stopped himself. Mma Ramotswe was looking at him over her teacup.

"Mr. Polopetsi," he said rapidly. "Yes, Mr. Polopetsi. I hope he's happy, Mma."

Mma Ramotswe looked at her watch. She would have liked to continue talking, but she had to get to the office and he to the garage.

Mr. J.L.B. Matekoni seemed to read her mind. "It would be good to talk all day," he said, adding, "To talk to you, that is — not to other people. Talking to you, Mma, is very . . . very restful, I think."

Mma Ramotswe looked at her husband and smiled. Life, she thought, was more or less perfect: here she was in her own house, in a country that she loved with all her heart — a good country, a peaceful country — and with a husband who was not only the finest mechanic in all Botswana but also a kind and generous man. What more could anyone want? she asked herself, and quickly came up with the answer: nothing. There was nothing more that she wanted, or would ever want; nothing at all.

But now, only a few hours after that early

morning conversation in which his happiness had been discussed, here was Mr. Polopetsi knocking at the door of the No. 1 Ladies' Detective Agency with that timid, self-effacing knock that he always used. It was so quiet, so hesitant, as to be almost inaudible, and it always made Mma Makutsi smile.

"It is like a rabbit knocking at the door," she whispered to Mma Ramotswe. "That is just how a rabbit would knock."

Mma Ramotswe put a finger to her lips; she did not want Mr. Polopetsi, who was slightly frightened of Mma Makutsi anyway, to hear her likening him to a rabbit. She could see what Mma Makutsi meant — there were times when he did have the appearance of a startled rabbit — but she would never want him to know that was how anybody saw him.

"Don't be unkind, Mma," she whispered back to Mma Makutsi, and then, in a much louder voice, called out, "Come in, Rra — the door is not locked."

Mr. Polopetsi entered the office. He was wearing a smart white shirt with a light blue tie. In the pocket of the shirt was an array of pens, their clips neatly lined up, ready for use. His trousers, into which a sharp crease had been ironed, were of a dark green shade, rather like the colour of the Limpopo, Mma Ramotswe thought. "Limpopo Green"; was there such a colour? Or should she call it "Polopetsi Green," a description that also seemed to suit the shade rather well?

"It's only me," said Mr. Polopetsi. It was not a very confident way of announcing oneself, thought Mma Ramotswe; as if the arrival of anybody else would have been a much more significant event. *Only me . . .* Her heart went out to him as he spoke. His life might not amount to very much — he was a man whom most people would hardly ever notice — and yet she knew that he was a decent man, a man who liked to help others, who would never be pushy or greedy, who did not expect very much out of life. It was men like that who were trampled over by ambitious, noisy men — men who wanted power and material wealth, men who boasted and bragged, men who, quite simply, often gave men in general a bad name. There were always plenty of those, it seemed, and not enough Mr. Polopetsis.

She gave him a warm welcome. "Mr. Polopetsi! I was hoping it was you. We were just talking about you, Rra, and here you are. That is very good."

Mr. Polopetsi looked alarmed. "Talking

about me, Mma?"

She was quick to reassure him. "Not gossiping, or anything like that, Rra. No, certainly not. I think it was just a case of Mma Makutsi saying something like, 'Here comes Mr. Polopetsi' — nothing controversial."

He seemed relieved. "I have just finished teaching for the day," he said. "I thought I would call in and see what was going on." Mr. Polopetsi had a part-time job teaching chemistry at Gaborone Secondary School. That occupied him, but only for a limited number of hours each week, which meant that he had the time to do some work for the agency. That he did on a voluntary basis, and even when Mma Ramotswe had offered him a token payment — all that the agency could afford — he had refused to take any money. His wife, he explained, was a senior official in a government department and earned more than enough for both of them. She was also entitled to a government car, which made a big difference to the family budget.

"It is sufficient reward for me to be involved in this work," said Mr. Polopetsi. "I would not like to sit about at home and think of chemistry all day."

Now, taking up Mma Ramotswe's invitation to sit down, he chose the rickety spare chair beside the filing cabinet.

"You should sit in the client's chair," said Mma Ramotswe. "It is more comfortable."

Mr. Polopetsi hesitated. "But what if a client comes in, Mma? What if a client comes in and finds me sitting in the client's chair? What then?"

Mma Makutsi snorted. "You shouldn't be so nervous, Rra. No client is going to come in."

"And if one did arrive," said Mma Ramotswe, "then the simplest thing to do would be to stand up and offer the client the chair. That would be the best way of dealing with an emergency like that."

Somewhat sheepishly Mr. Polopetsi moved to the more comfortable chair. Mma Ramotswe looked at him encouragingly.

"Is everything going well, Rra?" she asked.

He nodded. "Everything is going very well, Mma. Nothing much is happening, but I suppose that means that it is going well."

Mma Makutsi had views on this. "That is very true, Rra," she contributed. "I've always said, 'No sign of anything, then no sign of trouble.' That is what I've said."

Mr. Polopetsi considered these words of wisdom. "I don't think there are many people who would argue with that, Mma. They would probably all say that you're right. That's what I think, anyway."

A short silence ensued. Mr. Polopetsi looked down at his green trousers.

"I do like your trousers, Rra," said Mma Ramotswe. "Green is a good colour for men, I always say. What do you think, Mma Makutsi?"

Mma Makutsi peered round the side of her desk to get a better view of Mr. Polopetsi's trousers. "Yes," she said. "They are good trousers. I've tried to get Phuti to wear green, but he won't. I asked and he said, 'You wouldn't catch me in green — green is a good colour for women but not for men.' "

Mma Ramotswe threw a sharp, disapproving glance across the room. "That's nonsense, Mma. There are no colours that are just for men or just for women. That is not at all true. These days everybody can wear whatever they like."

Chastened, Mma Makutsi tried to correct the impression she had created, but it was too late. Looking miserable, Mr. Polopetsi fingered the crease on his trousers. "Why would Phuti say such a thing?" he asked. "He must know something about these matters."

Mma Ramotswe brushed this aside. "Oh,

Phuti wasn't being serious, Rra. Phuti is always saying things like that — just nonsense things, really." She threw another glance at Mma Makutsi. "Isn't that so, Mma?"

"Mma Ramotswe's right," said Mma Makutsi. "He wasn't thinking. He often makes these ridiculous remarks and then I have to tell him that he has it all wrong, and then he takes it all back. In fact, he took back that thing about green. He said that there's nothing wrong with green. He said he was mixing it up with some other colour — who knows which?"

It was a lame excuse, and most people would have realised as much, but somehow it seemed to reassure Mr. Polopetsi, who settled back in his chair and accepted the cup of tea Mma Makutsi had now poured for him. "My wife says these trousers are very smart," he muttered.

"But of course they are," said Mma Ramotswe, adding somewhat wistfully, "I wish I could get Mr. J.L.B. Matekoni to wear trousers like that."

Mr. Polopetsi looked anxious once more. "So, he wouldn't wear them either? Just like Phuti Radiphuti?"

Mma Ramotswe realised that she would have to take control of the conversation.

"Let's not talk about clothes," she said. "Mma Makutsi and I have talked enough about clothes for one day. Do you have any news for us, Mr. Polopetsi? Have you heard anything we ought to be aware of?" The request was clear enough, and it pleased Mr. Polopetsi, who suddenly perked up. He prided himself on the information that he picked up from what he described as his "sources." These were, in fact, his senior students at the school; teenagers, being the worst gossips of all, liked to pass on what they heard from their parents. Because the school was not far from the government quarter, many of these parents were party to the sort of information that did not get into the newspapers. Little nuggets of information about who was doing what, and with whom, and what might be expected to happen as a result, were regularly imparted to Mr. Polopetsi at odd moments in the school chemistry lab. Many of these were passed on to Mma Ramotswe, not in any idle, gossipy way, but as part of what Mr. Polopetsi saw as an intelligence briefing. A private detective needed to know what was going on, and he took the view that this information was safe in Mma Ramotswe's hands, as she would never use it for anything but good purposes. And in that respect, Mr.

Polopetsi was quite right: Mma Ramotswe sometimes complained that she could not choose her clients and must, of necessity, do her best by all of them, but she had never acted in such a way as to oppress or cheat anybody; never — and she never would.

Mr. Polopetsi took a sip of his tea. "There is something, Mma Ramotswe," he said.

They both waited for him to continue, but he simply took another sip of tea.

Eventually Mma Ramotswe broke the silence. "I'm listening, Rra, but take your time. There is no rush in these things."

"We have all day," said Mma Makutsi. "And tomorrow, if necessary."

This remark was meant humorously, but it unnerved Mr. Polopetsi. He glanced nervously at Mma Makutsi before he continued. "I do not want to take up too much of your time, Mma Ramotswe."

Mma Ramotswe sat back in her chair with the air of one for whom time was not of the slightest concern.

"There is somebody I know," began Mr. Polopetsi, "or rather, it is somebody I don't quite know, but who is the sister of somebody I know. She is a teacher at the Gaborone Secondary School. She is meant to teach games — you know, netball and running and things like that — but she is

36

interested in teaching chemistry too." He paused, and then shook his head. "I don't think it's a good idea to let the games teachers teach chemistry. This lady is very vague on her chemical symbols. You know, Mma Ramotswe, I discovered that she thought the symbol for salt was S. Can you believe that, Mma?"

From behind him, Mma Makutsi snorted contemptuously. "Hah! Salt is Sal. Everybody knows that."

Mr. Polopetsi spun round. He seemed almost distraught. "Oh, no, Mma Makutsi: whoever has told you that is very wrong. Salt is not Sal. Salt is sodium chloride. That is what you put on your food. S is sulphur."

Mma Makutsi looked puzzled. "You put sulphur on your food? Is that what you're telling us, Rra?"

Mma Ramotswe intervened. "No, he didn't say that, Mma. You didn't say we should put sulphur on our food, did you, Mr. Polopetsi? You said that the symbol for sulphur was S."

"That is quite correct," said Mr. Polopetsi. "Sodium is Na, and salt is therefore NaCl." He paused. "But if you go into a café and you want to ask the waiter for salt, do not say, 'Please give me the NaCl.' "

It was Mr. Polopetsi's little joke, and he

waited expectantly for their reaction.

"That is very funny, Rra," said Mma Makutsi. "I shall remember not to do that."

Mr. Polopetsi brightened. "And here's another funny thing, Mma Makutsi," he said. "There is a very funny poem that I learned when I was studying chemistry. I have never forgotten it. Would you like to hear it?"

"We should like that very much," replied Mma Ramotswe.

Mr. Polopetsi sat upright in his chair. "My old friend," he began, "is down below, his face we'll see no more, for what he thought was H_2O was H_2SO_4!"

There was silence, at least until Mma Ramotswe made an attempt at laughter. "Poor man," she said. And then, rather lamely, "Is your friend late?"

Mr. Polopetsi frowned. How could anybody not appreciate the poem? Was Mma Ramotswe being deliberately slow?

"He is late because he took the wrong pills, I think," said Mma Makutsi. "He was meant to take an H_2O pill and he took an H_2SO_4 pill. That is why he is late."

Mr. Polopetsi spun round again. "No, Mma," he said. "That is not right. H_2O is water and H_2SO_4 is sulphuric acid. My friend drank sulphuric acid rather than water and became late. That is what happened."

Mma Makutsi made a sympathetic noise of the sort that people make when they hear that others are late. "I'm very sorry to hear this," she said. "It is very sad."

Mr. Polopetsi stared at her. "It's not true, Mma. It's a poem; I told you that. It's a very funny poem."

"I am glad that he is not late," interjected Mma Ramotswe. "But returning to the person you were speaking about, the person you say you don't really know, is this the sports teacher who doesn't know the difference between sodium and sulphur?"

Mr. Polopetsi shook his head. "No, it's not her, Mma. It's her sister."

Mma Ramotswe digested this information. There were odd sideroads in any conversation with Mr. Polopetsi, and all that business about chemical symbols had been one such deviation. Once you got round all those, though, and were back on track in a conversation, he could explain things clearly enough.

"Perhaps you should tell us about this lady," she suggested. As she spoke, she glanced out of the window. The sun was on the acacia tree outside, throwing delicate shadows from the foliage. These shadows fell on the trunk of the tree, creating patterns of darkness and light, a mottled effect. A tiny creature, a lizard or gecko, moved suddenly from one of these shadows, clinging to the bark of the tree, becoming sunlit for a few seconds before retreating into the shade. *It is going about its business,* she thought; this small being had matters as large and important, to it, as our own human affairs. And most of the time, of course, we did not notice such things because it was our own business that we were concerned with, and our hearts were not large enough for things that were so much smaller than we were.

Mr. Polopetsi began. "This sister — that is, the sister of the teacher . . ."

"Yes, Rra," Mma Ramotswe encouraged. "This sister . . ."

"She lives not far from here, out towards Tlokweng, but not quite so far out. Maybe a mile or two; I have not been to her house, but it is somewhere over there." He gestured vaguely out of the window. "Her name is Charity Mompoloki. She was married to a man called Mompoloki, but he is late now. He was always smoking, you see, right from the time he was ten years old, they told me, and now he is late. Late from smoking."

Mma Makutsi made a disapproving noise

from her desk behind Mr. Polopetsi. "If you're smoking by the time you're ten, then you're not going to last very long."

Mr. Polopetsi nodded his head in agreement. "Your lungs are still growing then," he said. "What chance do they have if you're smoking? All those tars."

"You're a chemist," observed Mma Ramotswe. "You know about these things."

"Yes, I know about them, Mma Ramotswe, but I also know about these tobacco people who are always trying to recruit new smokers when the old ones give up — or become late. They say: now we must find new customers to buy these cigarettes of ours. How about ten-year-olds? How about young women? And so it goes on — more smokers to buy more cigarettes and then become late."

Mma Ramotswe did not like cigarette smoke and there was nothing here with which she was in disagreement. But she was keen to steer the conversation back to Charity Mompoloki.

"This Charity," she said. "Since she lost her husband, what does she do? Are there children?"

"I was told there are two children," said Mr. Polopetsi. "I do not really know these people, and so there may be more, but I

41

was told there are twins — both boys. They are still young. Maybe five or six — something like that."

"It is a shame for them," said Mma Ramotswe. "It is a shame for them to lose their daddy like that."

Mr. Polopetsi looked down at the floor. "There are many children like that, Mma. Remember?"

He did not have to explain further. There had been that disease and it had taken such a toll; mothers, fathers, uncles, aunts — the children had lost all these people, to such an extent that even the grandmothers, those resilient, uncomplaining women who could support the very sky on their shoulders, even they had buckled under the strain of looking after the children who were left behind.

"At least these children have their mother," pointed out Mma Makutsi. "There are many who do not."

Mma Ramotswe thought of Mma Potokwane. The children of Botswana still had Mma Potokwane, who had devoted her life to looking after orphans. "But this Charity lady," she pressed. "What does she do for money?"

"She had a job," answered Mr. Polopetsi. "It was quite a good job, Mma. I say 'was.'

She does not have that job any more, and that is why I am talking about her now."

"Ow!" exclaimed Mma Makutsi. "The economy. That's the problem. The economy. Everything is going well and people are very happy and then along comes the economy. Ow! And suddenly there are no jobs any longer and we're back to where we started."

Mr. Polopetsi did not respond to this, but continued with his story. "I heard all of this from the teacher, but I think it will be true. You see, she — that is, her sister — had a good job with a firm that sells office furniture." He turned to face Mma Makutsi. "It's not like the place your husband has, Mma. He sells beds, doesn't he?"

Mma Makutsi nodded; but correction was necessary. "Not only beds, Rra, but tables and chairs — for the dining room. And all the furniture needed for the living room: sofas, single chairs, coffee tables, wardrobes for the bedroom, chests of drawers for your clothes . . ."

Mma Ramotswe cut her short. "This other place, Rra — this office place — is it over near Kgale Hill?"

Mr. Polopetsi turned round again. "Yes, it is over there, Mma. Do you know it?"

"I have driven past it," said Mma Ramotswe. "It's called Office something, isn't it?"

Mr. Polopetsi frowned. "The Office Place, I think."

"That's it," said Mma Ramotswe. "It's a big warehouse. I know somebody who went in there once and said it was full of filing cabinets. As far as the eye could see, there were filing cabinets." She looked over towards Mma Makutsi, who was proud of her filing prowess. Filing, she understood, had been her strongest subject at the Botswana Secretarial College, from which Mma Makutsi had, of course, graduated with a final mark of ninety-seven per cent.

At the mention of filing cabinets, Mma Makutsi's glasses flashed in a beam of sunlight. "I must go there," she muttered.

Mr. Polopetsi continued with his tale. Charity Mompoloki had enjoyed her job selling office furniture and had been good at it. Then, quite out of the blue, she had been fired. There had been a pretext, of course: she had been rude to an important customer, who had complained and had pressed for her removal. Now she was without work and needed help.

"To get her job back?" asked Mma Makutsi.

"Yes," said Mr. Polopetsi.

Mma Ramotswe looked concerned. "But if she had been rude to a customer, Rra?

Will they not argue that her dismissal was justified — even if it was far too harsh?"

"Oh, they may argue that," said Mr. Polopetsi, "but the point is this, Mma Ramotswe: she wasn't rude at all."

"Ah," said Mma Ramotswe. "Then that makes a big difference."

"Yes," said Mr. Polopetsi. "It makes a very big difference."

Nobody said anything for a moment while they reflected on the case. Then Mma Ramotswe broke the silence.

"I think, perhaps, we should have another cup of tea," she said.

Nobody disagreed.

CHAPTER THREE:
YOU COULD FIND YOURSELF
SHAKING YOUR HEAD
SO MUCH

She picked up a fine piece of Botswana beef from the butcher before returning to Zebra Drive that evening. The butcher, whose own father had known her father, the late Obed Ramotswe, always gave her the best cut, just as he always managed to come up with some reminiscence of his father's dealings with Obed. There were not many stories to tell on the subject, but he made the most of those there were, recycling them every so often with additional details to add colour. Had her father ever told her about the time they saved a cow from drowning after a particularly heavy storm? Had he ever mentioned a man called Cephas Pilane who was a bit of a gambler and who had lost a donkey in a ridiculous wager? Had he ever told her about the time the two of them — his father and hers — were chased by a bull and had to climb a thorn tree, much to their discomfort? The stories were old ones, much embroidered, but they were typical of the skein of tales that kept people together, that reminded them of who their people were and what they meant to them. You might think they were just stories about cattle and the men who owned them, but of course they were much more than that: they were stories about Botswana and what it meant to be a Motswana. And she never tired of hearing about her father — that great man, that unrivalled judge of cattle, her daddy, as she called him, and of whom she thought at some point every day, every single day, and whom she had loved with all her heart. It did not matter if the butcher told her the same things time and time again — she would never tire of hearing what he had to say.

Back at the house, she parked her tiny white van in its customary place, put the beef in the fridge, and made herself a pot of red bush tea. She would drink the tea as she walked round the garden, carrying out her usual inspection of the vegetable patch — her beans were doing well, nurtured by the run-off water from the kitchen drain. In a dry country, no water is wasted, and Mma Ramotswe and Mr. J.L.B. Matekoni had stretched out a hose pipe that would take the water from the drain, across a stretch of dusty garden, to the raised vegetable beds towards the back of their plot. There the hose fed the water into an old oil drum that acted as reservoir and from which much smaller pipes led to the individual beds. The final stage in this engineering marvel was the trailing of cotton threads from a bucket suspended above the plants; water would run down this thread drop by drop to the foot of each plant's stem. No water thus fell on ground where nothing grew; every drop reached exactly the tiny patch of ground where it was needed.

Everything was in order. The beans were obediently ripening; the tomatoes were weighing down their stems; the melons, fat, lazy, and yellow, were half hidden by their leaves but would be ready any day now to be plucked, cooked, and served with gravy. In fact . . . She bent down and felt the largest of the melons. Then she tapped on it gently, as if to see if anybody was in. It was just right, and she now lowered herself onto her haunches and gently separated the melon from its stalk. She would cook it that evening, to go with the beef from the butcher. Mr. J.L.B. Matekoni's favourite meal of all was just that: good Botswana beef, fed on the sweet grass of the veld, accompanied by boiled melon from their very own soil. What could be better than that? What country, anywhere on the face of this earth, could deliver bounty as honest, as nourishing, and as delicious?

She had done much of the cooking by the time he came home. She had also collected Motholeli from school, where she had been at her girl guide meeting, started Puso on his homework, and generally tidied up the kitchen. Mr. J.L.B. Matekoni was slightly later than usual, as he had been dealing with a sophisticated modern car and had none of the diagnostic equipment that particular make of car needed. Something was wrong with the car's soul, he thought; a modern mechanic might put it differently, and might talk about malfunctioning sensors or a software problem of some sort, but in his view it was the car's soul. Somewhere deep in the electronic gadgetry orchestrating the engine, there was something wrong; and just as the failure of one organ in the human body may disrupt the performance of the whole, this little glitch had thrown the whole mighty engine into disarray. It had been a frustrating experience, but he had eventually solved the problem by disconnecting and then reconnecting as many wires as he could see. One of them had a faulty contact point and had responded to this shock therapy.

"It's only by chance that I fixed it," he said, lowering himself into a chair by the kitchen table. "What a fuss it was."

"Well, you did it," she said. "That's the important thing." She leaned forward and sniffed at the stew. Mma Ramotswe believed in using your nose while cooking; too many people, she thought, relied on taste, and were always dipping a spoon into a dish to see how it was faring. In her view, that was unnecessary — and unhygienic. You could find out everything you needed to know through the sense of smell. A good stew smelled like a . . . well, a good stew; it would remind you of that time when the sun has just sunk over the Kalahari, when the cattle have been brought back into their kraal against a background of gentle lowing, when the moon is floating up in the sky over Botswana and the children are sitting about the fire, waiting for their dinner. It smelled like that. It smelled like the world when, early in the morning, you made your way through the bush and the birds were just beginning to greet the world and the delicate leaves of the acacia trees were opening to the warmth of the gold with which the land was painted. It smelled like that, and all you

50

had to do was to train yourself to know when something was just right.

Mr. J.L.B. Matekoni was thinking of cars, though. He was thinking about the loss of soul in cars and what this meant for people like him — mechanics, who were priests of a sort. There would be no role for mechanics in the new world that was being created around them; a world in which you never fixed anything but simply replaced it with a new part. Look at what had happened to carburettors; look at what had happened to gearboxes; look at what had happened even to the lights that lit up the inside of a car when you opened the door. They used to have bulbs that you could take out and change — tiny, fragile things that came in flimsy cardboard boxes with the address of the factory printed on them — somewhere in England, or Germany, where he had heard the cattle were very well watered and were fat; and these bulbs, these little bubbles of impossibly thin glass, would fit just about any car that needed a replacement. Where were those bulbs now? They had gone, and now the lights in a car were whole units, square and chunky, that had to be specially ordered if they failed, which the manufacturers said they never would do, because they were meant to last for one hundred thousand hours, as he had seen claimed in the handbook of a car he had recently serviced. One hundred thousand hours . . . That sounded like a lifetime to him; it sounded like many generations of old bulbs, stretching off into the distance in a long line of little cardboard boxes.

He sighed, but privately and inaudibly. There was no point in bemoaning these things, because you could find yourself shaking your head so much that you would end up with a sore neck. And what was the point of that? You could not uninvent things; you could not bring back a world that had gone forever, even if you could remember it from time to time, and think fondly of what had been. It was important to be positive, and Mr. J.L.B. Matekoni was positive; he was. So he said, "I suppose you're right, Mma Ramotswe." This was always a good thing to say, and he meant it too, because she was usually right, and if there ever came a point when he could *not* say that, then that would be a sad day indeed. So, having said that, he went on to enquire about her day.

"And what about you, Mma? What about you?"

She replaced the lid on the pot in which the melon was being cooked.

"We had a visit from Mr. Polopetsi," she said. "Did you see him?"

He shook his head. "I was under that car. I was trying to work out what was what. You know, in the old days, if you went under a car . . ."

"Yes," said Mma Ramotswe. "It was simpler then." Everything had been simpler then, she thought — not just cars, but people and the world too. People knew what to do because they had the old Botswana morality to guide them, and that had never proved wanting. You respected your elders, you stood by those who were connected to you through friendship or family, you shared the things you had with those you knew and with those you did not know.

"So, what did old Polopetsi want?" Mr. J.L.B. Matekoni often called him that — old Polopetsi — although Mr. Polopetsi was only in his early forties. It was a term of affection, because he liked him, even if he found him slightly odd, with his frightened manner and his self-effacing comportment. "Is he doing some work for you?"

Mma Ramotswe joined him at the table. "He came to talk about a woman who is the sister of one of the teachers at the school."

Mr. J.L.B. Matekoni nodded. So many

things in Botswana started that way: somebody knew somebody who was a brother or sister of somebody else, and this person, or even this person's brother, needed your help, or even a loan. That was the way the country worked. "So, there is this woman . . ."

"She's called Charity Mompoloki."

He thought for a moment, but then shook his head. "I've never heard of her." He looked up at the ceiling, as if to find there some clue that would jog his memory. Mma Ramotswe had noticed his habit of doing this before, of looking to the ceiling for assistance, and had playfully said to him, "Yes, Rra, there could be something written on the ceiling — you never know." But now there was nothing, and he said, "I don't know of any family of that name — not personally, that is."

"She used to work at that office furniture place — the one near Kgale Hill."

Mr. J.L.B. Matekoni knew the place. "The man who owns that has a Mercedes-Benz. I have fixed it for him several times, but he does not drive it carefully. He is hard on the gearbox. A gearbox will not forget you if you are unkind to it. Gearboxes have a long memory — just like elephants."

Mma Ramotswe told him the story that

Mr. Polopetsi had recounted that morning. She told him how Charity had worked at the store for over six years and had done well. Then, without any warning, even as she was in the middle of taking an order for six filing cabinets and a receptionist's desk, she had been called to the manager's office and summarily dismissed. The pretext, Mr. Polopetsi said, had been rudeness to an important client. This had been denied vigorously, but the client had made it clear that he would not be bought off with a mere apology: he wanted the offender fired.

"That was all Mr. Polopetsi knew about the incident," said Mma Ramotswe.

Mr. J.L.B. Matekoni tutted in disapproval. He had heard that employers were getting tougher with their staff and were less tolerant than they used to be. It was not unconnected, he thought, with the desire to cut down the size of the workforce: find a pretext to dismiss somebody — any excuse would do — and slim down the payroll that way. He would never do that sort of thing, but there were many who would, and he strongly disapproved of the practice. "If you cannot afford to keep people on," he said, "then you should explain the situation to them rather than fire them for something else — something you've just made up."

Now, to Mma Ramotswe, he said, "She should have had a warning. I'm not excusing rudeness, but it's a bit extreme to get rid of somebody just because she forgot to be polite."

"I agree," said Mma Ramotswe. She knew that Mr. J.L.B. Matekoni would never do anything so harsh; on the contrary, he had always forgiven his apprentices for even the most exceptional mistakes and had never threatened to dismiss them. It was true that Charlie had lost his job at the garage, but that was only when financial stringency made it impossible to pay his wages, and since then he had been taken back, even if only on a part-time basis, the rest of his salary being made up by Mma Ramotswe. She had given Charlie a number of hours' work a week as an assistant in the agency — with mixed results.

Mr. J.L.B. Matekoni asked why Mr. Polopetsi had brought up the case of the dismissed woman. In response, Mma Ramotswe made a gesture of acceptance with her hands, the sort of gesture you make when there is no alternative. "He wondered whether I could help to get her job back." She looked apologetic, as if it were she who had made the awkward request.

Mr. J.L.B. Matekoni looked doubtful. "I

don't see what you can do, Mma," he said. "The labour court won't interfere in a case like that. They'd probably say that the dismissal was justified."

"Unless it's not true," said Mma Ramotswe. "Unless she was not rude in the first place."

Mr. J.L.B. Matekoni looked puzzled. "But you said she had been."

"No," said Mma Ramotswe. "I said that was the reason given for the dismissal. That's not the same thing as saying that she did what they said she did."

He looked up at the ceiling again, but only briefly. "You're suggesting that the client made it up?"

"No, I'm suggesting that the client may not know anything about it. I'm suggesting that the employer might have made it up."

"But why would he do that?"

Mma Ramotswe shrugged. "There are many reasons for wanting to get rid of somebody. I don't know what the reason might have been in this case, but what I do know is that if I were an employer in such a situation, and I wanted to get rid of somebody, my main worry would be the labour court. You can be taken to court, as you know, if you fire somebody without good reason. They may order reinstatement in the job. They may instruct compensation to be paid."

Mr. J.L.B. Matekoni had been aware of that. There had been a prominent case in the motor trade where a car salesman had been fired without good reason because he had been having an affair with the younger sister of one of the directors of the company. The director had considered the salesman unworthy of his sister, as the salesman came from a minority clan, and this element of animosity had been stressed in the newspaper reports of the case. The resultant bad publicity had its effect: sales had dropped because of public sympathy for the employee, and the firm had eventually filed for bankruptcy — all because of small-minded snobbery.

"It will be very difficult, Mma," he said cautiously. "If the original complaint is true, then there's not much you can do. If it is not true, then I don't see how you can prove it."

Mma Ramotswe appreciated his reservations, but they would not be enough to deter her from doing something for this woman — if she could. She could imagine nothing worse than being accused of something you did not do. There were few people in this world who would be able to do much for a person in that invidious position, but she felt that if anybody could do anything, it would be a private detective.

"I'm going to try to help her," she said. "We cannot leave her."

Mr. J.L.B. Matekoni took a moment to react. He had noticed the use of the word *we,* and he knew that she was right. If she did not take on this sort of matter, then there would be nowhere for an innocent woman — if she were innocent — to turn. That was clear enough, but there remained the question of payment. This did not sound like a paying proposition, and there was a limit to the number of cases Mma Ramotswe could take on without payment. Or was there?

"I don't suppose . . . ," he began, but stopped. She knew what he was going to ask.

"No, there isn't," she said. "Nothing was said about that."

Mr. J.L.B. Matekoni smiled. "That doesn't matter," he said, as cheerfully as he could. "The garage still makes a little bit of money and that will keep us going."

She nodded. "That's good of you, Rra."

"And all we need," he continued, "is to have enough money to clothe the children . . . and buy their schoolbooks and shoes and . . ." He waved a hand in the air. "And to eat, of course."

"Yes," said Mma Ramotswe. "And on that subject, Rra, I think this stew is about ready. Are you hungry this evening?"

She knew that she need hardly ask the question, but she did, out of politeness. Men were always hungry; they were hungry as boys, they were hungry as young men, they were hungry as mature men. It was part of being a man, and it was part of being a woman to observe this; not that women were never hungry — they were — but, thought Mma Ramotswe, they were hungry in a rather different way. One day, of course, these differences between men and women would disappear — there were signs of that beginning to happen already — but she did not think that day would come at all soon, and she was rather pleased that this was so. God had made things in a certain way, she felt; he had made Africa, he had made Botswana, he had made cattle — and then he made men and women; and he knew what he was doing and we should not be too quick to undo his work.

The reply to her question did not come in any words from Mr. J.L.B. Matekoni, to whom it had been addressed, but in chorus in two higher-pitched voices. "Yes, we are very hungry."

Puso and Motholeli had come into the room — Puso pushing his sister's wheelchair, both smiling broadly.

"Is homework finished?" asked Mma Ramotswe.

This was answered with a solemn nodding of heads.

"And done neatly?"

Again, nodding heads provided the answer.

Then Puso added, "I had to draw a map of the world, and then colour in the countries."

"He did it really well," observed Motholeli. "But he put Australia in the wrong place." She turned to her brother. "Australia is not at the top — it's down at the bottom, Puso."

"Then why don't they fall off?" asked Puso. "If Australia is at the bottom, then people would fall off. But they don't, do they?"

"It's because we're spinning round," said Motholeli.

Puso looked doubtful. "We're not spinning round." He looked to Mma Ramotswe for support. "We're not spinning around, are we, Mma?"

"I think we are, Puso, but gravity stops us

from falling off, I think. You know what gravity is?"

Puso looked knowing. "Everybody knows what gravity is," he said.

"And he made Botswana as big as South America," Motholeli continued.

Mma Ramotswe smiled. "I can see why he did that," she said. "Botswana's very important to us."

"See," said Puso, a note of triumph in his voice.

Both children looked pointedly at Mma Ramotswe. And then she said, "Dinner is ready now, I think."

She ladled stew onto four plates and placed these, one by one, on the table. Once seated herself, Mma Ramotswe lowered her head and said grace. "We give thanks for the food our country gives us, and we think of those who do not have what we have. We give thanks for Africa and for the good things that Africa gives its children. Amen."

"Amen," said Motholeli.

"Me too," said Puso.

CHAPTER FOUR:
IT IS VERY DIFFICULT
SOMETIMES TO KEEP UPRIGHT

"So," said Mma Makutsi the following morning; then, to make matters clearer, she added, "So, I see."

It was during their first tea break — the eight o'clock one, not to be confused with the mid-morning one, which took place as near to ten o'clock as was convenient — and rather than answer immediately, Mma Ramotswe took a sip from her cup of red bush tea. It was her favourite brew by far; she liked the taste of ordinary tea, but found that caffeine could make her heart race and had decided to switch to red bush instead. It refreshed without raising her heart rate and she had read that it had all sorts of other benefits. It was even good for the complexion, she had heard, and she had mentioned this fact to Mma Makutsi as tactfully as she could, knowing Mma Makutsi's sensitivity over her slightly difficult skin.

"I have read that red bush tea can be good for the skin," she said. "There are people who drink a cup of red bush tea and then, when what is left in the pot has cooled down enough, they apply it to their skin."

Mma Makutsi snorted. "They must look very foolish, Mma. Imagine picking up a teapot and pouring it over your head. Just imagine that. People would laugh at you if you did that."

"I'm not suggesting you pour it directly," said Mma Ramotswe.

Mma Makutsi's glasses had flashed a warning signal across the room. "Me, Mma? Are you saying *I* should pour this tea over myself?"

Mma Ramotswe was quick to reassure her. "I wasn't talking about *you,* Mma. All I was saying was that there are some people — and I don't know who these people are — but there are some people who use it for skin ailments. That is all. I do not know whether there is any evidence saying that red bush tea is good for the skin —"

"Is it on the packet?" interjected Mma Makutsi.

"No, there is nothing on the packet."

In Mma Makutsi's eyes, this settled the matter. "Well, there you are. If red bush tea really was good for people's skin, then they would put it on the packet. They would say something like: *This tea is very good for the skin too.* Or, *If you have problems with your skin, then this is the tea for you.*"

Mma Ramotswe had decided not to press the matter, but later that day she noticed Mma Makutsi surreptitiously dipping her finger into the teapot — the one reserved for red bush tea — and then dabbing it on her cheek. The message had been received; sometimes it was necessary to be indirect in getting through to Mma Makutsi, as there were defences to be negotiated. These defences could appear in unexpected places, not just when you were talking about Bobonong or some other already identified area of sensitivity, but at other times too. Yet once these had been circumvented, then Mma Makutsi would listen, and would take to heart what you had to say. Some people never did that, thought Mma Ramotswe — they either did not listen, or they listened and then dismissed what they heard. Mma Makutsi was not like that; she had her pride, but she knew when to put those feelings to one side.

But now, on that morning, there had come a slightly ominous "So" from the other side of the office, and that meant Mma Ramotswe should tread warily.

"So," Mma Makutsi repeated. "So you think that Mr. Polopetsi should go with you to see this woman, whatever her name is."

"Charity Mompoloki."

"Yes, this Charity Mompoloki. You think he should go, Mma?"

Mma Ramotswe took another sip of her tea. "Well, it's his case, in a way, Mma. Charity's sister went to see him about it."

Mma Makutsi shook her head. "No, Mma. She did not go to see him. She was talking to him at the school. It was just one colleague talking to another colleague — like me talking to you. She did not consult him as a detective, because Mr. Polopetsi is not a detective, is he? He is a chemistry teacher."

Mma Ramotswe let her finish.

"And there is a big difference," Mma Makutsi concluded, "between being a chemistry teacher and being a detective."

Mma Ramotswe made light of this. "Of course there is, Mma. You're absolutely right. I would not like to be taught chemistry by a detective."

"Nor ask a chemistry teacher to carry out an investigation," said Mma Makutsi. "It is the same thing, really."

Mma Ramotswe wondered whether to let this pass, but decided not. She had to defend Mr. Polopetsi, who had, after all,

66

once been a full-time employee of the agency, and who, for all his timidity, often came up with helpful suggestions. "No, Mma," she said. "I think that Mr. Polopetsi is a perfectly good detective." She sensed that Mma Makutsi was going to interrupt, so she raised her voice to complete what she had to say. "And in this case, he is the person who brought the matter to our attention, and so he should come with me to see this woman."

Mma Makutsi looked deflated. "I was only trying to help, Mma. I didn't want Mr. Polopetsi to be a burden to you."

Mma Ramotswe hesitated. For all her occasional bluster, Mma Makutsi was vulnerable. She had come from nothing — although Mma Ramotswe would never openly refer to Bobonong as nothing — and she had achieved so much; yet in the background there remained all the uncertainties and insecurities that everyone felt, no matter who they had become. Inside every one of us, thought Mma Ramotswe, there is the child we once were, the child that was unsure about the world and our place in it. And she understood something else, too: if she were in Mma Makutsi's shoes, she would be equally keen to be in on this rather unusual and intriguing enquiry, not to mention being eager to set right a manifest injustice. Who could resist the prospect of doing that? There was so much unfairness in the world that the chance of correcting just one small bit of it seemed attractive indeed.

She took a deep breath. "I have been thinking, Mma Makutsi," she said. "I think it would be very helpful if you came too."

Mma Makutsi was cautious. "Me as well, Mma? All three of us?"

Mma Ramotswe nodded. "Yes. Because I think you have a very good nose . . ." She paused as it occurred to her that this might not be the most tactful of expressions; Mma Makutsi's nose had slightly enlarged pores at the side — hardly noticeable, but there nonetheless, and for a moment Mma Ramotswe imagined her colleague applying red bush tea to her nose, dabbing it on gently with that lace-edged handkerchief she loved so much. "You have a very good nose for these things, Mma. When it comes to judging people . . ."

It had worked. Mma Makutsi, visibly enlarged by the praise, was smiling broadly. "Thank you, Mma. I would very much like to come and see this poor woman. Anything I can do to help."

"Then that's settled," said Mma Ramotswe. "Mr. Polopetsi will be coming in at nine — he's not teaching today. Then all three of us can go to that lady's house and speak to her about what happened."

"I think I shall be able to tell pretty quickly," said Mma Makutsi.

"Tell what, Mma?"

"I'll be able to tell whether she's rude. You can always see these things, Mma. A rude person trying to be polite is always polite in a rude sort of way. You can always tell."

Mma Ramotswe finished her tea. "Well, since we have a bit of time to wait until Mr. Polopetsi arrives, perhaps . . ."

Mma Makutsi foresaw the request. "A very good idea, Mma. I shall refill the kettle straightaway."

Charity Mompoloki's house was neatly kept. On each side of the front door was a planter made from a sawn-in-half oil drum, and in these grew two flowering aloe plants, their blossom the same colour as the red tin roof.

"A very pretty house," said Mr. Polopetsi, as they drove up in Mma Ramotswe's somewhat overloaded van. The size of the van was an issue: Mr. J.L.B. Matekoni had long ago installed an old-fashioned bench seat that would allow the seating of two passengers, along with the driver — or, rather, would allow that where all three were of moderate size. Mma Ramotswe, however, being traditionally built, required slightly more room than the average driver — in fact, a full eight inches more room, and this meant that she overflowed — in the nicest possible sense — into the space that would be occupied by the passenger in the middle. In this case that was Mr. Polopetsi, who, being the smallest, had been invited to sit between Mma Ramotswe and Mma Makutsi, in which position he was inevitably pushed over into the portion of seat occupied by Mma Makutsi.

As they approached Charity's house and Mma Ramotswe began to turn the steering wheel, Mr. Polopetsi found himself being pushed inexorably in Mma Makutsi's direction. The upper part of his leg was now pressed firmly against Mma Makutsi's own leg, which, rather than yielding, seemed to be being pushed back against the intrusion.

"Yes," said Mma Makutsi, looking sideways at her neighbour. "Yes, the house is certainly very pretty. But Mr. Polopetsi, would you mind moving over a bit — there is not much room in this van and we must all keep to our allotted place."

They were words of unmistakable censure, and Mr. Polopetsi, who at the same time admired and feared Mma Makutsi, struggled to find the right response. Eventually he said, "I am doing my best, Mma. It is very difficult sometimes to keep upright."

Mma Makutsi laughed. "Hah! That's a very good remark, Rra. Don't you think so, Mma Ramotswe? 'It is very difficult sometimes to keep upright.' That could be a motto for many people. How do you keep upright when there are so many bad things happening in the world?"

"And temptations too," added Mma Ramotswe, reaching for the handbrake. "There are many people who simply cannot keep upright when they are faced with a strong temptation."

"That's right," said Mma Makutsi. "It is particularly hard for men."

Mr. Polopetsi bit his lip. There certainly were many men who were weak, but surely that did not justify saying that all men yielded to temptation.

Mma Ramotswe switched off the ignition. "I do not think we should be too hard on men, Mma," she said.

"I am a man," began Mr. Polopetsi. "And I think . . ."

He did not finish; Mma Makutsi had dug

him in the ribs playfully. "So you are a man, Rra," she said, with a laugh. "Perhaps you can tell us why men give in to temptation so easily."

"Come now, Mma Makutsi," said Mma Ramotswe. "I know many women who give in to temptation just as readily as men. I know how I feel when Mma Potokwane offers me a slice of her fruit cake. Do I give in to temptation? I'm afraid I do, Mma. Every time."

"There you are," said Mr. Polopetsi mildly. "We are all weak — all of us."

"And what about you, Mma?" Mma Ramotswe continued. "I believe you find it hard to resist new shoes."

The question had not been posed in any hostile way, but the temperature in the car suddenly seemed to fall. "I need shoes," said Mma Makutsi reproachfully. "We all need shoes, Mma Ramotswe. Unless I'm missing something; unless there are people who are happy to walk about barefoot, as if they were out in the bush."

Trapped between the two women, Mr. Polopetsi did his best to bring the discussion on temptation to an end. "I think we should go in now. Somebody has come to the door. We cannot sit here and talk about temptation and such things while that lady is waiting for us."

They got out of the car and made their way up the short path that led to Charity Mompoloki's gate. Politeness required that they call out before entering, even if the householder was standing, as she was, at the front door.

"Ko! Ko!" called Mma Ramotswe. "We are here to see you, Mma — may we come in?"

Charity came out to meet them. She shook hands first with Mma Ramotswe, then with Mma Makutsi, and finally with Mr. Polopetsi, then gestured for them to follow her into the house. "It is cooler inside," she said. "I have a fan and I shall turn it on."

It suddenly occurred to Mma Ramotswe that this was a house in which the electricity bill might be an issue. "I'm sure that we shall be cool enough once we're inside," she said.

"A fan will make us even cooler," said Mma Makutsi.

Mma Ramotswe shot Mma Makutsi a glance. This was intercepted by Mr. Polopetsi, who immediately understood. "I would prefer not to have the fan on," he said. "Please do not bother, Mma."

Mma Makutsi frowned. "You like to sit

near the fan in the office," she pointed out. "You always turn it on."

Mma Ramotswe cleared her throat. "I'm hoping there'll be some more rain soon," she said. "I know we've had some good rains, but there's always room for more. The cattle will like it."

In Botswana, that was the most uncontroversial of comments. Nobody would disagree with any sentiment in favour of rain, nor could they express anything but sympathy for cattle. Cattle had no vote, nor the words to express a view, but their feelings ranked above just about everything else in the country.

"I will give you water," said Charity. "You must be thirsty."

Again this was the practice of politeness. In a hot country, not to offer water would be impolite.

As she raised her glass of water to her lips, Mma Ramotswe glanced at the room into which they had been led. It was a combined kitchen and living room, furnished simply, but comfortably. While there was no sign of luxury, it was clean and tidy: it was not the room of one who had no resources at all — poverty, as everybody knew, had a very recognisable smell.

Mma Ramotswe spoke first. "I should

explain who we are, Mma," she began. "I am Mma Ramotswe and this is Mma Makutsi, and this is Mr. Polopetsi."

Charity nodded. "I know who you are, Mma. My sister told me that you would be coming."

"I see," said Mma Ramotswe.

"And I am very grateful to you," Charity continued. "This thing that happened to me is the worst thing I have ever experienced in my life — ever." She paused, watching the effect of her words on her visitors. Then she continued, "That is why I am so glad that you'll be able to get my job back."

Mma Ramotswe exchanged a glance with Mma Makutsi.

"Excuse me, Mma," said Mma Makutsi, turning to face Charity. "We cannot guarantee that, Mma. At the moment we have no idea whether or not we'll be successful."

Charity's face fell. "But I heard that you always manage to sort things out," she said. "That is why you're number one — the No. 1 Ladies' Detective Agency. They told me that you have never failed."

Mma Ramotswe put down her glass of water. "I wish that were true, Mma," she said. "But we are only human, and there have been many times when we have not been able to find out what we needed to find out."

Charity appeared to interpret this as modesty. "Oh, I'm sure that's not true. I mean, what you say is not true; what other people say *is* true."

Mma Ramotswe shook her head vigorously. "No, Mma, what I said about what they said — that's true, I'm afraid. What *they* said is not true, even if it's very kind of them to say it."

Mr. Polopetsi, who had been silent up to this point, now intervened. "Mma Ramotswe's right," he said, raising a finger to emphasise his point. "She's right about being wrong."

Charity looked at him blankly. "I didn't say anybody was wrong, Rra."

"No," replied Mr. Polopetsi. "You did not say that, Mma. I did not say that you said it. I said that Mma Ramotswe was right in saying that sometimes she gets things wrong."

This was too much for Mma Makutsi. "Mr. Polopetsi, I don't want to say that *you're* wrong, but I think that you are wrong here. Mma Ramotswe very seldom gets things wrong." She fixed him with a challenging stare. "I should know, Rra. I have worked with Mma Ramotswe since the very beginning, since the first day. I have been there at her side in all these investigations, right from the beginning."

Mr. Polopetsi looked confused. "But I thought you were just the secretary in those days."

Even if he had tried, Mr. Polopetsi could not have chosen a more dangerous form of wording. Mma Makutsi stiffened, and her glasses caught the light from the room's only window. "Just . . . ," she muttered. "*Just* the secretary . . ."

Mma Ramotswe took matters in hand. "Let's not get tied up with something that isn't really at all important. Let's not bother about whether the No. 1 Ladies' Detective Agency does this thing or that thing." She paused, giving Mma Makutsi a discouraging look. Then, turning back to Charity, she said, "The point is this, Mma: we shall do our best to help you, but you must understand that we cannot work miracles. Detective work is not like that — it is the slow uncovering of information; it is talking to people; it is thinking about the meaning of what you know — and what you don't know. It is all of those things, Mma."

Mr. Polopetsi agreed. "That is what it is," he reassured Charity. "Very slow — like a tortoise."

Charity understood. "I can imagine that. Small facts, big facts; looking here, looking there; listening to what the wind is saying."

Mma Ramotswe clapped her hands together. "Oh, Mma!" she exclaimed. "That is a very good way of putting it. 'Listening to what the wind is saying.' Yes! That is just what you have to do."

Not to be outdone, Mma Makutsi revealed that this was what she had always thought. "The wind hears everything," she said.

"That's true," said Mma Ramotswe, and then, to Charity, "But now, Mma, we need to know what happened."

Charity sighed. "I lost my job. I had worked in that place for over six years, Mma. I started just after my boys were born."

Mma Ramotswe had seen the signs of children; the crayon drawing pinned to the wall — a picture of that universal childhood vision: a house, a tree, a smiling sun above. It was how they saw the world, she thought; it was how we wanted the world to be, what we wanted of it, at whatever stage in life we were at. "You have two boys, I hear, Mma," she said. "I hear they are twins."

Charity smiled with pleasure. "Two little boys. They are with their grandmother for a few days. She lives out at Mochudi."

The mention of Mochudi brought an exclamation of surprise from Mma Ramotswe. "That is my village, Mma. That is where I come from."

"My mother is from there, too, Mma. She was a nurse in the hospital when it was the Dutch Reformed place. She worked with Dr. Moffat."

"I know him," said Mma Ramotswe. "I sometimes have tea with his wife, now that they are living in Gaborone." She paused. "I do not think I've met your mother. There are so many people in Mochudi these days."

"Everywhere is larger today," contributed Mma Makutsi.

Charity turned to her. "Are you from Mochudi too, Mma?"

"Bobonong," Mma Makutsi replied.

"That is a very nice place," said Charity.

No encomium could have been better chosen. "Yes," said Mma Makutsi, "Bobonong is a good place."

"So," said Mma Ramotswe, steering the conversation back to Charity's problem. "So, you worked there for six years and then this thing happened."

Charity closed her eyes briefly, as if reliving a painful moment, and then opened them to look directly at Mma Ramotswe. "I've never been rude to customers," she said quietly. "I have never, ever spoken to them sharply. I've always, always tried to give them the best possible service. That is what I am like, Mma Ramotswe. That is the way I have done the work that God called me to do. When God called me to sell office furniture, I said to myself, 'I shall do this to the best of my ability.' That is what I said, Mma, and I hope that you believe me when I tell you that is what I did."

Mma Ramotswe assured her that she believed every word she had said. That led to the conclusion that somebody had lied.

"The customer lied," said Charity. "That is the only possibility."

"Yes," said Mma Makutsi.

Mr. Polopetsi, who had been staring out of the window while Charity spoke, now turned round. "No," he said. "I don't think so."

Mma Makutsi looked at him accusingly. "I don't think you're getting it, Rra. If Mma Charity said that she wasn't rude — and we know that she's telling the truth — then it must have been the customer who lied."

Mr. Polopetsi shook his head. "No, Mma. There is another possibility."

Mma Makutsi smiled mockingly. "I don't think so, Rra. I think —"

Mr. Polopetsi, who rarely, if ever, interrupted anybody, now cut Mma Makutsi short. "The employer might be lying, Mma Makutsi. Have you thought of that? The boss may have made the whole story up as an excuse to get rid of Mma Charity."

Mma Ramotswe, who had of course already considered this possibility, turned to Charity and asked her how she had got on with her boss during those six years.

"There were no problems," said Charity. "My boss never had any reason to be dissatisfied with my work. I was given a bonus every year — my sales record, you see, was very good. I could sell office furniture to . . . to people who didn't even have an office. That's what they said about me, Mma: I'm not making that up."

"Then why would he tell those lies about you?" asked Mr. Polopetsi.

Mma Makutsi was still smarting from having been contradicted — convincingly — by Mr. Polopetsi. "We don't know that he told lies, Rra," she admonished. "There is no proof of that."

Mr. Polopetsi looked to Mma Ramotswe for support. He himself was surprised that he had openly disagreed with Mma Makutsi, and he had no stomach for further argument with her.

"You are both right," said Mma Ramotswe

tactfully. "We don't know who's telling the truth here." She stopped, and then corrected herself quickly. "Except Mma Charity, of course. She is obviously telling the truth."

"Whoever is not telling the truth," said Mr. Polopetsi, "the end result is the same, isn't it? This poor lady has lost her job although she did not deserve to lose it."

"What will you do now, Mma?" asked Mma Ramotswe. "Is there another job you can do until this is all settled?"

Charity made a gesture of helplessness. "What can I do, Mma? You know how difficult it is to get jobs. I'm forty-six, and that is not an easy age if you want to get a new job. People say, 'Oh, I see you're forty-six, Mma, and there are many twenty-year-olds after this job. I hope you'll understand, Mma.' "

This struck a chord with Mr. Polopetsi. "It is very unfair," he said. "I encountered the same thing when I was looking for a job. They never told me to my face, but I knew that they wanted a much younger person."

"Soon the whole world will be run by teenagers," said Mma Makutsi. "We will be allowed to work, but only if the teenagers are in control. We shall all be working for the teenagers."

Mma Ramotswe laughed. "We think they should be working for us, do we?"

Mma Makutsi saw nothing amusing in that. "But of course, Mma. We know so much better than they do."

Mma Ramotswe raised, as delicately as she could, the issue of money. There were so many people who seemed to survive even if they had no job; somehow they made do, supported by friends and family, caught in the invisible nets that people create for one another. Was that how it would be with Charity? "It will be hard for you," she said. "Without a job, will you be able to —"

Charity interrupted her. "To get by? I have some savings, Mma. It's not very much, but it will keep me going for a few months."

Mma Ramotswe lowered her eyes. After that, she would have to go back to the grandmother, as people always did when they reached the end of the road.

"This house?" asked Mma Makutsi. "Do you own it, Mma, or do you pay rent?"

"Rent," replied Charity. "But the man who owns it is a good man. He knows what has happened and he will not be unkind to me."

"But he is a landlord," muttered Mma Makutsi. "And eventually landlords have to get rent."

Charity looked at her reproachfully. "I know that, Mma. Don't think I haven't thought of that."

Mma Ramotswe asked about the client who was said to have complained.

"He is the head of a firm of accountants," she said. "He has big offices in Lobatse and Francistown, as well as Gaborone. Then he has smaller offices in many other towns. He is up at Maun. He is over in Ghanzi. He is a very successful accountant, and all his furniture comes from our . . . from their depot here in Gaborone."

"So he is a rich man?" asked Mma Makutsi.

"Yes, Mma, he is a rich man."

"So he would have been unlikely to lie about something like this," said Mma Makutsi. "I can see no reason why he should. If you're rich you don't have to get mixed up in things like this."

"But you'll be very good at complaining," interjected Mr. Polopetsi. "Rich people like to complain about small things. If something is not quite right, then a rich person may make a very big fuss. You'd think the skies were falling."

Mma Ramotswe was interested to find out whether Charity had seen this man since the incident was said to have taken place. She had not. "I was dismissed the day afterwards," said Charity. "So if he has come in, then I would not have been there."

"His name?" asked Mma Ramotswe.

"Mpho. George Mpho."

Mma Ramotswe nodded. She had seen the name before, but had never met him. He had his picture in the newspapers from time to time: George Mpho presenting the prizes; George Mpho standing outside his new office in Francistown. He was not unknown.

"Did they say what you were meant to have done?" asked Mma Makutsi.

"They said I had shouted at him. They said I had told him to go and build a desk himself if he didn't like what was on offer." She stared at Mma Ramotswe. "That would have been very rude, Mma."

Mma Makutsi laughed. "That's very ridiculous. Who would say a thing like that?"

"Well, they said that I did," muttered Charity.

Mr. Polopetsi was shaking his head. "Sometimes these things boil down to the word of one person against another."

This brought agreement from Charity. "And what is my word worth, Rra? How much is it worth when you put it beside the word of somebody like Mr. George Mpho?"

"The value of a person's word doesn't depend on who they are," said Mma Ramotswe evenly.

"No," said Mr. Polopetsi. "Mma Ramotswe is right. A very rich man can tell very big lies. A very poor man can tell only the truth. It all depends on what's inside somebody."

Mma Makutsi was not convinced. "That's a nice thought, Rra, but I'm not sure that it's true. People listen to those who are rich and powerful. They nod their heads all the time. They say, 'Oh yes, that is quite true.' That is what people are like."

It was clear from Charity's defeated expression that this was how she saw the matter. Her earlier optimism that Mma Ramotswe could bring about the rectification she desired seemed to have entirely evaporated. "I am finished," she said.

"Nothing is finished until it is finished," muttered Mr. Polopetsi.

They all looked at him. Then Mma Ramotswe brought the visit to an end. "Mr. Polopetsi is right, Mma," she said to Charity. "We shall go now, but we shall be thinking very hard. And we will get in touch with you and tell you if we have come up with anything."

"You're very kind," said Charity. "But my heart is very cold now."

"That is why we are going to think so hard," said Mr. Polopetsi.

As they left the house, Mma Ramotswe turned to Charity and asked her whether she had enemies. The question seemed to surprise her. "I don't think so, Mma. None that I know of, at least." She paused, and then appeared to remember something. "There is one person, though, who dislikes me. I wouldn't want to call her an enemy, but perhaps that's what she is."

"And who is that person, Mma?" asked Mma Ramotswe.

"She is called Violet Sephotho," answered Charity.

Mma Makutsi gave what sounded like a cry of triumph. "Her!"

"You know her, Mma?" asked Charity.

"Oh, I know her only too well," said Mma Makutsi. "So docs Mma Ramotswe. And even Mr. Polopetsi here knows her, I think."

"I met her a long time ago," said Charity. "It was when I was studying at the Botswana Secretarial College."

This brought forth another cry from Mma Makutsi. "The Botswana Secretarial College? You were at the Botswana Secretarial College?"

"Yes. I was there at the same time that Violet Sephotho was."

Mma Makutsi's eyes narrowed. "I thought I'd seen you somewhere. I thought your face was familiar, Mma."

Mma Ramotswe decided to give an explanation: "Mma Makutsi is a graduate of that college, Mma. You two must have been there at the same time. She . . ." She hesitated, but decided to continue. "She graduated with ninety-seven per cent in the final examinations."

This proved to be the key to memory. "Ninety-seven per cent! So, you're that Grace . . . that Grace . . ."

Mma Makutsi gave the necessary nudge. "Makutsi."

"Of course," said Charity. "You used to sit in the front. I sat at the back."

"There were many ladies there," said Mma Makutsi. "I don't think we got to know one another very well."

"Well, well," said Charity. "I'm sorry that I didn't recognise you, Mma."

Mma Makutsi answered warmly. "That doesn't matter, Mma. Remember Mma Moswaane? Remember her? The shorthand teacher?"

Charity burst out laughing. "How can I forget?"

"And Mma Mamelodi, who did that funny thing with her hair? She taught us accounts."

"Of course. Poor lady." Charity shook her head at the memory. Then her expression changed, and she was serious once again. "Violet cheated, you know."

"That doesn't surprise me," said Mma Makutsi. "Not that it did her much good. Her final mark was very low, you know — barely fifty per cent."

"She took one of my essays and copied it," said Charity. "I was very annoyed when I discovered this and I gave her a piece of my mind. She was furious and she threatened me if I did anything about it. I think she couldn't stand the idea that I knew she was a cheat. That's what turned her against me."

"That's because she felt guilty," said Mma Ramotswe.

"She has hated me ever since," said Charity. "If I see her in the street, she looks the other way. She cuts me dead. It's as if I didn't exist."

"I know how you must feel," said Mma Makutsi. "She does that to me too."

"Well," said Mma Ramotswe. "This is an extraordinary coincidence. We shall have to think about it some more." She looked at her watch. "But not now, I think. Later."

In the van on the way back to the office, Mma Makutsi reflected on their meeting. "One thing is certain," she said. "We have to help that poor lady."

"Do you think that Violet has anything to do with it?" asked Mr. Polopetsi.

"I'm not sure," said Mma Ramotswe.

"Oh, I'm certain she has," said Mma Makutsi.

Mma Ramotswe thought that this might be loyalty speaking — the two graduates of the Botswana Secretarial College had embraced one another with particular warmth when she, Mma Makutsi, and Mr. Polopetsi had finally left. But emotions and detective work did not always mix; there was something about that in Clovis Andersen's *The Principles of Private Detection.* What had he said? Emotions have the same effect as a magnet has on a compass . . . Yes, that was it. The needle swings around in a confusing way and you lose direction. Yes, exactly. Clovis Andersen had such a way with words — and he was usually, if not always, absolutely correct.

CHAPTER FIVE:
GOOD DAY, MMA CHARITY

Mma Ramotswe drove up to Mochudi by
the old road, because that was the road she
had used with her father. They had travelled
between Mochudi and Gaborone, a journey
of just over twenty miles, in Obed Ramotswe's old truck — a vehicle which, for all
its rattles and tendency to belch smoke,
never let them down. It was, people said, a
travelling pharmacy, with its cartons of
cattle remedies — drenches and pills — that
he would deliver to the cattle posts on the
outer reaches of the Kalahari. In the back,
among pliers and screwdrivers and fencing
tools, there were hessian sacks and salt licks
still in their packaging. It was a working
vehicle — the transport of a man whose
business was cattle.

She missed him so — still, after all these
years, there was so much she wanted to ask
him. She wanted to talk about Botswana in
the old days, a long time ago — even before

Seretse Khama took over; she wanted to know what it had been like to grow up in Mochudi when there was only one shop and one butchery. She wanted to know where her grandmother came from and what had happened to her grandfather's cattle; he was said to have owned the finest bull in Botswana — so great a bull that there had even been talk of raising a statue to it when it died, the patriarch of several hundred cattle families, its progeny spoken about even over the border in Mafeking. There was so much she would have liked to have found out, but, as was the case with so many questions, they are only asked when it is too late and they can no longer be answered.

On this road, driving by herself in her white van, she sometimes imagined conversations between her and her father. She could almost hear his voice, his deep, considered tones. She could hear him address her, as he often did, as "my Precious." And that voice, she thought, came from somewhere very far away, some place that was Botswana but not quite Botswana; a place beyond the hills, behind the clouds, where the late people of Botswana kept watch over those who were not yet late.

The old road went past the graveyard where her parents were buried. She had never known her mother, having been an infant when she died, but she visited the grave once a year and attended to whatever needed to be done. And wept. It was possible, she thought, that one wept more for those one did not know than for those one did, because there was more to regret; to lose somebody without the chance of ever showing love was a heavy loss indeed.

Today, though, she had no time to stop at the graveyard; she would make that trip the following week, or the week after that. A week or two is nothing to the dead, but to those busy with running an office and a home it was time not easily spared. Now she had to get to Mochudi in time for a meeting at the school of those who had attended it in the past and who would be prepared to support a plan for a new school library. It was an ambitious project, and although the government was giving money, it was up to the local community — and past students of the school — to raise the shortfall. Along with many others, Mma Ramotswe had been invited to a meeting at which the library plans would be revealed; then, she was sure, they would be asked to make a contribution. She was happy to do that, even if she could not afford to give a great deal, and she had ideas, too, about money-making schemes. There could be a fashion show in Gaborone, she thought, with the proceeds going to the library project. Mma Ramotswe did not normally attend fashion shows, but this one, she thought, would be special. It would be a fashion show for traditionally built ladies, in which all the outfits would be modelled by ladies like that and would be for people exactly like them. So there would be none of those skinny, stick-like models who tripped along the fashion catwalks in impossibly skimpy frocks; there would be, rather, comfortably padded ladies in loose-fitting dresses made of good, solid material.

This traditionally built fashion show would be a great success, as there were many ladies in Gaborone and its immediate surrounds who would recognise themselves in all this. They would flock to the show and make donations with a generosity that matched the generosity of their figures. Mma Ramotswe was already making a mental list of such ladies, starting with Mma Potokwane, who was traditionally built however you looked at it. Mma Potokwane tended not to spend money on herself, and was mostly content with dresses that she had worn for a very long time, often concealing them, anyway, behind a pink-and-white quilted housecoat that she wore when doing her rounds of the Orphan Farm. But her husband could be worked upon, and persuaded to treat her to a new outfit from the traditionally built fashion show.

Mma Ramotswe drove directly to the school. It was school holiday time, so there were no children around, other than a few who had been brought by mothers attending the meeting. There was a large crowd assembled in the school hall — almost one hundred people — and the hubbub of conversation reached the tree under which Mma Ramotswe parked her van. The pitch of this increased as she approached the hall, and once she was inside it became a roar of chatter and laughter. Mma Ramotswe immediately understood why: this may have been a school meeting but it was also a reunion of old friends, and people had a great deal of catching up to do. What happened to him? What happened to her? Where are you living now? There were so many questions to be asked and answered that it seemed unlikely there would be time for the real business of the gathering.

But there was, and this business was conducted with firmness and dispatch by the principal. She explained the plans, and showed a small cardboard model of the new library. There were many suggestions as to improvements: the addition of a window here and a door there, the insertion of an extra basin for the children to wash their hands before they handled the books — "An excellent, practical suggestion," said the principal — and then several views were expressed as to the colour of the walls, the roof, and the shelving. Mma Ramotswe's own suggestion — that there should be a fashion show for the traditionally built — was received with acclaim, and noted down by the school secretary. "And I take it, Mma Ramotswe," said the principal, "that you will be happy to chair the committee for this event?" There were murmurs of agreement, and before Mma Ramotswe had the chance to demur, her agreement was minuted.

Mma Ramotswe returned to her van. She had expected the meeting to last longer and had intended to go straight back home rather than to call in at the office. Now she found herself with several hours on her hands; she could make good use of this in Mochudi, where there were numerous people she could visit — elderly relatives, for instance, whom she liked to see from time to time; her cousin, who ran a small grocery store on the edge of the village; her blind great-aunt who lived with another set of cousins behind the hill and who always welcomed visits from relatives. But then she remembered Charity had mentioned that her mother still lived in Mochudi, or just outside; there would be time to visit her if she could find out where she lived.

She knew exactly what to do. The woman who ran the post office in Mochudi knew everybody, and where they lived. Mma Ramotswe had obtained information from her before, and it had always been reliable; if anybody could direct her to Charity's mother, it was Mma Mangole. And that was how it turned out: Mma Mangole knew exactly where the old lady lived, and assured her that she would be in. "Mma Lentswe hasn't left her house for years," she said. "She sits there reading all the papers — ow! That lady reads and reads — and keeps a note of everything. Everything."

Mma Ramotswe had no specific questions to ask of Charity's mother; what she wanted to do was to get to know the family a bit better. At the heart of Charity's case — in as much as she had a case — was the assertion that she simply would not have done what she was alleged to have done. Mma Ramotswe had to be satisfied about that, as the worst thing for any exponent of a cause is to find out that the cause is flawed; that the innocent are, in fact, guilty as charged. Mma Makutsi was convinced that Charity was in the right, but Mma Ramotswe could see where that conviction came from. That was a matter of a shared attachment to the Botswana Secretarial College and a shared enemy in the shape of Violet Sephotho. Mma Ramotswe wanted to be sure herself; she was tending to the view that Charity was, as she claimed, the wronged party, but she wanted to know a bit more, just to be sure.

She found the house without difficulty. Mma Mangole had directed her past the My Darling Fresh Produce Store, past the large new house with a green roof, to the point where the tarred road stopped and became, like a river reaching a confluence, three separate, meandering tracks. The right-hand track was the one to take, past a clump of thorn bushes stripped bare on the lower branches by goats, and then skirting a small gully, along the side of a *donga* frequented by herd boys ignoring their sheep. This eventually led to a cluster of traditional houses, round and thatched, each ringed with a neatly kept *lelapa,* the courtyard marked out by low, mud-constructed walls.

"*Dumela,* Mma Charity," said Mma Ramotswe. *Good day, Mma Charity* — Mother of Charity; this was a traditional term of address in which a woman's name was linked with her firstborn.

The elderly woman to whom she had directed this greeting had been sweeping the yard, and looked up with surprise at her unexpected visitor.

Mma Lentswe peered at Mma Ramotswe through a pair of round tortoiseshell glasses, obviously trying to retrieve a name from memory. "*Dumela,* Mma," came the clearly spoken reply. "You are well, I hope."

Mma Ramotswe completed the formal greetings, and then went on to say, "You do not know me, Mma, but I am Precious Ramotswe . . ."

She did not get any further. "Oh, then I know who you are, Mma. You are the daughter of Ramotswe — I'm sorry, I cannot remember his name, and he is late . . ."

"Obed Ramotswe. Yes, he was my father, Mma."

Mma Lentswe invited her through the opening at the front of the *lelapa.* "You must come in, Mma, and I shall make some tea. On a hot afternoon like this, it is best to drink tea, I think."

Mma Ramotswe laughed. "That is what I

always say, Mma. Tea is very important in this weather."

"I have electricity here," said Mma Lentswe. "You wouldn't think it, would you, as we are just outside the village boundary. But we have it now, Mma, and so I can see much better at night and I can boil a kettle."

"That's very good, Mma."

"When I think of what this country has done," continued Mma Lentswe, "I feel very proud. All these things we have made for ourselves. We've built a whole country from the ground up."

"That is true, Mma."

Mma Ramotswe was shown to a wooden chair that had been placed under an acacia tree in the yard. Sitting here while Mma Lentswe made tea in the kitchen behind the house, Mma Ramotswe looked up into the boughs of the tree. There was an air of peace about the place that took her back to her childhood in Mochudi. That had been a period of quiet, of calm; there had been no traffic noise then, no hurry to do anything very much — just the sound of birdsong and cicadas and the lowing of cattle coming in from the lands. This was the heart of her country — the very heart.

Mma Lentswe returned with the teapot and two old-fashioned white enamel mugs.

"I was a teacher, Mma," she said. "Not here in Mochudi, but down in Lobatse, where my husband worked. He is late, like so many people these days. He worked for the Meat Commission. I taught in a school there."

Mma Ramotswe mentioned the name of friends in Lobatse, and Mma Lentswe nodded; she knew them, although she had lost touch with them since she had moved back to Mochudi. For a few moments there was silence. It would have been impolite for Mma Lentswe to ask Mma Ramotswe the purpose of her visit; in the old Botswana one did not have to have a reason to visit others, even strangers.

"I have met Charity," said Mma Ramotswe.

Mma Lentswe looked at her over the top of her spectacles. "You have heard what has happened?"

Mma Ramotswe nodded. "It is very sad. She told me she had worked there for —"

"For six years," interjected Mma Lentswe. "And then this business with a customer."

"It is very unfortunate," said Mma Ramotswe. "And unfair too, since she did not say what they said she said."

Mma Lentswe frowned. "Are you sure about that, Mma?"

"Charity told me she didn't say that."

Mma Lentswe looked into her teacup. "Children say these things. They never admit they did anything. I was a teacher, Mma — I know that."

Mma Ramotswe was puzzled. What had this to do with children?

"Of course she isn't a child," continued the older woman. "But when you are the mother of somebody, then she will always be your child. That is just the way it is, Mma."

"I see."

"My daughter is a headstrong woman," said Mma Lentswe. "For most of the time she is very easy — a very polite person — and then suddenly, just like that, she can say something very rude. It does not happen very often, but it happens."

Mma Ramotswe sat quite still. This was not what she had expected to hear, and she felt dismayed. Now she knew that it had happened. Charity had done what she had been accused of doing — her own mother, who should know her better than anybody else, had just confirmed it.

"Oh well," said Mma Ramotswe. "It is a great pity."

"Yes, it's a great pity, but I wasn't really surprised, Mma. I think that they are being very harsh in dismissing her just for one bit of bad behaviour, but I suppose that is the way things are these days. The world is a very strict place now." She looked out over the bush beyond the *lelapa* wall. "You know, Mma Ramotswe, in the school that I taught in down in Lobatse, there was a teacher who was actually spitting at the children. Can you believe that? If she got cross with a badly behaved child, she would spit at them. And do you know, when there was a complaint made about this, they gave her another chance. She did not lose her job, but was given a chance to mend her ways."

"That was kind."

"Yes, but do you know what happened? A few months later this teacher had a big row with the principal over something or other, and do you know what she did? She spat at the principal." Mma Lentswe grinned. "And that was the end of her teaching career."

Mma Ramotswe laughed. "That lady should never have been a teacher, Mma."

"No. She found another job. She became a policewoman. She did very well in the police, I think. Last time I read about her in the papers, I saw that she was in charge of one of the bigger police stations. I hope that she was not spitting on the criminals."

Mma Ramotswe laughed again. "I hear that you read the papers, Mma."

Mma Lentswe nodded. "I keep scrap-books. There is nothing else to do here. I keep scrapbooks of any news about people from Mochudi and Lobatse too. The two places I have lived in for a long time." She paused, as if she had remembered some-thing. "There was a picture of your father in one of the papers a long time ago. I think it was something to do with an agricultural show. He won something for one of his bulls."

Mma Ramotswe remembered the news item. It had been cut from the paper and framed. Somehow it had been lost in the intervening years.

"And there was another mention of a Ramotswe," continued Mma Lentswe. "A couple of years ago, I think."

"A picture of my father?"

"No. Not your father. Some lady."

"Of me?" asked Mma Ramotswe. "When I started the agency they had an article about it."

"No, not you, Mma; of some other lady. It will be in my scrapbook."

Mma Ramotswe was puzzled. Her name was an unusual one, and she thought that she knew of everybody called Ramotswe. They were cousins, some close, some dis-tant, but they did not number more than seven. And of those seven, five were men and two were women. So this other Ramotswe would have to be either Bontle Ramotswe or Gladys Ramotswe, both of whom now lived up in Francistown where they were married to two brothers. That was the sort of thing that could end up as a news item, so perhaps that was it. "Sisters marry brothers" was exactly the sort of thing that the press liked to report on a day when there was little or no other news.

"Could you show me this thing, Mma?" she asked.

"Of course," said Mma Lentswe. "I shall fetch it, Mma, while you pour yourself more tea."

Chapter Six:
My Goodness, Mma,
Look at the Names

Mma Ramotswe observed speed limits for two reasons. One of these was that she believed that laws were there to be obeyed, and that if everybody drove as fast as they liked there would be mayhem on the roads. That was a good, sound reason, and one that was fully endorsed by Mr. J.L.B. Matekoni if not by Charlie, for whom a speed limit tended to be an irritant. "They don't really mean it," he said. "They know you can't drive that slowly all the time. The Government knows that."

Her second reason for sticking to the speed limit was more prosaic. Even had Mma Ramotswe wanted to drive faster, her tiny white van, with its underpowered engine, was incapable of going any faster than a sedate twenty-eight miles an hour, which fell comfortably below the limit prescribed for most roads in Botswana. And that was on a flat road and with a reasonable tail-wind. Hills and head-winds were another matter altogether, and brought the van's speed down even further; so much so, in fact, that bicycles, and on one occasion even a donkey, could overtake Mma Ramotswe. She did not mind this, of course. "I have no desire to drive past anybody," she once said to Mma Potokwane. "What does it matter if you take two hours to do a journey that everybody else takes one hour to do? What does it matter, Mma?"

And Mma Potokwane had agreed. "You're quite right, Mma Ramotswe. Where's the rush? The places we're going to will still be there when we arrive. I don't see any reason to hurry."

This sort of backing up from Mma Potokwane pleased Mma Ramotswe greatly. The two women had always seen the world in much the same way, and it was encouraging to hear that one's views were supported, more or less unconditionally, by at least one other person. There were minor differences of approach, of course: Mma Potokwane had a tendency to take advantage of some people — notably Mr. J.L.B. Matekoni, whom she regularly inveigled into doing any repairs that the Orphan Farm needed — but if this was a fault, it was a very minor one, and she always acted with the welfare of the children in mind. When it came to the real issues, to questions of value, to questions of right and wrong, then she and Mma Ramotswe were always in complete agreement. That we should share with other people — yes, of course we should; that we should think about how other people are feeling — again yes, of course we should do that; that men should let ladies sit down if there are not enough chairs to go round and that they, the men, should stand — well, who would disagree with that? To the surprise of both Mma Ramotswe and Mma Potokwane, it appeared that there were people who felt that this was an old-fashioned way of behaving and that if a man reached the chair first he should sit down, even if a woman ended up standing. These people argued that offering a lady a chair implied that she was weak and that men and women should be treated differently. Well, said both Mma Ramotswe and Mma Potokwane, of course women should be treated differently. Of course they should be treated with respect and consideration and given the credit for all the hard work they did in the home, looking after children (and men), and in the workplace too. Offering a lady a chair was one way of showing that this work was appreciated, and that strength and brute force — at which men generally tended to excel — was not the only thing that counted. Respect for ladies *tamed* men, and there were many men who were sorely in need of taming; that was well known, said Mma Ramotswe.

But now, heading back into Gaborone after her visit to Charity's mother, Mma Ramotswe was eager to get back to the office as soon as she possibly could. She wanted more than anything else to have a word with Mma Makutsi and, if she could prise him away from his car repairs, Mr. J.L.B. Matekoni. There were two things she was eager to talk to them about: she wanted to tell Mma Makutsi about what Charity's mother had said about her daughter suffering from outbursts, and she wanted to talk to Mr. J.L.B. Matekoni about what she had seen in the somewhat tattered scrapbook produced by the elderly woman. The cutting she had been given from that was safely tucked in the pocket of her blouse, ready to be shown and discussed.

So it was with her foot pressed firmly down on the accelerator that she made the return journey into Gaborone. The traffic was light, and although she never exceeded twenty-five miles an hour, she found herself driving up to the shared premises of the No.

1 Ladies' Detective Agency and Tlokweng Road Speedy Motors well before it was time for either of the businesses to close for the day.

She found Mr. J.L.B. Matekoni under a car parked over the inspection pit. The light from his lamp, like the torch of a speluncean explorer, moved about in the darkness, at one point illuminating the grinning face of Charlie, who was in the pit with him.

"No, Charlie," she heard him say, "that is nothing to do with the brakes. It's . . ." She did not hear the rest because Charlie had started to sing a few bars of a popular song of the time.

"I am up here, Rra," she called out. "I don't want to disturb you in the middle of something important, but I need to talk to you."

The torch beam flashed about and shortly thereafter Mr. J.L.B. Matekoni emerged from the inspection pit. He wiped his hands on the flanks of his overalls, and looked apologetically at Mma Ramotswe. "I don't have a cloth, Mma. I try to use a cloth."

"Don't worry about that, Rra," she reassured him. "There is so much grease on your working clothes that it makes no real difference."

He took this as an invitation to wipe his

hands again. As he did so, he looked at her quizzically. "Has something happened?" he asked.

She nodded. "Can we go into my office, Rra. I want to show you something."

Mma Makutsi was busy shuffling papers when they entered the office. She had not expected Mma Ramotswe back, and letters and other documents were strewn about both desks — hers and Mma Ramotswe's.

"I am catching up on my filing," said Mma Makutsi. "I'm making very good progress."

"Is there any chance of tea?" asked Mr. J.L.B. Matekoni. "I've been on the go since eight this morning and I've had no lunch."

Mma Makutsi immediately switched on the electric kettle and began to prepare the two teapots — one for ordinary tea and one for Mma Ramotswe's special red bush tea. As she did this, Mma Ramotswe discreetly pushed some of the papers to the side of her desk. Then she took the newspaper cutting from her pocket, unfolded it, and laid it down on the desk.

"Read that, Rra," she said. "And look at the photograph."

Mr. J.L.B Matekoni extracted his reading glasses from his chest pocket and began to examine the newspaper cutting. He still moved his lips slightly when he read — an ancient habit that gave an impression of close, considered attention.

"Three local women win an award for their performance in their nursing exams," he read aloud. "Lobatse can be proud of these three ladies whose nursing prowess has been widely recognised."

He looked up at Mma Ramotswe. "They are all operating theatre nurses, Mma. They're the ones who help with the operations, aren't they? Sewing things up, removing some of the blood, and so on? That's what a nurse like that does, isn't it?"

"Yes, it is, Rra," she replied.

From the other side of the office, Mma Makutsi had a contribution to make. "I read in a magazine somewhere that these nurses sometimes know more about operations than many junior doctors. There was a case where somebody was having an operation and the doctor had to go out to the bathroom. He couldn't wait, and so he had to go out."

"That can happen sometimes," said Mr. J.L.B. Matekoni.

"Yes," continued Mma Makutsi. "So this doctor went out, but when he came back he discovered that the nurse had completed the operation in his absence — and had done it very well."

Mr. J.L.B. Matekoni whistled. "That is very worrying." He frowned. "But I don't suppose the patient knew anything about it. And as long as it was a success . . ."

"Which it was," said Mma Makutsi, as she brought them their cups of tea. "Often the people who are number two in any set-up are the ones who know the most."

There was a sudden silence. This remark, intended to refer to theatre nurses and perhaps co-pilots and the like, had a strong resonance closer to home. It could equally refer, everyone realised, to assistant detectives or indeed to those who, although no longer assistant detectives, now being associate directors, or even co-directors, were, nonetheless, still number two in an organisation such as the No. 1 Ladies' Detective Agency — just for the purpose of example, of course.

For a few moments, the silence weighed heavily. But Mma Ramotswe did not mind; someone more inclined to take offence would have undoubtedly done so, but she understood how Mma Makutsi felt, and so she said, "You are absolutely right, Mma. The number two person is often better at things. That is well known, I think."

Mr. J.L.B. Matekoni had picked up the veiled reference and was keen to move the conversation away from potentially difficult waters. Pointing to the photograph in the cutting, he asked, "These ladies, Mma — these special nurses — do you know them?"

Mma Makutsi now picked up the cutting and glanced at the photograph. "The one on the left looks exactly like somebody who was in my group at the Botswana Secretarial College. It could be her sister, in fact . . ." She trailed off. She had read the inscription below the photograph. "My goodness, Mma, look at the names."

Mma Makutsi read them out. "Pearl Badi (28), from Lobatse. Nayna Baipidi (31), also from Lobatse. And . . ." She looked up in surprise. "Mingie Ramotswe (43), from Lobatse, formerly from Mochudi."

Mr. J.L.B. Matekoni frowned. "Mingie what?"

"Mingie Ramotswe," said Mma Makutsi. "Look, here it is. Mingie Ramotswe. That is her — this one on the side." She paused. "And look at the face, Rra. Who does that remind you of?"

The resemblance, once pointed out, was undeniable. Mr. J.L.B. Matekoni put the cutting down on the desk and looked at Mma Ramotswe in confusion. "But I thought you only had those two female cousins, Mma — those two who went up to Francistown. I forget their names."

"Bontle and Gladys," supplied Mma Ramotswe. "Yes, those are the only two — that I know of."

"So who is this woman?" asked Mma Makutsi, almost disapprovingly. "Who is she to call herself Mingie Ramotswe?"

"That must be her name," said Mma Ramotswe. "Why else would she call herself that?"

Mma Makutsi shook her head. "But you have always said that there were very few people with the name Ramotswe, Mma. It's the same with Phuti's name. There are no other Radiphutis — just him and a couple of cousins. That's all."

"And your little Itumelang, Mma," said Mma Ramotswe with a smile. "Do not forget your little boy."

Mma Makutsi put a hand to her mouth. "Oh, I forgot about Itumelang. Yes, there is him. Him, Phuti, and those three cousins. That is all the Radiphutis there are in the world."

Mr. J.L.B. Matekoni repeated Mma Makutsi's question. "So who is this lady, Mma?" He tapped the newspaper cutting. "If she comes from Mochudi, why have we not heard of her?"

Mma Ramotswe hesitated before replying. "Comes from," she said. "But that may only mean she was born there. You come from the place you were born, don't you?"

Mma Makutsi pointed out that this was true. "I say that I come from Bobonong," she said. "But it's a long time since I was there."

"But if I met you in the street," argued Mr. J.L.B. Matekoni, "and I said to you: 'Mma, where are you from?' you wouldn't say Bobonongong . . ."

Mma Makutsi corrected him. "Bobonong," she said. "People often add a few extra *ongs.* It is very careless of them." She looked reprovingly at Mr. J.L.B. Matekoni, who made an apologetic gesture. You had to be careful about Bobonong when Mma Makutsi was present; he had learned that over the years. You also had to be careful about what you said about the Botswana Secretarial College; that was another area of sensitivity — along with Mma Makutsi's job title, whatever that was; it was so difficult to remember whether she was a co-director or an associate director, or simply a director.

He persisted. "You'd say, 'I'm from Gaborone,' because that's where you live. That's what you'd say, wouldn't you, Mma

Makutsi?"

"It's an interesting question," she said. "There must come a time when you change these things. Perhaps it depends on how long you have lived in a new place. You forget old places when you move from them. They fade away."

No, thought Mma Ramotswe, they do not fade away. Those images of those old places, the places you come from, never completely disappear. They remain with you, those scraps of memory; those pictures somewhere in your mind of how things were, of what the sun looked like when it shone through the window of your childhood room and caught floating specks of dust in its rays; of how you looked up at the ceiling above your sleeping mat; of the faces of an aunt or a grandparent or a friend; of all the things that once were, in that place that was home to you then, and perhaps are no longer.

But this was not the time for such thoughts, and she steered the conversation back to the issue of this Ramotswe person, or *alleged* Ramotswe person.

"Do you think it's possible that she has just found the name?" Mma Ramotswe said. "People change their names, you know. They're allowed to do it. You see those

117

notices in the paper: 'Mr. So-and-So wishes to inform the public that he will in future be known as Mr. Something Else.' And you think, why is this man changing his name? What has he to hide? Perhaps this Mingie Ramotswe is like that."

Mma Makutsi considered this for a few moments and then pronounced it perfectly possible. "There are many people who do not like their names. There was a girl at the Botswana Secretarial College whose real name was Virtue but who called herself Daisy."

Mr. J.L.B. Matekoni laughed. "Maybe she didn't want to be virtuous," he said. "Maybe she thought that no man would ever ask her out if she was called Virtue."

Mma Makutsi looked disapproving. "I don't see what that has to do with it," she said. "Why would a man not ask a girl out if she's called Virtue?"

Mma Ramotswe glanced at Mr. J.L.B. Matekoni. "If she preferred Daisy, then that is her business, I think. But going back to this Mingie Ramotswe, I must say I'm curious about her."

"Then ask who she is," said Mma Makutsi. "We can find her easily enough. I know the lady who is in charge of the Nursing Association. She has a register of everybody and will easily find her." She paused. "Phuti sold her a new suite of furniture. Large leather chairs. That is how I know her."

"She will be very comfortable," mused Mr. J.L.B. Matekoni. "Sitting in those large leather chairs — she will be very comfortable after a busy day at the Nursing Association."

"That is very true," said Mma Ramotswe. "People who work hard deserve comfortable chairs." She drained her teacup. "So that is that," she continued. "Now there is the question of Charity Mompoloki. I have met her mother now."

"Poor woman," said Mma Makutsi. "She must be very sad about her daughter's problem."

Mma Ramotswe wondered how to phrase her response. She did not want to do Charity's mother an injustice and to accuse her of indifference, but the fact remained that she had failed to back up her daughter's story, and this led to the conclusion that she simply did not believe her protestations of innocence. And if your own mother did not believe you, then did you deserve to be believed by anybody?

"She was very sorry about what had happened," Mma Ramotswe began. "But I don't think she was surprised."

"Perhaps not," said Mma Makutsi. "These days nobody should be surprised by people who do unkind things like making up reasons for firing employees they don't like."

Mma Ramotswe realised that she would need to be direct. "No, it wasn't that, Mma. It was more a case of her not being surprised by her daughter. She said that she could have outbursts from time to time."

"Well, who can't?" Mma Makutsi asked.

"She believed that Charity probably was rude to the customer."

This was greeted with silence.

Mma Ramotswe waited. "Did you hear what I said, Mma Makutsi?"

"I heard you, Mma," Mma Makutsi replied. "You said that the mother did not believe the daughter. That is what you said."

"That's right."

Mma Makutsi spoke quietly. "Well, I am glad that lady is not my mother. If that is her idea of loyalty, then what has Botswana come to?"

Mr. J.L.B. Matekoni joined in. "I don't see what this has to do with Botswana," he said.

"I do," snapped Mma Makutsi. "If that is the way that mothers behave, then this country is in serious trouble, believe me."

Mr. J.L.B. Matekoni looked towards the door. "I cannot leave Charlie under that car much longer," he said. "If he gets bored, he starts fiddling around in the engine, and that is very dangerous."

Mma Ramotswe understood. The Charity issue was not something that concerned him directly, although his judgement was usually sound and he could be very helpful. So she said to him that he should get on with his work and she and Mma Makutsi would decide what to do about Charity.

"She's not lying," said Mma Makutsi as Mr. J.L.B. Matekoni left the room. "I hear what you say about her mother, Mma, but I'm not convinced. That woman" — she pointed vaguely out of the window in what Mma Ramotswe presumed to be the direction of Charity's house — "that woman is a victim. It's written all over her."

Mma Ramotswe sighed. "Well, Mma Makutsi, what do you suggest we do?"

Mma Makutsi looked at her blankly. "But you're running this enquiry, Mma. You and Mr. Polopetsi. You must decide that — I am only voicing an opinion here."

Mma Ramotswe looked down at her desk. Life was becoming complicated. There was this curious information about Mingie Ramotswe — that was not really something she felt obliged to investigate, but she knew that if she did not satisfy her curiosity about this new Ramotswe she would forever wonder about who this woman was. So there was that to deal with, and then there was this unfortunate Charity affair, and she frankly had no idea as to how to take that further. She sighed again. A deep sigh can be cathartic, and when Mma Ramotswe sighed, she sighed from the very depths of her body. The effect of such a sigh was very much the same as the effect of a deep breath, although the air was going the other way. Such a sigh somehow concentrated the mind. And then it expressed something that was hard to put into words: an acceptance of the complexity and difficulty of the world.

"You're sighing," observed Mma Makutsi.

"Yes, Mma, I'm sighing."

Now Mma Makutsi sighed too. This sigh caused Mma Ramotswe to look up, catch Mma Makutsi's eye, and smile. The smile was returned. Then they both sighed once more.

CHAPTER SEVEN:
IT IS VERY IMPORTANT
TO HAVE CLEAN FLOORS

Mma Ramotswe did not need an invitation
to visit Mma Potokwane, old friend, dis-
penser of wisdom and encouragement,
maker of profoundly tempting fruit cake,
and matron of the Orphan Farm at the end
of the Tlokweng Road. That last qualification was the most important — at least in
Mma Ramotswe's eyes. Our childhood
always has its significant figures, adults
whom we admire with all the enthusiasm of
youth — a popular school teacher, a favourite aunt or uncle, a neighbourhood leader
of some sort. When Mma Ramotswe was a
girl, there had been a matron of the hospital
in Mochudi whom she regarded in this way;
to be a matron struck her as being something magnificent. Matrons were looked up
to by everybody — by the ranks of nurses
whom they commanded, by the hospital
patients whose welfare she guarded, and by
any young girl who appreciated the example

of a woman exercising power and authority.

Matrons ran hospitals. There may have been doctors around, and some of these doctors may have been allowed to use titles that suggested that they were in charge, but everyone knew that the person doing the real work of running the hospital was Matron. It was Matron who saw to it that the wards were clean, that the patients received their pills and their food on time, and that everybody behaved in a fitting and proper manner. Woe betide anybody who fell foul of Matron; matrons had ways of dealing with people like that, and they always won — always.

Mma Ramotswe had been dismayed when she read in the papers that all over the world matrons were being replaced by people described as administrators. She had discussed this with Mma Potokwane, who had heard similar reports, and even knew a matron over the border — a distant relation of hers — who had been replaced not by an individual bureaucrat, but by a committee. That had rubbed salt into the wound, and nothing good could come of it, said Mma Potokwane.

"It is almost beyond belief," said Mma Potokwane. "Everybody knows that the best person to run a hospital, or any institution

— a boarding school or a retirement home or whatever — is a matron. That is the way it's meant to be."

Mma Ramotswe could not agree more. So she said, "Exactly," and encouraged Mma Potokwane to elaborate.

"When I was a junior nurse," continued Mma Potokwane, "we had a very fine matron in charge of us. Oh, that lady, Mma Ramotswe, she was what every matron should try to be. She was a traditionally built lady, of course . . ."

"Of course," said Mma Ramotswe. "It is very important for a matron to be traditionally built. It adds authority."

Mma Potokwane looked thoughtful. "Yes, I see what you mean, Mma. It is definitely an advantage for matrons to be traditionally built, but I have known some matrons who are not blessed in that way. There was a matron at the hospital in Molepolole who was not at all traditionally built. She was as thin as a goat, Mma, and she was not very tall either. You'd describe her as wiry, I suppose. But my goodness, Mma, she was a very good matron. You wouldn't see her coming — she would just suddenly be there."

"That is a great talent," said Mma Ramotswe. "It is very useful if people cannot see you coming. That may be one disadvantage to being traditionally built: people will see you coming and will stop whatever it is they are doing that they should not be doing."

Mma Potokwane agreed that this was so. "This matron out at Molepolole would sometimes pop up in a ward as if she had been hiding in a cupboard or something. And if she found any of the nurses slacking or any of the patients misbehaving, there would be terrible trouble. I heard of one occasion . . ." She laughed at the memory, and Mma Ramotswe had to prompt her to continue.

"I heard of this occasion when some people came to visit one of the patients. It was the rainy season and apparently they brought mud in on their shoes. Now matrons do not like mud . . ."

"They certainly don't," agreed Mma Ramotswe. "Your floors in your own place are always spotless, Mma Potokwane. I've noticed that."

Mma Potokwane acknowledged the compliment. "Thank you, Mma. It is very important to have clean floors. If you have clean floors, then it is likely that everything else will be clean. It is a question of attitude." She paused. "Anyway, there was this young man in hospital — he had had his appendix removed, and two of his friends came in with mud all over their shoes. Matron saw this mess and she told one of the nurses to fetch a broom. When this arrived, Matron went up to the two young men and made them sweep the whole ward — under the beds, around the cupboards, everywhere. These were two young men who had probably never been made to clean up, and they certainly learned a lesson."

"She must have been a very good matron, Mma," said Mma Ramotswe.

"One of the best ever," said Mma Potokwane. "But now, Mma, what do we see? Matrons being abolished. Abolished, Mma!"

"It's very foolish," said Mma Ramotswe. "The whole world is getting very confused. All sorts of people are introducing change here, there, and everywhere. And is it change for the better, Mma?"

Mma Potokwane shook her head vigorously. "It is not, Mma. It is not change for the good. People who run hospitals and schools and whatnot do not need other people to tell them how to do it. They should be left to do it in the way they have always done it."

Mma Ramotswe agreed. She felt there were far too many busybodies trying to destroy the authority of parents, of teachers, and, of course, of matrons.

"Some people would say that I'm old-fashioned," said Mma Potokwane. "They say this is the future — a future where there will be no matrons."

"Old-fashioned?" Mma Ramotswe exclaimed. "You're not old-fashioned, Mma. Just because you do things the way you've always done them — and the correct way, if I may say so, Mma — does not mean that you're old-fashioned."

"Well, that's what they say, Mma."

Mma Ramotswe was usually very even-tempered. She rarely allowed matters to rile her, and only very occasionally expressed a strong opinion. She could see the world as others saw it — she understood if people took a different view of things — but there were limits, and Mma Potokwane had just described one of them. "These people," she said, with a note of irritation creeping into her voice, "what are they thinking of? They spend all their time criticising the good things we have — the old Botswana morality, for example, as well as matrons, of course — but what do they say should be put in their place? They have nothing to offer, Mma. They say that life will be better if we get rid of our traditions, but if we did that, all that would come would be selfishness, Mma. It would be every person for himself, or herself. People would forget about other people because there would be nothing to bind them together: none of the memories, songs, greetings, or customs that make people into a nation. We would have plenty of shiny cars, Mma — plenty of Mercedes-Benzes — but inside we would be as empty as an old ant-hill. You wouldn't care if somebody was starving, because that person would mean nothing to you. That person would not be your brother or your sister, as they always are in the old Botswana morality; they would just be strangers. Think of that, Mma. Just think of that."

It was a long speech for Mma Ramotswe, but it was one delivered with feeling. And Mma Potokwane found nothing in it with which she disagreed. It expressed, she thought, everything that she felt about her own job in this life, which was to look after children and make what were often rather sad little lives into something better. And in doing this, she sought to bring the children up to believe that there was more to life than just having the material things you saw that others had, and that even if you had these things, it was better to share them with others. Was that old-fashioned? If it was, then she would be proud to call herself old-fashioned.

No, Mma Ramotswe needed no invitation to visit Mma Potokwane, possibly for the very reason that in an old-fashioned view of things, a friend would always be there to receive you, invited or not, announced or unannounced. And on the day following that rather disquieting visit to Mochudi, that day of unexpected disclosures about Mingie Ramotswe and about the character of Charity Mompoloki, Mma Ramotswe decided to pay a visit to Mma Potokwane at roughly eleven o'clock in the morning, a time when she knew her friend would be in her office, enjoying the mid-morning cup of tea and, with any luck, a slice of fruit cake.

Parking her van under the tree that she always favoured for these visits, she stretched her legs before making her way over to Mma Potokwane's office. In the nursery playground, under the shade of a well-established acacia tree, the children who were too young to go off to the local school were playing some game that involved a mixture of shouted Setswana counting and whoops of glee. Mma Ramotswe stood still for a while as she listened to the children's voices; there was something vaguely familiar about the words of this game, and after a few minutes she realised that she had herself as a child played this game, with its accompanying chants; and she saw the dusty playground in Mochudi, around the school on the hill, and the teacher watching from the verandah, ready to deal with any excessive roughness. And it gave her pleasure, real pleasure, to think that such things had been handed down from one generation to the next and were still performed under trees that were the sons and daughters, the grandchildren too, of the trees under which previous generations had played.

Mma Potokwane had seen her from her window and had switched on the kettle even before Mma Ramotswe crossed her office threshold.

"I see you, Mma Ramotswe," she called out.

"And I see you, Mma Potokwane," replied Mma Ramotswe.

They sat down, each in her accustomed chair.

"I don't want to disturb you," began Mma Ramotswe. "I know how busy you are." It was the way she started every conversation with Mma Potokwane, and it brought the usual protestations from her host. "Everyone is busy these days," said Mma Potokwane. "Do you know anybody who isn't?"

Mma Ramotswe thought. She was busy; Mma Makutsi was busy; Mr. J.L.B. Matekoni was certainly busy. Mr. Polopetsi was busy too, in a part-time sort of way. Were there any idle people left? In the past, there had seemed to be plenty of those, but they had either stopped being idle or had managed to conceal their idleness behind a façade of being busy.

"But even if I have plenty of things to do," continued Mma Potokwane, "it is very important to be able to sit down and talk."

There were a few minutes of general chat until tea was poured. Then, without saying a word, Mma Potokwane opened an old biscuit tin to reveal half a fruit cake. She did not need to ask Mma Ramotswe whether she would like a piece, but cut a large wedge and put it on a plate.

"There will be more if required," she said, smiling, as she passed the plate to her guest.

Mma Ramotswe thanked her. She closed her eyes as she took her first bite of the cake; Mma Potokwane's baking, she found, was strangely therapeutic. You might be very tense, you might have all sorts of worries, and then you popped a piece of cake into your mouth and all your issues seemed to disappear — as if they had never been there in the first place. Tea could achieve the same result, but much less reliably and on a smaller scale; fruit cake could be prescribed by doctors trying to relieve anxiety in their patients: *a slice of fruit cake three times a day until further notice.* The results would be impressive; depression would lift, and the body, always sensitive to mood, would respond accordingly. Of course, these remedies always came with warnings, and so there might be one on the cake tin, reading, "Do not eat this cake while driving or operating machinery . . ."

"I'm glad you came, Mma Ramotswe," began Mma Potokwane. "I was going to telephone you about something."

Mma Ramotswe looked up from her contemplation of her plate of cake. "And I was going to call you too, Mma."

Mma Potokwane looked interested. "There are things to be talked about, Mma?"

Mma Ramotswc nodded. "There are two matters that have been worrying me."

Mma Potokwane laughed. "I may have one to add, I'm afraid . . . But, tell me, what's on your mind, Mma."

Mma Ramotswe broke off a small piece of fruit cake and washed it down with a sip of tea. Her curiosity had been aroused by the mention of a third worry, and she asked whether they could talk about that first.

Mma Potokwane looked out of the window. This was a bad sign: when Mma Ramotswe looked out of the window, it was usually because there was a problem that defied internal solution. And if no solution could be found in the office, then what alternative was there but to look outside, out into the bush with its almost unbroken panoply of acacia trees and its dusty paths wandering this way and that?

"This is not very good news, I'm afraid," said Mma Potokwane.

Mma Ramotswe sat quite still. Somebody was ill — very ill. That was what that sort of preface usually announced. She shivered.

"I have a friend who works in the Standard Bank in town," said Mma Potokwane. "She is one of their tellers."

Mma Ramotswe nodded. Her first feeling was one of relief; this was not about illness but about a different danger: money. She had her savings — such as they were — in a deposit account in the Standard Bank. Did Mma Potokwane know something about the bank's solvency?

"I hope the bank is all right," said Mma Ramotswe. "I have a savings account there."

"The Standard Bank is a very good bank," Mma Potokwane reassured her. "It is perfectly sound."

"That is good news, Mma."

Mma Potokwane continued. "This friend said to me the other day that she had seen somebody come into the bank whom she recognised. She told me who it was. I asked her whether her friend was quite sure, and she said that she was. She had served as a clerk in the police before going into the bank, and she had been trained to be very good at identifying people. She said she would not have mistaken this person, and anyway, when he came into the bank to change some South African rands into pula he had to sign a slip, and she saw his name on it."

Mma Ramotswe frowned. She was not sure why this man in the bank should be of concern to her. Was it somebody she had exposed in the course of one of her investigations — Charlie Gotso, for instance — the ruthless businessman and sponsor of witchcraft, whom she had exposed all those years ago.

Mma Potokwane delivered the blow in lowered tones. "Note Mokoti."

Mma Ramotswe had not been prepared for this. She had last seen her abusive first husband some years ago, and she had by and large stopped thinking about him. Of

course, he came to mind every so often —
it is hard to write trauma completely out of
your life — but he was not somebody she
worried about. On his last visit to Gaborone she had given him some money and
told him that she did not hate him. She had
forgiven him, in effect, and sent him on his
way saying that she did not wish to see him
again. Forgiveness was never easy, but Mma
Ramotswe believed in it because she knew
that without forgiveness we cluttered our
lives with old business. Not forgiving was
like scratching at a sore to keep the healing
scab from forming.

It took her a few moments to regain her
composure. "Note?" she said.

Mma Potokwane inclined her head. "I had
hoped we would never again have to discuss
that man," she said.

"So had I," muttered Mma Ramotswe.

"I had to warn you," said Mma Potokwane.

Mma Ramotswe agreed, and thanked her.
"It is better to know when there is something like that," said Mma Ramotswe. "The
worst thing is bumping into somebody like
that without any notice. It must be like stepping on a snake."

"That's a very good way of putting it,
Mma," said Mma Potokwane. "But the

question we have to ask ourselves is this: What is Note Mokoti doing in Gaborone?"

"Is there a concert?" Note was a trumpeter and occasionally toured with a group of better-known jazz musicians. His own career had stalled; he made a living, thought Mma Ramotswe, but only just.

Mma Potokwane said that she had asked somebody who knew about these matters and he had told her that there were no jazz concerts that month. The next one, he said, would be in six weeks' time and featured a band from Zambia. There was nothing from South Africa, where Note now lived.

Mma Ramotswe became silent. Memories had faded, but could so easily be reactivated, as they were now, and her memories were of fear. Mma Potokwane, watching her, guessed at this, and sought to reassure her. "He can't harm you, Mma — not any more. You are a married woman and you have a husband who will not allow that. And you have a position — you have a detective agency, you have been mentioned in the *Botswana Daily News;* you are not the vulnerable girl you were back then."

It was some consolation, and Mma Ramotswe did her best to put on a brave face.

"And another thing," said Mma Potokwane. "Note has not tried to contact you.

That is a good sign. It means that he is here for some other reason — he is not here to make life difficult for you."

Mma Ramotswe thought that Mma Potokwane was probably right. "Let's not talk about him," she said. "There are other things to think about." But although she said this — and tried to feel it at the same time — there was a cold knot of dread somewhere within her. Note . . . even the name, uttered inside her, without speaking, could do its icy work.

Mma Potokwane seemed relieved to be able to change the subject. "You said that there were some matters that were preying on your mind, Mma. What are these matters?"

It took Mma Ramotswe a moment or two to compose herself. *Forget Note . . . forget him. Forget.*

"Mma?" pressed Mma Potokwane.

"I'm sorry, Mma. Yes, we have a rather tricky matter on our hands."

She told her about the Charity Mompoloki case.

"I'm afraid that Mma Makutsi and I have opposite views on this," Mma Ramotswe said. "She thinks that Charity is telling the truth; her mother thinks the opposite."

"Mothers always know," said Mma Poto-kwane.

Mma Ramotswe confessed her suspicions. "I think that Mma Makutsi is being swayed by her loyalty to the Botswana Secretarial College," she said. "You know what she's like. She's not looking at it in a sensible way."

Mma Potokwane made a disapproving sound. "It's very important to be detached," she said. "When I'm dealing with a problem out here, I always try to pretend that I don't know everybody involved. I look at it as if I'm a stranger."

"Mma Makutsi is not doing that," said Mma Ramotswe. "And I think that she'll influence poor Mr. Polopetsi."

Mma Potokwane looked thoughtful. "Yes, Mr. Polopetsi has many merits, but he is easily led," she said. "Perhaps, Mma, you need to run a parallel investigation. You can let Mr. Polopetsi and Mma Makutsi investigate in their way, while you investigate in yours. Then, when they get stuck or go up the wrong path, you will quietly sort the whole thing out in your way. They will then see the advantages of being detached."

Mma Ramotswe looked at her friend. Was there something underhand about this, or was it simply a way of defusing a disagree-

139

ment? A moment's thought convinced her: there was no need for anybody to be deceived — she could follow her own line of enquiry, and Mma Makutsi, along with Mr. Polopetsi, could follow theirs. Not only would this prevent arguments, but it would mean that more possibilities were explored. No, Mma Potokwane, in her inimitable way, had come up with a solution.

"You know, Mma Potokwane," she said at last, "I think that's exactly what I need to do."

"Good," said Mma Potokwane, sounding businesslike. "Now, what is this other matter you were talking about?"

Mma Ramotswe looked pointedly at her empty plate.

The unspoken request was picked up immediately. Old friends know one another's weaknesses, and Mma Potokwane knew exactly how Mma Ramotswe felt about cake — and many other things too, but particularly cake. "Of course," she said. "Here, let me give you another slice of this."

Mma Ramotswe did not demur, and fortified by a further helping of fruit cake, she told the matron about how she had discovered the existence of Mingie Ramotswe. Mma Potokwane listened with interest, and closely examined the newspaper cutting when Mma Ramotswe produced it.

Looking up from the cutting, she fixed Mma Ramotswe with an enquiring gaze. "Are you wanting my advice, Mma?" she asked.

Mma Ramotswe nodded. "I would like to hear what you think, Mma. I always like that. But I do have some views on what I should do."

"Oh, and what are those views, Mma?"

"I could find out about this lady from the nursing authorities. They should know where she is."

She became aware that Mma Potokwane was shaking her head rather vigorously. "Is there something wrong?" she asked.

"I wouldn't," said Mma Potokwane.

"You wouldn't try to contact her?"

"That's right — I wouldn't."

Mma Ramotswe was puzzled. "But why, Mma? Surely if there is a relative you don't know about and then you discover this person, surely you would want to get to know her."

Mma Potokwane started to shake her head again. "I think there are big risks in doing that without first making enquiries," she said. "What if such a person is not the sort of relative you want?"

From her generous perspective, in which

people were invariably given the benefit of the doubt, it had not occurred to Mma Ramotswe that this Mingie Ramotswe might not be the sort of person she would wish to know. But now, with that possibility bluntly articulated by Mma Potokwane, she saw that this could well be so.

"There may be a way of doing this," said Mma Potokwane. "If you were to find out something about this person *before* you met her, then you could decide whether or not this is a relative you want to find — if she is, in fact, a relative."

"Which she might not be," said Mma Ramotswe.

"That's right. And of course, if she isn't, then it doesn't matter at all what she's like."

"Except for one thing," said Mma Ramotswe. "Even if she isn't a relative, people might still think she is and that could reflect badly on me — and the family in general." She paused, as she mulled over the possibility. She had known of a case where a well-known family in Mochudi had been grossly embarrassed by a person who had arrived in the village and claimed to have the same name as them. He had been a drunkard and a womaniser and had brought nothing but shame until he eventually disappeared — in unexplained circumstances, some mur-

mured, although others believed he had fallen into an old ant hole while staggering about drunk. There was much to be said for a common name — the sort of name that many hundreds, if not thousands, of people bore. In those circumstances, if some namesake did something wrong, one might escape embarrassment simply because the name was so ubiquitous and nobody would associate you with the wrongdoer.

"Well," said Mma Potokwane, "whatever you decide to do, I'm sure that you'll be very careful." She paused. "There aren't any other problems at the moment, are there?"

"No," said Mma Ramotswe. "I don't think there are."

"In that case," said Mma Potokwane, "there's a small slice of cake left in the tin. It would be a pity to let it become stale."

"A very big pity," said Mma Ramotswe.

Mma Potokwane reached for a knife. "I shall divide it, Mma, and then you choose. That is always a guarantee of fairness, don't you think?"

CHAPTER EIGHT:
NOT A GOVERNMENT-LOOKING PERSON

Mma Makutsi was surprised by Mma Ramotswe's suggestion.

"You mean, you want me to take charge of this Charity business, Mma? As . . ." She took off her spectacles as she searched for the right words. ". . . as Principal Investigating Officer?"

It was an entirely new term, never before used in the No. 1 Ladies' Detective Agency, and it took Mma Ramotswe by surprise. Principal Investigating Officer: it had an impressive ring to it, there was no doubt about that, but was it too official? As a private detective one had to be careful not to give the impression that one was in some way working on behalf of the Government. Would people think this of a Principal Investigating Officer?

Mma Makutsi replaced her spectacles as she waited for Mma Ramotswe's reply.

"You'll be in charge," said Mma Ramotswe guardedly.

"As Principal Investigating Officer?" pressed Mma Makutsi.

"You'll be the one in the driving seat," Mma Ramotswe reassured her.

Mma Makutsi appeared satisfied. "As Principal Investigating Officer I shall do my best," she said.

Mma Ramotswe decided that perhaps it did not matter too much. If Mma Makutsi wanted to be a Principal Investigating Officer — if it meant so much to her — then she should be allowed to call herself that. People were sensitive about how they were described, and if it gave Mma Makutsi pleasure to create new titles for herself, then there was no real harm in that — as long as she did not mislead anybody.

"It's important that we remember we're acting in a private capacity," she said.

Mma Makutsi nodded. "Yes, that's very important."

"So if you introduce yourself as a Principal Investigating Officer, make sure that nobody thinks you're from the Government."

Mma Makutsi laughed. "Nobody would think that, Mma. Do you think I look as if I'm from the Government?"

Mma Ramotswe was not sure how to answer. Admittedly there was an official

145

look that some government people culti-
vated — a sort of stern, rule-bound look —
but there were plenty of civil servants who
were indistinguishable from the general pop-
ulation.

Mma Makutsi repeated her question. "Do
you think that, Mma?"

"No," said Mma Ramotswe. "You are not
a government-looking person, Mma."

"I am very relieved to hear that, Mma,
because it is important in our line of work
not to look like anything in particular."

Mma Ramotswe frowned. "But we have
to look like something, Mma. We can't look
like . . ." She shrugged. ". . . like nothing."

Mma Makutsi smiled. "Of course, Mma.
What I meant is that we should not look
unusual. We mustn't stand out."

Mma Ramotswe agreed with the aim of a
discreet appearance. "I think there is something in *The Principles of Private Detection*
about that. I think Clovis Andersen had
something to say about not —"

Mma Makutsi interrupted her with chapter and verse. "It is in his chapter entitled
'Watching and Waiting.' That is what the
chapter is called, Mma. Page eighty-five."

Mma Ramotswe was impressed. "That is
very good, Mma. You know that book back-
wards."

Mma Makutsi clearly appreciated the compliment. Taking off her spectacles again, she gave them a further polish. "There is so much in that book, Mma. Every page has some bit of important information. It is one of the very great books of our times."

"That is true," said Mma Ramotswe. "He is a great man, Mr. Andersen."

Mma Makutsi replaced her spectacles. "A very great man. And he says, if I remember correctly, that you should always try to be *typical*. That is the word he uses, Mma — typical. If you're typical, then nobody will notice you."

Mma Ramotswe nodded. "I think that's right."

"It is definitely right, Mma," continued Mma Makutsi. "So if people see you in the street, Mma Ramotswe, they probably just think, *There goes another traditionally built lady.* And they don't think: *Who is that woman, and what is she doing?*" She paused. "We don't want them to think that, do we, Mma?"

"We do not, Mma," Mma Ramotswe replied. But she was thinking that Mma Makutsi, for all her claims to invisibility, was quite a striking-looking person, particularly with her large glasses. And it was all very well for her to dismiss Mma Ramotswe as just another traditionally built lady, but what was Mma Makutsi herself? She was taller and more large-boned, but there were definitely parts of her that were traditionally built, although Mma Ramotswe did not feel it appropriate to think about these matters.

Mma Ramotswe smiled. This odd conversation had made her remember something that Mr. Polopetsi had done. It had been some time ago, when he first became associated with the agency; he was helping with an investigation that involved watching a married man who was suspected, quite rightly as it turned out, of meeting a lover in his parked car, and Mr. Polopetsi had been detailed to keep watch in the car park in which these trysts were thought to be taking place. Mma Ramotswe had driven him there in her tiny white van and had noticed that he had an unusually large hat with him. It was the sort of hat cattle ranchers liked to wear — as wide brimmed as a verandah — and circled round the crown, where a leather hat-band might once have been, with a strip of zebra skin.

Mma Ramotswe had found it difficult to keep her eyes off this hat, even while driving. Eventually she had asked him about it. "This hat of yours, Rra, is a very fine one. Where did you get it?"

Mr. Polopetsi explained that a friend had given it to him. "He said he no longer wore it, Mma, and that it was too good a hat to be thrown away."

Mma Ramotswe's gaze drifted to the zebra-skin hat-band. "No, I can see that. There are not many hats like that."

"So I am going to wear it today as a disguise," said Mr. Polopetsi.

The van swerved, but was quickly brought back under control.

"As a disguise, Rra?"

He explained that he normally wore a small grey hat with a narrow brim; this wide-brimmed hat would be a very effective way of hiding his identity. "Nobody will think *Oh, that's Polopetsi standing there,* will they, Mma? They will think I am somebody else altogether — perhaps somebody down from the Okavango, from Maun, or somewhere like that, where they wear hats like this."

Mma Ramotswe felt a strong urge to laugh, but managed to control herself. That hat, she thought, would attract the attention of anybody who went near that car park; all they would see, she imagined, would be that extraordinary hat with a small man underneath it; and anybody planning to do something risky — planning a clandestine meeting — would immediately be put on guard.

Eventually she found the words to express her doubts. "What you say is very true, Rra," she said. "They will not know it's you, but they may see you, don't you think? They may wonder who has such a fine hat. They may even come up to you and ask you where they could get a hat like it."

Mr. Polopetsi fiddled with the brim of the hat. He ran his fingers along the zebra skin, disturbing the fall of the pile. Mma Ramotswe could see that he was disappointed. "On the other hand, Rra," she said, "people who have reason to be wary — people who are up to no good, for example — they may think that anybody wearing a hat like that could not be somebody trying to appear inconspicuous . . . Do you follow me, Rra?"

"I think so . . ."

"And so these people — like this man who is seeing yet another girlfriend while his wife stays at home and looks after the children *and* their business — these people would never imagine that the man in a hat like that could be watching them."

She waited for his reaction; now they were approaching the car park where he was to be dropped off to begin his observations, and, as they drew up just short of it so that he could get out of the van, he said, "I think, on balance, I shall leave the hat in the van, Mma."

She was relieved, and as she drove away, leaving him to his task, she thought of how important it was to go halfway in any disagreement — to see the other person's point of view and to find the positive side of it; this little discussion with Mr. Polopetsi had been yet further proof of that. If you did that, if you expressed their viewpoint rather than your own, then you found that they often came round to seeing things as you saw them. If only everybody would do this, she thought; if only the leaders of countries, politicians and people like that, would adopt the same approach, then how much more peaceful and harmonious would be our world. Rather than threatening one another with this, that and the next thing, they would say to one another, "What good ideas you have! And how well you put them!" And this would draw the response, "Well, your ideas are very good too, and you are so right about just about every-thing!"

Or if they simply said to one another, "I like you." That was all that was required. "I like you."

But now, she was interested in finding out what Mma Makutsi — the Principal Investigating Officer — was planning to do. It would be important, she felt, not to duplicate effort; not only was this wasteful, but she did not want Mma Makutsi to discover that she was asking the same questions of the same people as she was.

In response to her enquiries, Mma Makutsi revealed that she and Mr. Polopetsi would be speaking to the people who were working in The Office Place at the time when the incident took place. "Not that it actually took place," said Mma Makutsi dismissively. "But we need to find out whether these people know anything. If they do, why have they not spoken out?"

Mma Ramotswe thought that it was unlikely that any employee would deliberately cross their boss. "They would not want to put their own jobs in peril," she said. "That is often the reason why people don't speak out."

Mma Makutsi thought otherwise. "Yes, Mma, but in any business, any business at all, there will always be at least one person who does not like the boss and who will be happy to — how do they put it? — blow the whistle." She paused, as if for emphasis, and then concluded: "There will always be one. Always. No matter how small the business is."

Mma Ramotswe listened to this without comment. Mma Makutsi sometimes made remarks that she had not thought out fully before she made them. This might be just such an occasion. It would have been bad enough had she stopped short of mentioning small businesses, but her singling out of such concerns was the height of tactlessness. If there was always one person who disliked the boss, then who was it in the No. 1 Ladies' Detective Agency? The choice was not very wide: there was Mma Makutsi herself, there was Mr. Polopetsi, and there was Charlie, who worked part-time in the agency and part-time in the garage. Then there was Fanwell, who, although employed by Tlokweng Road Speedy Motors, took his morning break in the agency, sat on the lower of the two filing cabinets while he drank his tea, and could loosely be considered to be associated with the agency. Which of these would Mma Makutsi choose if she had to apply her generalisation this close to home?

Mma Ramotswe was not sure how she would ask this question, but in the event she had no need to pose it. Mma Makutsi suddenly gasped, and put her hand to her mouth.

"Oh, Mma Ramotswe," she blurted out,

"I've just realised what I've said. I didn't mean to say that there would be anybody like that in *this* business. Oh no, Mma — I certainly did not."

Mma Ramotswe made light of it. "Think nothing of it," she said lightly. "I did not imagine you were applying that rule to the No. 1 Ladies' Detective Agency." And then she added, "It was a slip of the tongue, Mma."

Mma Makutsi took off her glasses and gave them a wipe. "That is definitely what it was, Mma. It was a slip of the tongue." She sniffed. "I would never say anything to hurt you, Mma Ramotswe. I hope you know that."

Mma Ramotswe did her best to reassure her. "I know that very well, Mma Makutsi."

"Because everything I have, Mma — everything — I owe to you, and your kindness."

Mma Ramotswe was touched, but she did not think it was true. "No," she said. "You owe it to your hard work. You don't get ninety-seven per cent in this life without working very hard. And that is what you did."

Nothing more was said, nor needed to be said. Mma Makutsi prepared to leave the office, and Mma Ramotswe buried herself in a copy of the *Botswana Daily News,* always an antidote to any difficult situation. There was an article about a new government plan to help small farmers, and she began reading that. She did not get far, as her mind was wandering, and the details of the stock support scheme that would help the owners of cattle in drought-stricken areas were overtaken by thoughts of Mingie Ramotswe. She was recalling the advice Mma Potokwane had given her, and she was now on the point of deciding to make some enquiries about what sort of person Mingie was. Then, if what she heard was encouraging, she would seek her out and find out just who she was and why she should claim to be a Ramotswe.

But where to start? Sister Banjule, she thought. She was the nurse at the Anglican hospice, and was she not known as Sister Elephant because of her memory? She would know something about this Mingie Ramotswe because Sister Banjule knew just about every senior nurse in the country, had trained half of them, and had brought the other half into the world during her years as a midwife. She would know.

The Holy Cross hospice was on Mboya Close, a modest white building set a short

155

way back from a side-road in one of the poorer parts of town. Mma Ramotswe knew about it because she knew the people who had set it up. Her friend Dr. Moffat had been one of these, and then there was Sister Banjule herself, who on Sundays came to the Anglican Cathedral, where she always wore an elaborate hat, as if she were attending a wedding. It was Sister Banjule who had nursed Mma Makutsi's brother, Richard, when he had been at the end of his illness, and Mma Ramotswe remembered the dignity that she had lent to his final days, when his body seemed to be in such open and implacable revolt. The new medicines came too late for Richard — he would have had a chance now — but not then, and he had eventually been released from his suffering.

She parked the van at the edge of the road outside, finding some shade from a rather dispirited-looking acacia tree. It was not much, but even a scrap of shade could make the cab less furnace-like after some time in the direct sunlight. Once inside the compound, she stepped onto the verandah and knocked at the door marked "Office."

A young man answered. He was dressed in a pair of loose-fitting blue trousers and a white smock-like shirt. Mma Ramotswe recognised these as the working clothes of the nurse or the ward assistant. She introduced herself and asked whether Sister Banjule was available.

"She is very busy at the moment," said the young man. "I don't know when she will finish. It depends on . . ." He looked away.

Mma Ramotswe waited for him to say something further, which he eventually did. "It depends on when the patient becomes late, Mma."

Mma Ramotswe caught her breath. "Oh, I wouldn't want to disturb her. I can come back some other time. I'm very sorry."

The young man seemed unaffected. "Oh, that doesn't matter. You know this is a hospice, Mma. We are here to help patients who are very ill. Many of them will soon be late."

Mma Ramotswe lowered her voice. "I know that you people do very good work," she said.

"Thank you," said the young man. He cocked his head in the direction of a corridor. "I'll go and tell her you're here, anyway."

She protested. "You mustn't disturb her."

"It will not be a disturbance. I'll just tell her." He looked at her enquiringly. "What is your name, Mma?"

She told him, and he left. A minute or so later, he reappeared. "Sister says that I can take you through there."

Mma Ramotswe shook her head. "I mustn't disturb her. I really must go, Rra."

"No, Mma. She wants to see you. She says that the patient she is with is from Mochudi originally. She says you should say hello to her. It will be good for her to talk to you."

He led the way down the corridor, stopping outside a half-open door.

"She is in there, Mma," he said. "You may go in."

Mma Ramotswe entered the room. It was not very large, and much of the space was taken by a narrow bed on which a woman was lying, a sheet drawn up to her chin. At the bedside was a chair on which Sister Banjule was seated. She was holding the hand of the woman on the bed. There was an additional chair against the wall.

"Mma Ramotswe," said Sister Banjule. "It is very good to see you." She gestured to the other chair. "You must sit down, Mma — then I can introduce you to this lady."

Mma Ramotswe sat down. She looked at the figure on the bed; it was hard to tell much about her, but she was clearly very ill. The skin of her face was drawn tight; her arm, emerging from under the sheet to hold

158

Sister Banjule's hand, was like a stick.

Sister Banjule leaned forward as she spoke so that her patient might hear her. "This lady has come to see you, Mma," she said. "She is from Mochudi too."

"A long time ago," said Mma Ramotswe.

"You'll have to speak up," said Sister Banjule, and, as a whispered aside to Mma Ramotswe, "Hearing goes towards the end."

"I have not lived in Mochudi for many years, Mma," said Mma Ramotswe, her voice raised.

The woman's eyes opened a little wider. It was hard to see what lay behind the folds of the eyelids, but there was a sudden glint of light, as if something had been reawakened. "Mochudi," she said, her voice distant, cracked with age and frailty.

"My father was Obed Ramotswe," said Mma Ramotswe. "He is late now."

"They're late now," said the woman. "All of them."

Mma Ramotswe exchanged a glance with Sister Banjule, who smiled. "You are still with us, Mma," she said to the patient. "And that is the important thing. One day, God will call you, but it is not going to be today."

The woman wheezed, and Mma Ramotswe realised that this was a laugh. When

159

she spoke again, her voice seemed stronger. "I knew your father," she said. "He was a good man. Good with cattle."

Mma Ramotswe nodded encouragingly. "He knew a great deal about cattle, Mma. I think there was nobody else in Botswana who knew as much about cattle as he did."

The woman shifted slightly in the bed. Her expression now seemed more animated — as if the conversation had stirred her from her somnolent state. "And I knew your mother."

Mma Ramotswe leaned forward. "I never knew her, Mma. She died when I was very young."

The effect of this was unexpected. The woman shook her head. "No, Mma. I don't think so. She was a dressmaker. She moved over the border. She went to one of those places over there." She attempted to wave her hand in the direction of South Africa, but did not manage more than a slight movement.

Mma Ramotswe was puzzled. "I think that is somebody else."

But the woman said, "Ramotswe. She was the wife of Ramotswe. She never came back, but I think you did."

"I never went away," said Mma Ramotswe.

Sister Banjule now intervened. "I think

we are thinking of different people. And it doesn't matter, Mma." She turned to Mma Ramotswe and whispered, "They can get confused. There's no point in upsetting them."

Sister Banjule made it clear that the visit was over. Tucking her patient's hand back under the sheet, she rose from her chair and gestured for Mma Ramotswe to follow her. Once outside, she said, "I think she was happy to see you. They like to meet new people."

"She seemed to pick up," said Mma Ramotswe. "I think that she was a bit confused, though. That business about going over the border and so on. That was very odd."

"They get confused," said Sister Banjule. "And that lady is on a powerful dose of morphine. She is mostly sleeping now because this is probably her last day. She may have one more, but it will not be long now."

Mma Ramotswe said nothing. She was thinking about how we measured out our days: for much of the time, this was in years, but there must come a stage when it was in months, and then, at the end, in hours and even minutes. But even when our span was so reduced, the thought was always present that although we might be going, the things and places we loved would still be there. So it must be a consolation to know that there would still be Botswana; that there would still be a sun that would rise over the acacia trees like a great red ball and would set over the Kalahari in a sweep of copper and gold; that there would still be the smell of wood fires in the evening and the sound of the cattle making their slow way home, their gentle bells marking their return to the safety of their enclosure. All these things must make leaving this world less painful.

Sister Banjule now offered her a cup of tea, but Mma Ramotswe declined. "I can see how busy you are, Mma," she said. "If you do not mind, I shall not have tea this time. But I would like to ask you something, if I may."

Sister Banjule inclined her head. "Anything, Mma — although I might not know the answer, and . . ." She hesitated; something was worrying her. "I know that you're a private detective, Mma. So if you want to ask me something about one of our patients, I must warn you that I cannot speak. We must observe the patient's confidence, you see. We cannot tell you things about the people we look after."

"Oh, I did not have anything like that in

mind," Mma Ramotswe reassured her. "I wanted to ask you about a nurse."

Sister Banjule frowned. "But that might also be something I cannot talk about," she said. "I can give a reference, of course, if the nurse in question asks for it."

"It is nothing to do with that," said Mma Ramotswe. "In fact it's nothing to do with anything."

Sister Banjule tried to work that out. "Nothing to do with anything . . . I'm sorry, Mma, I don't understand. How can something have nothing to do with anything? Surely everything has to do with something . . . if you think about it."

Mma Ramotswe made a cancelling gesture. "That is not what I wanted to say. What I meant was that this is purely private. I want to know something for strictly personal reasons."

Sister Banjule relaxed. "Then that's fine, Mma. I shall tell you what I know about this . . . about this *something*."

Mma Ramotswe posed her question. "Do you know of a nurse who has the same name as mine: Ramotswe? She is an —"

"Operating theatre nurse," supplied Sister Banjule. "Yes, I know that nurse — a little. I don't know her personally all that well."

Mma Ramotswe waited for her to continue.

"She came up here for a while," said Sister Banjule. "Then she was in Lobatse. I think she may still be there. In fact, I think she is. I think I saw something about a meeting down there and she was on the list of those attending."

"Do you know anything more about her?" asked Mma Ramotswe.

Sister Banjule's brow furrowed. "Not really, although I seem to remember that she trained over in South Africa. It may even have been down in Cape Town. They have that big hospital there — you know the one? It's where they did the heart transplant many years ago. That famous doctor. She trained there and then must have come back home to Botswana afterwards."

"So if I wrote to her at the hospital down in Lobatse, she would get the letter?"

Sister Banjule seemed amused by this. "I wouldn't trust the hospital to deliver the letter," she said. "You know how these big organisations can be when it comes to passing things. No, I'd go and see her. I could get her address for you, if you like. I have a good friend in the hospital office who'll give it to me."

Mma Ramotswe might have pointed out

that this was exactly the sort of breach of confidentiality that Sister Banjule had earlier on been keen to avoid, but she said nothing.

She had a final question for Sister Banjule. "What's she like?" she asked. "Not as a nurse, but as a person: What's she like?"

Sister Banjule hesitated before replying. "As I told you, Mma, I don't know her all that well. It's hard to judge people if you don't know them well."

Mma Ramotswe picked up the note of reservation. "You're not sure about her, Mma?"

"I didn't say that. I said that I don't know her all that well . . ." She faltered. "She's different, Mma. She's not the same as everybody else."

Mma Ramotswe stared at her. "How is she different, Mma?"

Sister Banjule seemed embarrassed. "I don't really know, Mma. I just don't know."

Mma Ramotswe did not press her. She suspected, though, that Sister Banjule *did* know, and just didn't care to reveal what she thought. She would not make it more embarrassing for her; she would not try to elicit information — if it was even that — from her; she would be satisfied with an address in Lobatse — that was all she needed at this stage.

"I would like to meet this lady," said Mma Ramotswe. "You said you could get me her address."

But now something seemed to come over Sister Banjule. She shifted her weight on her feet, awkwardly, as if she had thought of something. She did not reply immediately.

Mma Ramotswe pressed her. "I would be grateful if you could, Mma. I can assure you I only want to meet her. There is nothing else."

Sister Banjule shook her head. "I don't know, Mma. Yes, I said I could get her address, but if you don't mind . . ." She now looked quite uncomfortable. "You see, these days people are so fussy about what you say. You tell somebody something and the next moment you have the Nursing Council shaking their fingers at you and saying, 'You have no right to say this thing, or that thing . . .' It is very difficult even to breathe these days — you have to do it in the right way or somebody will come and complain about you."

The absurdity broke the tension. "Don't worry, Mma. I don't want to embarrass you. I'll go down to Lobatse . . ."

Sister Banjule looked relieved. "I can tell you one thing, Mma. There's a man at the

hospital gate down there who knows everybody. He operates the barrier that lets cars
in and out. He is one of those men who cannot stop talking — all the time, talk, talk,
talk." She paused to imitate with her hand
an overactive jaw. "Men say that some
women talk too much, but they haven't met
this man. He makes up for all the silent men
in Botswana." Again she paused, this time
to give an impression of a strong, silent
look. "We know those men, don't we, Mma?
Those men who think they can melt your
heart just by looking at you like this."

Mma Ramotswe laughed. "Yes, all women
know those men. The men think that women
will think, *Here is a man who is thinking
deep, strong thoughts,* but in fact, Mma,
those men are not really thinking about
anything at all."

Sister Banjule agreed. "I like men to say
something from time to time," she said.
"But not all the time like this man down in
Lobatse. Anyway, Mma, if you speak to him,
he will tell you where this Mingie Ramotswe
lives; if she has a car, what make it is; where
she goes to church; whether she has children, and so on. Everything, Mma."

"He sounds like a gossip," said Mma
Ramotswe.

"That is an unkind word," Sister Banjule

said, "but sometimes unkind words are the only ones we can use. Yes, he's a gossip, Mma — one of the biggest gossips in Botswana. Champion Gossip. No. 1 Gossip, like your No. 1 Ladies' Detective Agency — the best in Botswana."

CHAPTER NINE:
WHY ARE YOU ALWAYS FILING?

Charlie drove Mma Makutsi and Mr. Polopetsi to The Office Place. Mma Makutsi knew how to drive, and had taken over a car that had previously belonged to Phuti's Double Comfort Furniture Store, but she preferred to be driven. As for Mr. Polopetsi, he was in possession of a driving licence, but usually left any driving to his wife, who was the more decisive member of the partnership and, unlike her husband, would not wait timidly and for far longer than necessary at any intersection until all possible traffic had passed by.

Four-way stops, where drivers took it in turn to proceed, were a special challenge for Mr. Polopetsi. By and large the system worked, with every driver taking it in turns to go through the intersection, depending on who arrived first at the stop sign. But when Mr. Polopetsi drew up, he would then, out of overabundant caution, yield to everybody — even those who arrived after him — thus causing uncertainty and confusion for all the other drivers. Having seen this once or twice, Mma Makutsi had decided that she would no longer drive with Mr. Polopetsi.

Charlie, of course, was a different sort of driver altogether. He had to be reminded that nobody was in a hurry, that there were other drivers on the road, and that if he took any more corners at speed Mma Makutsi would report him to Mr. J.L.B. Matekoni.

"It is better to be late than *the* late," Mma Makutsi said to Charlie as they set off that morning. "Remember that, Charlie."

"That is very funny, Mma," said Charlie, smiling. "*The* late rather than late. That is a very funny thing. You're very clever, Mma."

"I didn't say I made it up," said Mma Makutsi. "But you just remember that. We're in no hurry to get to this office furniture place; so no speeding, Charlie."

"Are you buying a new filing cabinet, Mma?" asked Charlie. "Is that why we're going to this place?"

"We are not," said Mma Makutsi. "There is nothing wrong with the filing cabinets we have. They may be old, but they work very well."

Charlie grinned. "File, file, file," he said.

"Why are you always filing, Mma Makutsi?"

"Because I believe in tidiness, Charlie," Mma Makutsi answered. "Unlike some people."

Mr. Polopetsi had been silent until then. Now he said, "That is so, Charlie. Mma Makutsi is very good at office procedures. She has a reputation for that."

Mma Makutsi appreciated the compliment. "Thank you, Rra. Now we must set off."

"But why are we going?" asked Charlie. "If it's nothing to do with filing cabinets, then why are we going to this office place, or whatever it calls itself?"

Mr. Polopetsi took it upon himself to answer. "It's an enquiry, Charlie — an active enquiry."

"About?"

Although Mma Makutsi had harboured her misgivings about Charlie's part-time employment in the agency, she recognised that she had some responsibility for training the young man, and so, as they set off, she laid out the bare facts of the case. Charlie listened intently as he drove. Then, when Mma Makutsi had finished, he laughed.

"Simple," he said. "This is a very simple case."

Mma Makutsi gave him a sideways look.

"No case is simple, Charlie. That's something you should learn. No case is simple — that's right, isn't it, Mr. Polopetsi?"

From the back of the car, Mr. Polopetsi voiced his agreement. "Nothing is simple in this life, Charlie. If you think something's simple, then you haven't looked at it properly."

Charlie was not deterred. "This case is. Would you like me to tell you what's going on here?"

Mma Makutsi gave an irritated snort. "Your trouble is you didn't listen. Mr. Polopetsi has just told you: nothing is simple. You think you know better than Mr. Polopetsi? He's a chemistry teacher. You think you know better than him?"

"I'm not saying that," replied Charlie. "All I'm saying, Mma, is that this case is simple. The answer is sticking out five miles. Anybody can see it."

"Well, if you're so smart," said Mma Makutsi, "you tell us what's really going on."

They speeded up to pass a slower car. Charlie waved to the other driver as they shot past.

"You know that person, Charlie?" asked Mma Makutsi.

"Know her, Mma? No, I don't know her.

But she's a girl, you see, and I always wave to girls as I go past."

Mma Makutsi made a disapproving sound.

"It's just a question of manners," Charlie continued. "But you wanted me to give you the answer to this case of yours? Well, here's what I think. If somebody has been fired for no reason at all, then one thing you can say for definite is: the boss didn't do it because he didn't like the person he fired. That's definite."

Mma Makutsi looked scornful. "Oh yes? And how do you work that great theory out?"

"Because if a boss doesn't like somebody, he'll make up a good reason to do what he really wants to do because he doesn't like the person."

"But that's exactly what we have here," Mma Makutsi pointed out. "This lady was fired because she was said to have been rude to a customer."

"Hah!" exclaimed Charlie. "And is that meant to be a good reason? I said *good* reason, Mma. You don't fire somebody just because they've been rude once. You make up something really bad — probably something dishonest — like stealing. That's what you'd make up first. You'd put something in her locker and then announce that everything's going to be searched. And what do you find? You find some company property in the person's locker."

There was silence while this was digested. It was difficult to refute the logic of what Charlie had said, but Mma Makutsi would not admit that just yet.

"So if he didn't fire her because he disliked her," she said, "then why? Do you have some big theory about that, Mr. Sherlock Holmes?"

The irony was lost on Charlie. "Mr. Sherlock Holmes, Mma? I like that. That's kind."

"Well?"

Charlie thought for a moment. "The real reason is very obvious, Mma. The boss fired this lady to give her job to somebody else."

"Oh yes?"

"Yes. And why would he want to give her job to another lady? Because that other lady will be his girlfriend, Mma — that's why."

From the back Mr. Polopetsi made a contribution. "That's perfectly possible, I suppose."

Mma Makutsi, though, would not concede that easily. "How do you know that?"

Charlie laughed. "Because that's what I'd do if I were him. He's a man — I'm a man. I know what a man would do."

Mma Makutsi looked out of the car window. Her lips were tight in disapproval. She turned back to face Charlie. "Not everybody's like you, Charlie," she said.

"No, not everybody," said Charlie brightly. "But most men are, aren't they, Mr. Polopetsi?"

Mr. Polopetsi said nothing. He was not like Charlie — he knew that — but part of him wished that he were perhaps just a little bit like Charlie. Women looked at Charlie — he had noticed that on so many occasions — and yet they had never looked at him, even when he was a young man; they had looked past him, or had glanced at him and then looked away again as if the first glance had been a mistake, which he thought it probably had been. Not that it mattered too much now: he had a kind wife who had a very good government job and he had a house with new furniture, purchased on his wife's salary, and a car that went with his wife's job. All of that was far more important than being noticed by women, and yet, and yet . . .

They were nearing their destination. Outside The Office Place there was a large car park. "Go in there," said Mma Makutsi curtly. "And I'm sorry, but you can't come in, Charlie. This is a very delicate investigation. You must wait outside, please."

Charlie shrugged. "I'm only trying to be helpful, Mma Makutsi. But you know best, Mma — you know best."

The Office Place occupied a large, square building of the sort constructed by builders whose aim is pure functionality. If there were windows, there was no evidence of them on the building's façade. That was dominated by a large door surmounted by a sign that said WAY IN. Above that, in large red lettering, was another sign proclaiming that ALL YOUR OFFICE NEEDS could be met within.

"This is a very ugly building," sniffed Mma Makutsi as she and Mr. Polopetsi approached the front door. "The Double Comfort Furniture Store has flowers at the front. Phuti is very particular about that sort of thing. He says that the Garden of Eden had no concrete in it."

Mr. Polopetsi frowned. "There were no buildings in the Garden of Eden, Mma. There are no references to buildings of any sort."

Mma Makutsi adjusted her spectacles. "I know that, Mr. Polopetsi. That's the point that Phuti was making."

They went in. Stretching out before them

176

was a large sales floor on which office furniture — desks, tables, chairs — was displayed in bewildering profusion. Against the walls on every side were shelves carrying smaller items, including computers and screens, printers, and all the paraphernalia of the modern office. For all her scepticism, Mma Makutsi caught her breath in admiration, and then she saw the filing cabinet section, and she gasped.

"Look," she whispered to Mr. Polopetsi, lowering her voice as one might on entering a cathedral. "Look at those filing cabinets, Rra."

Mr. Polopetsi followed her gaze. He remarked that with filing cabinets like that, one would never want for space.

"And ease of access," said Mma Makutsi. "That is the trouble with older filing cabinets: you have to pull hard on the drawers. I've even worked with one that needed to be kicked to open."

As she spoke, she reflected on how far the secretarial profession had come since that luminous day when she had first enrolled in the Botswana Secretarial College and seen her first filing cabinet. Such was human progress; and to think that they were even talking now about filing papers in something called the Cloud. She was not sure how good an idea that would be in a country like Botswana, where the skies were always clear and empty, but that did not seem to be too much of an issue. She did not think, though, that there would ever be any substitute for a proper filing cabinet with its hanging drawers and its clear alphabetical layout. That was what she had learned on, and that was where she felt most comfortable.

Mma Makutsi looked about her. There was an office at the far end of the sales floor, and she could see through a glass partition that there was somebody in it, sitting at a desk and talking on the telephone. Now, a woman appeared from this office, and then another emerged from a door to its side.

"You go over there," Mma Makutsi said to Mr. Polopetsi. "Go over to the desk section. I'll go and look at chairs."

They went their separate ways, and each made an elaborate show of inspecting a desk and a chair. One assistant approached Mma Makutsi and another Mr. Polopetsi. The woman who went to Mma Makutsi greeted her politely and enquired whether there was anything in particular she was looking for.

"I'm interested in chairs," said Mma Makutsi. "My desk is a bit high, you see, and the chair I have is too low."

The assistant, a neat-looking woman in

her late forties, nodded. Mma Makutsi noticed her dress, which was made of a cloth popular with women in Botswana — a cotton print in brown and ochre. There was a reassuring air of respectability about this woman: she could easily have been a Sunday-school teacher or a senior social worker. Mma Makutsi liked her immediately, and decided to introduce herself.

"I'm Grace Makutsi," she said. "I'm a director of a . . . firm." She almost revealed her association with the No. 1 Ladies' Detective Agency, but decided not to, remembering Clovis Andersen's advice: *Say who you are, but not exactly who you are.*

"My name is Flora Mbeli," said the woman. "Please call me Flora, Mma."

"And you must call me Grace," Mma Makutsi responded.

Flora smiled. Her manner was friendly, but not unctuous. "May I ask where you work, Mma?"

Mma Makutsi waved a hand vaguely in an easterly direction. It was an expansive gesture that could have included Johannesburg, Maputo, and even Hong Kong, but was limited by her adding, "Over on the Tlokweng Road."

Flora did not enquire further. "There is nothing worse than a chair that's too low,

Mma. You see, your arms have to reach up and that strains the muscles down your side. It also means your neck is at the wrong angle, and that can be very uncomfortable."

Mma Makutsi said that it was important to be comfortable at work. "Good working conditions are vital, Mma," she said. She looked at Flora before continuing, "If staff are happy, then the business is happy. That is a very important rule in any business."

Flora nodded. "That's very true, Mma — very true." There was a certain wistfulness in her voice that was exactly what Mma Makutsi wanted to hear.

"You sound a bit sad, Mma," she said.

"No, I'm not sad, Mma. I was just thinking about how true your comment was."

Mma Makutsi waited, but it was clear that if the conversation were to progress along these lines, she would have to guide it where she wanted it to go. Looking about her, she said, as casually as she could, "I should imagine this is a good place to work, Mma. It looks . . ." She searched for the right word. "It looks like a contented company."

Flora did not respond.

"It looks as if people are happy working here," Mma Makutsi persisted, trying to make her comment sound casual and inconsequential.

This time Flora rose to the bait. "They used to be," she said. "I'm not so sure about now."

Mma Makutsi waited a moment before she said anything. Clovis Andersen had taught her this. *Don't ask one question after another — bang, bang, bang. People don't like to be subjected to a barrage of questions.* There would be no barrage now, just a general remark and then a gentle probing — so gentle, she hoped, that Flora would not suspect an ulterior motive.

"A happy workplace is really important," said Mma Makutsi. And then, on the tail-coat of this observation, "So what changed things, Mma?"

Flora hesitated. Glancing over her shoulder, she dropped her voice. "When I first came here, Mma, about eleven years ago, it was just after they had opened this place. I was the only person doing sales then, so it was just Mr. Gopolang . . ."

"He's the owner?"

"Yes — or, rather, he owns it jointly with his brother. But the brother is . . . what do you call such a person . . ."

"A sleeping partner?"

"That's it. I always thought that was an odd expression, Mma. I always thought of a sleeping partner as being somebody who sat

181

with his head on his desk and slept."

Mma Makutsi laughed. "Some of them probably do."

Flora resumed her story. "The business became bigger — it did quite well, Mma. After four years they took on another sales person. That was fine. She was called Bonnie. I liked that lady — she came from up north somewhere, but she was a very hard worker and would always stand in for me if I needed time off for something. We were very good friends. It was all very nice in those days."

She became silent as she reflected on what once had been.

"And then?" asked Mma Makutsi.

"Oh, the business expanded. Mr. Gopolang employed a woman called Charity Mompoloki. I liked Charity, but shortly after she took the job, Bonnie left because her husband was in the police and he had been posted up to Maun. It was a promotion — he was made inspector — but I don't think she was very happy going all that way up there. Anyway, she left and that was when . . ." Flora looked over her shoulder again before finishing the sentence. "That was when a certain person was given a job." She inclined her head towards the other side of the sales floor, where Mma

Makutsi could see Mr. Polopetsi in conversation with the other assistant. "That person, I'm afraid, Mma. She came."

Mma Makutsi reached down to stroke the top of an office chair.

"It's not real leather," said Flora. "But it's very easy to clean."

"It must be hard to work with somebody you don't get on with," said Mma Makutsi.

"Oh, it is, Mma. I tried at the beginning — I did my best, but she is too ambitious, that one. You see, we get paid on commission here. We get a salary, yes, but the rest is based on our sales. And she tries to get to customers when they come in. She tries to get to them before they have a chance to speak to me. That way she gets more sales. More sales, more commission."

Mma Makutsi clicked her tongue in disapproval. "It's best to share these things, Mma."

Flora gave Mma Makutsi a look whose meaning was quite clear: *you understand,* it said.

Mma Makutsi now ventured the question she had been hoping to ask. "And this other lady, Mma? Charity, did you say?"

Flora's expression now became one of annoyance. "She's gone." She lowered her voice. "Fired."

Mma Makutsi pretended to look surprised. "For what?"

"For nothing, Mma," hissed Flora. "I thought you couldn't get fired in this country for nothing — with the Labour Act or whatever they call it. I thought those days were over, but no, I was wrong."

Mma Makutsi shook her head in disbelief. "But they must have given some reason. They must have used some excuse."

"Oh, they did. They said she had been rude to one of our customers. That was the reason they gave."

"And she hadn't been rude at all?"

For a moment Flora did not reply. Then she said, "No, I wouldn't say that."

"Say what?"

"I wouldn't say that she hadn't been rude." She paused. "Charity was a very nice woman, Mma — she was my friend. But she believed in speaking her mind. And then she could say things that people don't expect other people to say to them."

Mma Makutsi's eyes opened wide. "Even to a customer, Mma?"

Flora wrinkled her nose. "He's a very unpleasant man, that man. We've all been tempted to speak our minds to him. She did. But it was only once — and I don't think she deserved to lose her job just because of that." She paused. "We should all be allowed a second chance, Mma, don't you think?"

Mma Makutsi did think that. But her mind was not on issues of fairness or unfairness; it was on the information she had just been given about the dismissal. So it was justified. This was not what she had wanted to find out, and she could not conceal her disappointment. "Did you see this taking place, Mma? Were there any other witnesses?"

At first Flora seemed unwilling to answer. "These things happen very quickly, Mma. Things are said and then it's all over and the damage is done."

"Yes, I know that," said Mma Makutsi. "But did you see it, Mma? Were you in the shop at the time?"

Flora nodded reluctantly. "I was in the shop."

"But did you see it?"

"I was close by . . ." Flora broke off. Her suspicions had been aroused, and now she was looking at Mma Makutsi through narrowed eyes. The Sunday-school teacher had disappeared, to be replaced with something more calculating. "Why are you asking all these questions, Mma? Are you here to buy a chair or are you here for some other reason?"

It was a direct challenge, and Mma Makutsi did not dodge it. "I am here in my official capacity," she said. "I am here as Principal Investigating Officer."

Flora repeated the title. "Principal Investigating Officer? From the Government?"

Mma Makutsi was ready for that. "No, but on behalf of an interested party."

"On behalf of Charity?"

Mma Makutsi had not expected this, and she answered it truthfully. "You could say that."

Flora's suspicions seemed to melt away. "Why didn't you tell me, Mma? Why didn't you ask me? If she's bringing a case, then I would be prepared to give evidence. I would be prepared to say that she was not rude to that man."

Mma Makutsi was taken aback. "But you've just told me she was, Mma."

"Yes, I told *you*. But I could tell a very different story to help my friend."

Mma Makutsi drew back. The No. 1 Ladies' Detective Agency did not tolerate lying, and still less would it be party to perjury. "That is out of the question, Mma," said Mma Makutsi coldly. "We would never condone lying — even on behalf of our client."

Flora pouted. "But you said you were looking for a chair," she pointed out. "That must have been a lie. You came here to ask me questions."

Mma Makutsi could not accept the accusation. "Detectives require cover," she said. "And there is a big difference between cover and lying."

"Such as?" challenged Flora.

"Cover harms nobody; lies do."

It was just the note on which to end their conversation, and with that she turned away and went to fetch Mr. Polopetsi, who had just finished his conversation with the other assistant. They left in a silence that remained unbroken until they reached the car, where Charlie was waiting for them. As she got into the car, Mma Makutsi turned to Charlie and told him that the explanation he had advanced a short while ago was wrong. "I'm sorry to say," she began, "but that lady was indeed rude to their client. So your idea that she was fired because the owner wanted to give the job to a girlfriend cannot be right."

Charlie turned on the engine and looked in the driving mirror. "Unless . . ." He waited for another car to move out of its parking place. "Unless . . ."

Mma Makutsi waited. Eventually he continued, "Unless the man she was rude to — this big client of theirs — was a friend of the owner and the owner asked him, you see, to say that she was rude, you see, and she really wasn't. You get how that works, Mma?"

Mma Makutsi dismissed this out of hand. "You have a very big imagination, Charlie. You should start writing stories. Perhaps you could get a job in films over that side, over in Johannesburg or somewhere like that." She laughed. "Lots of girls in the film industry, Charlie. Glamorous girls." She turned to address Mr. Polopetsi in the back of the car. "What do you think, Mr. Polopetsi? Would Charlie make a good movie director?"

Mr. Polopetsi laughed nervously. "He would be better than me, Mma. I wouldn't make very good movies."

Charlie looked in the mirror. He saw Mr. Polopetsi sitting in the back, too small for his seatbelt, and he smiled. "Stranger things have happened, Rra," he said. "I can see you doing something really exciting, Rra. You could be my assistant director."

Mr. Polopetsi smiled at the compliment. "I don't know, Charlie. I'm not very good at telling people what to do."

Mma Makutsi laughed. "You men," she

said. "Your time is up, I'm afraid. All the big jobs are going to be done by women soon. You just watch out — the women are coming!"

"Coming in my direction, I hope," said Charlie. "Come on, girls — I'm over here. Kiss, kiss! That's the way. Big kisses for Charlie: one, two, three! Ow!"

"Concentrate on your driving, Charlie," snapped Mma Makutsi.

When they got back to the office, Mma Makutsi and Mr. Polopetsi discussed what they had been told. Mr. Polopetsi listened intently to Mma Makutsi's account of her conversation with Flora, and told her about what the other assistant had said to him. He did not reveal, though, everything he had heard. He had decided that he would have to speak to Mma Ramotswe in private because of the nature of the information he had received — some of which bore directly on Mma Makutsi in a way that he felt she very probably would not like.

Chapter Ten:
One of Those Who
Did Not Have the Look

While Mr. Polopetsi and Mma Makutsi were conducting their individual conversations in The Office Place, Mma Ramotswe was driving down the road that led from Gaborone to the southern town of Lobatse. It was a road that she knew well, and it occurred to her that her van knew it well too. Of course cars had no memory — one should not attribute human qualities to them — but even so . . . *if* cars were to know anything, then her van would know this road, and *if* we were talking about such a world, it would be quite capable of finding its own way down this particular highway. The landmarks were familiar: there was Kgale Hill, on the right shortly after they left the confines of the town, a great sentinel of granite pushed up by some ancient geological hiccup. That had happened when all Botswana was still a vast inland sea, and the hill would have been an island then, surrounded by the waters of that now vanished lake, a refuge from the strange aquatic creatures that must have ruled the roost in those days: crocodiles far larger and more frightening than any of the denizens of the modern Limpopo; creatures for which there would simply be no name, so terrible and so hungry as to intimidate even the crocodiles . . . She stopped herself. She did not like to think of such times; the world was problematic enough as it was, without dwelling on what things were like before Botswana existed.

She glanced at Kgale Hill. It was benign enough in the middle of the day, even if you could make out places where there were caves and fissures in the rock that one would have to be careful about; at night, though, it would not be a place to linger. She shivered. A long time ago, when she had first come to Gaborone, she had gone on a church picnic at the foot of the hill. It had been the afternoon, and there had been some thirty people at the event, including children from the Sunday school. The Ladies' Guild had been responsible for the catering and had prepared baskets of sandwiches and cakes; the men had undertaken the making of a fire for the *braai,* and there had been chains of sizzling sausage, the *boerewors,* as it was called because it had been so popular with the Boers over the border in the old days; they liked their meat, those people, almost as much as the Batswana did. In fact, thought Mma Ramotswe, everyone in these parts liked their meat, and Mr. J.L.B. Matekoni was a good example of that. Stew was his favourite, but he was very happy with chicken, ostrich, and steak of any description; bacon was another weakness of his — served with sausages, if available, and fried tomatoes. In fact, Mma Ramotswe reflected, she herself liked all of the above, as well as fat cakes, another Botswana delicacy, and pastries of every description.

At that picnic, with the smell of the *braai* drifting through the acacia trees, she had gone for a walk with a couple of other young women from the church. The picnic site had been at the base of the hill, and they had walked as far as the first jumble of boulders that marked the sudden ascent of a rock face. They sat down on one of the smaller boulders and surveyed the scene around them. Off in the direction from which they had come, they saw the members of the party milling about — the children running around as they played some game or other, the women talking in small groups, the men clustered about the smoking fire. And then one of the young women turned to Mma Ramotswe and asked her if she had heard something. There had been a hissing sound, she said.

Mma Ramotswe listened. From a distance she heard the sound of the children's voices; somewhere behind, an orchestra of cicadas was striking up; but there was no hissing. Another woman heard it, though, and said that yes, there was a hissing sound. They stood up and looked around them. "We should go," said the woman who had first heard the noise. "It's not safe to stay here."

They moved away, glancing behind them as they did, everyone aware of the fact that they had been in the presence of danger. It could have been a rock python — a snake that, although massive, you could usually avoid — or it could have been something even more sinister: a black mamba, the most feared and ferocious snake in Africa, capable of outstripping a galloping horse, they said; remorseless in defence of its territory, its dark head coffin-shaped — appropriately enough for a snake that could kill a large man within minutes. As they retreated, they were seized by a sudden panic and they began to run, shouting out as they did and alarming the men, who left their fire and their sizzling sausages to find out what was amiss.

The men had made a joke of it, saying that all sorts of creatures made noises like that and they could have been frightened of something as innocent as a bullfrog, or a mongoose perhaps, or any number of friendly residents of the hill. Even a monkey, it was suggested, could make a hissing sound to enjoy the sight of a group of scared young women tripping over themselves to get away.

But now, driving past the hill, she remembered the momentary terror, even after all those years. That fear was something that was always with you in the bush, and it was only the foolhardy who would ignore it. There were things that it was perfectly right to be scared of — because they were, in themselves, frightening things. Some of them you could see, others were not so visible; some you could hear; others you sensed in some other, indefinable way.

The hill falling away behind her, she drove past the turn-off to Mokolodi, and thought of her friend who lived there, who painted the plants and flowers of Botswana, and whose husband and son had worked so hard to make the animal sanctuary at the edge of their land. She smiled as she thought of her friend, Neil, who had worked there and who knew equally well, it seemed, every humble tortoise as well as every lumbering rhino.

There were other landmarks as she travelled down the road. The turn-off to the farm where she had, a few years previously, helped to solve one of those family disputes that can poison relations between those who should love one another rather than argue about who is entitled to what. And after that, another gate that marked the small farm of yet another client whose neighbour had been stealing his cattle and who had eventually turned to Mma Ramotswe for help. Both of these matters had been resolved satisfactorily, which meant, in Mma Ramotswe's view, that all those concerned had been persuaded to see reason. That, she felt, was the key to the solution of any problem: you did not look for a winner who would take everything; you found a way of allowing people to save face; you found a way of healing rather than imposing.

And then, just before reaching Lobatse, she passed a farm that evoked a particularly poignant memory. This was not a place she had become involved in professionally; this went back to a time well before that, when as a young girl she had gone there with her father to buy a bull for their herd of cattle.

It was a big purchase, as a good strong bull could cost many thousands of pula. And this one was a beauty, her father said; this one was a paramount chief among bulls, a bull in whose veins ran the blood of great bulls of the past — bulls revered among cows, the progenitors of whole lines of fine cattle.

They had seen him standing under a tree to keep out of the sun, his cow-wives all relegated to less favourable positions in the cattle enclosure. Approaching him with the breeder, they had been treated to a breathless account of his finer points. They would have noticed, said his owner, the size of the hump on his back — for he was Brahman; they would have seen his broad, fine face — the large eyes, the floppy ears that drooped down on either side of his head; and the evident strength, of course, of his forequarters. They would have seen all these things, the breeder said, and he hesitated to mention them to somebody as knowledgeable as Obed Ramotswe was, but he thought it might be helpful just to list them anyway.

"You see, Precious," said Obed, drawing her aside, "this bull will be a very good daddy for hundreds of calves. He has that look about him, you see. It's hard to say why he has that look, but he just has, and half the work in being a good judge of cattle is learning to detect that look."

She smiled at the memory. Her father, her dearest daddy, had become late many years ago now, but she still thought of him every day. Now she remembered his words about "the look" and reminded herself that she used that expression about people too. Some people had "the look" and others did not. It was something to do with confidence, she thought. You had the look if you knew who you were, what you were doing, and why you were doing it. That bull had the look because he knew that he was good at being a Brahman bull; he knew what was expected of him, and he was not plagued by any doubts. Doubts were the enemy of the look — that was very clear. If you were not sure that you should be doing what you were doing, it showed — and you then became one of those who did not have the look.

She saw the sign pointing to the hospital, and she composed herself, putting aside the rambling thoughts that she had allowed herself to think as she drove down the road. Now was the time to concentrate on the task in hand. And that involved finding the man who had been mentioned by Sister Banjule. She had called him the No. 1 Gossip, and Mma Ramotswe would now find out whether that label was justified. She would give him the benefit of the doubt, as she always did: her experience had taught her that the names we gave to others, and the things we accused them of, often said more about us than they did about them. She liked Sister Banjule, whose work was good work, but it might be that she herself wished that she had more time to talk and could talk more freely than her job allowed. Medical people carried a lot of secrets, and by and large kept these to themselves; they could be excused if every so often they felt the desire to be able to talk to others about what they saw, to unburden themselves of the weight of confidences. Mma Ramotswe, at least, had Mma Makutsi to talk to about the secrets she learned in her job — that was perfectly permissible; but what would it be like if she had nobody with whom to discuss these things?

The Athlone Hospital in Lobatse was directly off the main road into town, a collection of neat brick buildings occupying grounds that were dotted with trees. The main gate was an impressive, rather-too-heavy arch in the vernacular style; to its side was a small cabin for security guards. As Mma Ramotswe turned, she saw that there was nobody in the box, which had a generally deserted air about it. Nor was there a sign of anybody when she parked in the visitors' car park. For a few minutes she sat in the van, the windows open to allow for the circulation of air. It was a hot afternoon, and the beating down of the sun on the stationary vehicle's roof would soon force her to seek shelter, but she was able to stay until she saw a couple of nurses come out of one of the buildings and begin to walk towards the car park.

The nurses were dressed in smart blue-and-white uniforms and had small caps neatly pinned into their hair. This, thought Mma Ramotswe, was a hospital where a good matron still held sway: you could tell immediately from the demeanour of the nurses that they were used to having a watchful, matronly eye upon them. It was the same with soldiers and policemen, and mechanical apprentices, come to think of it — with anybody, really; take away authority and things soon fell to pieces. Mma Potokwane would be proud of nurses such as these, thought Mma Ramotswe.

Mma Ramotswe got out of the van and approached the two nurses. They smiled at her when she came up to them, and greeted her courteously, in the traditional Botswana way, enquiring after her health and then waiting politely for her to ask whatever it was that she wanted to ask.

"There used to be a man at the gate," she began. "He was quite a fixture here, I believe, but I didn't see him when I came in."

One of the nurses laughed. "Oh, Stephen. Yes, they've transferred him to the blood department. He's the —"

"We call him the blood man," the other nurse interjected. "He's the porter there, really. He puts things away and tidies up — that sort of thing. He's not a proper technician."

"Do you know him, Mma?" asked the first nurse.

"Not really. But I want to talk to him about something."

Both nurses laughed. "He'll like that," said one. "That man is a very big talker, Mma. Botswana Talking Team at the Olympic Games."

They all laughed. "Could you direct me?" asked Mma Ramotswe.

Armed with their directions, she made her way into the warren of buildings that constituted the hospital, eventually arriving at a doorway marked with the sign "Blood Bank." The door was open and she could see beyond it a desk with a telephone and a half-empty bottle of water. "If not in, push bell button firmly" said a small notice. Mma Ramotswe located the button and pushed it in a way that she hoped was firm enough. This produced a ringing somewhere within and, after a minute or so, a middle-aged man, dressed in what Mma Ramotswe would describe as hospital blue, appeared from around a corner.

"Now then, Mma," he said. "What can I do for you?"

Mma Ramotswe smiled. The man's manner was friendly — even breezy — and she knew that she had found the right person.

"You're Stephen, aren't you, Rra?"

He nodded. "That is the person you're talking to, Mma. I'm Stephen, and this is the Department of Blood. I am the Blood Executive."

Mma Ramotswe suppressed a smile. It seemed that virtually everybody had some grand title now, what with Mma Makutsi announcing herself as Principal Investigating Officer and Stephen conferring on himself the grandiose office of "Blood Executive."

"This isn't about blood," she said. "I wanted to find something out, Rra." She paused. It was her policy to be as direct as possible, and she felt that this was a man who would rather like the idea of talking to a private detective. "You see, I'm Mma Ramotswe — Precious Ramotswe — and I'm the owner of the No. 1 Ladies' Detective Agency."

Her instinct was right. Stephen's eyes widened. "The No. 1 Ladies' Detective Agency!" he exclaimed. "But, Mma, I know that place! I saw it when I went up to Gaborone last time. I was visiting my uncle who lives along the Tlokweng Road, and I went right past your office."

"Well, there you are," said Mma Ramotswe. "Many people —"

He cut her short. "Yes, there was your sign with that very name on it. And I thought: What's this? What's a detective agency doing on the Tlokweng Road? That's what I thought, Mma."

"Well, Rra, we need to have —"

She did not get the chance to finish. "Oh, I'm sure you have every reason to be there, Mma — away from prying eyes. And when I arrived at my uncle's place — he has this big place, Mma, seven bedrooms, would you believe it? When I arrived at my uncle's place, I said to him, 'Uncle, what is all this about a ladies' detective agency? What's going on?' And he said, 'Stevie' — that's what he has always called me, Mma — he said, 'Stevie, there are many mysteries in this town. That fat lady' — that's what he said, Mma, I'm quoting him directly — 'that fat lady is very good at sorting out the problems people have.' I am not making that compliment up, Mma — that is exactly what my uncle said."

"He was very kind, Rra. And you — you're very kind too."

Stephen shrugged. "It is better to tell people good things, Mma — if you can. Of course, there are many people it would be very difficult to say anything good about. I'm sure you know who I'm talking about." He looked at her conspiratorially. "I think you do know, Mma — in your job you must find out many things."

"We do. But I try —"

Once again she was not allowed to complete her sentence. "The things one sees, Mma, working in a place like this!" He cast his eyes up towards the ceiling. "Of course, we have to be very confidential, but I see it all, Mma — and then some more after that." He paused, and then, looking over his shoulder, he continued, "You know what I say, Mma? I say that if you know somebody's blood group, then you know the person. You may not believe that, but I tell you it's absolutely true. This horoscope business is all a lot of nonsense — you know, star signs and all that. How can the stars influence us, Mma? They are miles and miles away from us. So, it doesn't matter if you are the sign of the fish or the bull or whatever, it makes no difference in my opinion, Mma." He paused to draw breath; Mma Ramotswe, wisely, decided it was pointless to interject. "But your blood group, Mma — that's a different matter, because your blood is *inside* you, Mma. It's going round and round and, I'll tell you something, it goes into your head, into your brain. And if something goes into your brain, Mma, it affects your ideas. That stands to reason, Mma."

"I see," said Mma Ramotswe. Somehow, she could not find the energy to say much more than that; this man was just too exhausting to contradict.

"So," Stephen continued, "if I know your blood group, then I can tell you what sort of character you have. And you know how I can do that, Mma? The answer is independent research. I've carried out a major research project, Mma, right here in Lobatse. When people come to give blood, I get to know their blood group. But I do something else: I talk to them, and while the blood is draining out of them — don't worry, Mma, we don't take it all, we just take a pint or so — I talk to them and I find out what sort of person they are. Then, when we get their blood types, I relate their personality type to their group. I then average everything out and find out if there is a connection between a particular sort of personality and a particular blood group."

He stopped, and looked at her in triumph. "I have had some very good results, Mma. What blood group are you? Do you know?"

Mma Ramotswe laughed. "I have no idea, Rra, I've —"

"My guess would be that you are type O, Mma. That is very common. And it fits your personality type, which must be strong and sensible if you are a private detective. I myself am a very rare type, Mma. I'm AB negative. There are very few of us — just a handful in Botswana. That type is very sensitive and intelligent, Mma — not that I would say that about myself, but that is what we are."

And prone to talk too much, thought Mma Ramotswe.

She decided to take matters into her own hands. "I wanted to ask you something, Rra."

He was about to say something more, but

the firmness with which Mma Ramotswe now spoke, and the volume of her voice, seemed to have an effect.

"What I want to ask, Rra, is this: Do you know where I can get in touch with one of the nurses who works down here — one Mingie Ramotswe?"

Stephen's eyes lit up. "Mingie Ramotswe? Yes, of course. She is one of the sisters. She doesn't work in this hospital all the time — she is in one of the other clinics, I think. But she's here from time to time. I think she's part of a team that's based here. She used to be a theatre sister, but now I think she's doing community nursing. She goes out to those clinics off in the bush — way, way away."

"Do you know her, Rra?" asked Mma Ramotswe.

Stephen nodded. "Yes, of course I do, Mma."

"And do you know where she lives?"

"Yes. She is in one of the new houses two blocks east of the main road — the road you will have come in on. Those new houses are on Khama Way. She is in the house at the top of that street — I saw her in the garden of that place when I drove past once. She has a big bougainvillea at the gate."

Mma Ramotswe made a note in her notebook. Stephen watched. "Why do you want to see her, Mma?"

There was only one answer she could give. "It's because she shares my name, Rra. I am curious to see if we are related in some way."

Stephen thought about it. "Yes," he said. "You are both called Ramotswe. It's possible." He paused. "You've never met her, Mma?"

"No, Rra. I've never met Mingie."

He hesitated. "She's an interesting lady," he said.

"Oh yes?"

He hesitated again. There was a smile playing around his lips. "She's not like the average lady," he said. "She is not average."

Mma Ramotswe waited. Sister Banjule had alluded to something similar, but had not explained what she meant.

"We are not all the same," said Mma Ramotswe. "Life would be very dull, Rra, if we were all the same. It would be the same as our all having type O blood. That would be very dull for somebody like you, I would have thought."

If there was a touch of reproach in Mma Ramotswe's comment, it was lost on Stephen. "Yes, it would be very dull," he agreed.

"In what way is this lady interesting, Rra?"

Stephen made a gesture that Mma Ramotswe found hard to interpret. "Interesting? Did I say interesting? Well, I suppose she is. It is interesting that she is not interested, shall I say?"

"I don't follow you, Rra," Mma Ramotswe said.

"I am not sure that she is a lady who likes men very much," he said, lowering his voice. Then he added, "Why is there no husband, Mma? There are plenty of good men in Botswana — what excuse does a woman have for not having one of these men as her husband?"

Mma Ramotswe held his gaze. "Oh, Rra?" she said. "Surely you are not saying that it's the duty of every woman in Botswana to have a husband. Surely not."

Stephen drew back. His ebullience faded now, and he spoke less rapidly. "I'm not saying that, Mma."

"But I think that's exactly what you did say, Rra," she said gently.

"I didn't mean —"

She looked at him reproachfully. "Don't you think that it's best if we don't worry about what other people are, Rra?"

He stuttered a response. "Yes, Mma; of course, Mma. I am not one of those people who say that we all have to be the same. I would never say that . . ."

"I am glad to hear it, Rra. I didn't think that you were an unkind man."

He was saved by the ringing of the bell. His relief was very evident. "I'm sorry, Mma, but that is somebody come to get some blood. I must deal with this immediately."

She thanked him, and made her way out of the blood department. She thought of an expression she had heard — one that was used when it was difficult to get information from somebody. People said in those circumstances it was like trying to get blood out of a stone. Well, was there an expression for when somebody gave out too much information? If not, then perhaps somebody should invent one. Getting a word in edgeways with Stephen was like . . . what was it like? Trying to stop the Limpopo in full flood. That was it, she thought. And perhaps she should write it down in her notebook before she forgot it. Often the interesting things you said were lost for all time if you did not write them down in your notebook.

When she returned to the van, she did not drive away immediately, but stood beside it for a few minutes while she decided what to do. When she was younger, she had never experienced any difficulty in making up her mind: you saw what needed to be done, and then you did it. It was as simple as that. Now things were different; life was perhaps not quite as straightforward as you once thought it to be — things that would previously have been quite clear could be clouded by a slew of possibilities. The old Botswana morality, of course, could be a helpful guide — you could never go wrong if you stuck to that — but it seemed that sometimes it had nothing to say about a problem or dilemma. And that was the case right now: What guidance did the old Botswana morality have in circumstances where you wanted to satisfy your curiosity about somebody who had the same name as you did but where, at the same time, people seemed a bit wary of the person in question? The answer was that the old Botswana morality was silent on this and it was entirely up to you to decide what to do.

Mma Ramotswe decided to go back to Gaborone but, at the hospital gate, where a left-hand turn would have taken her back in the direction of home, she turned right. She did it deliberately, and it involved a reversal of her plan: she would make a detour onto Khama Way and see — just take a look from the outside — what sort of place Mingie Ramotswe lived in. Stephen had given fairly specific information: Khama Way, at the top of the street, with a big bougainvillea bush at the gate.

It took no more than a few minutes to reach Khama Way, and once she was there, Mingie's house was immediately identifiable. There was the large bougainvillea, riotous and unclipped, a splash of deep red against the washed-out browns of the rest of the garden. Behind it, at the end of a short driveway lined with red cannas, was a neat whitewashed house of the sort that bureaucrats called a "middle-income dwelling." There was no car outside, and the windows were all shut; Mingie was out, perhaps at one of the remote clinics that Stephen had mentioned. That at least settled that: she would not be meeting her on this occasion.

But then she thought: neighbours. If she could engage one of the neighbours in a brief conversation it would enable her to form a better impression of what Mingie was like. There had been these curious reservations — if one could call them that — from both Sister Banjule and Stephen. A neighbour would settle it one way or the other, although . . . Mma Ramotswe reminded herself that neighbours could be unreliable witnesses. There were people who simply did not get on with those around them, and such people could not be trusted to give an unbiased view. On the other hand, Mma Ramotswe thought she could see through that sort of thing easily enough and would not be swayed by any spitefulness.

She drove slowly past Mingie's gate. The house immediately next door looked unattended, but the one on the other side of the road had a small pickup truck parked outside it and there were several children in the garden. To the side of the house was a washing line, and a woman in a red dress was engaged in hanging up washing. Pulling in to the verge, Mma Ramotswe stepped out of her van and approached the woman attending to the washing.

Greetings were exchanged.

"A woman's work is never done, is it, Mma?" said Mma Ramotswe.

The woman smiled. She had a broad, open face and Mma Ramotswe had taken an immediate liking to her. She suspected that this woman had a lot of work to do — there were at least four children in the garden — and some of the clothes she had been hanging up looked as if they belonged to a young infant. So there was another one indoors, out of the sun. Five young children: she could only just imagine what that did to your day.

"Washing in particular," the woman said. "You finish one load, and there's another one waiting."

"You could get a girl to do it, Mma," said Mma Ramotswe.

This was a perfectly reasonable thing to say. Anybody in any employment in Botswana was expected to engage somebody to help in the house. There was nothing extravagant about this; it was, in fact, a form of sharing: if you had a job, you had money, and money needed to be spread around. The people who helped in the house were often paid a pittance and expected to work long hours, but they were desperate for any job and were pleased to take on what came their way. Mma Ramotswe did not subscribe to this exploitation; she paid Rose, who helped her in the house, much more than she would get elsewhere, and treated her with decency too. Mma Makutsi took the same view. Since her marriage to Phuti Radiphuti she had been given help in the house, but she never took advantage of the people who did that work. She remembered what it was to be poor, and she acted accordingly.

The woman looked at her. She was bemused. "I am the girl, Mma," she said.

Mma Ramotswe put her hand to her mouth. "I'm sorry, Mma. I didn't mean . . ."

The woman laughed. "It doesn't matter, Mma. I have a girl who helps me with my children — we are all in the same position. One person helps another and that other person helps another person, and so on."

Mma Ramotswe was pleased that there was no awkwardness. "I was wondering, Mma," she said. "I was wondering when Mingie will be back." She pointed to Mingie's house. "Is she off at one of the clinics?"

The woman nodded. "Yes, she went off yesterday. Usually, it's two or three days at the most."

"Do you know her well?" asked Mma Ramotswe.

The woman finished the hanging up of a child's brightly coloured dress and then turned to face Mma Ramotswe again. "I know her better than many," she said. "So, yes, you could say I know her quite well."

It was a strange reply. *Better than many . . .* What was implied by this? That Mingie kept to herself?

"She doesn't have many friends, then?"

said Mma Ramotswe.

The woman reached for a handful of clothes pegs. "She has her friends," she said evenly. "But some people don't like her, I think."

Mma Ramotswe allowed a few moments to pass. A hoopoe, its russet crest topped with dots of black, had alighted on the grass not far away and was watching them. The woman noticed it and remarked that the same bird often presented itself when she was hanging out the washing. "I know somebody who believes that the birds are our ancestors," she said. "She thinks that ancestors come back to watch over us, and they take the form of birds, especially hoopoes and hornbills. I don't believe that, Mma — do you?"

"No," said Mma Ramotswe. "And sometimes I think it's a pity that we can't believe things that would make us feel much better." She paused. "But what you said interests me, Mma — why do some people not like Mingie?"

The woman started to hang out a shirt, separating the arms with pegs to allow the cloth to dry more evenly. "I don't know, Mma. People are strange. That lady — Mingie Ramotswe — is one of the kindest ladies I know. She is a very good woman, Mma."

"Oh?"

"Yes," said the woman. "My husband is late, you see, Mma. When he became late, she did so much for me, Mma — I can't tell you how much, because her kindness was like a very deep well. There was so much of it. And I know she's helped other people too, Mma. She is a very good woman."

Mma Ramotswe felt relieved. This was the sort of informal, sincere testimonial that was infinitely more useful than any muttered reservations or cryptic remarks. When somebody lost a wife or a husband, then the true colours of others came out. She was sure now: if Mingie Ramotswe was some sort of relative, then she would be proud to have her.

She looked at her watch. "I must be going, Mma," she said. "I shall leave her a note."

"I can tell her you called," said the woman. "I'll see her when she comes back. I can tell her then." She looked at Mma Ramotswe quizzically. "What did you say your name was, Mma."

Mma Ramotswe did not hesitate. "Precious Ramotswe," she said.

The woman expressed surprise. "What relation are you?" she asked.

Mma Ramotswe waved a hand vaguely. "I'm not sure," she said. "But I think I'd like to find out."

She said goodbye to the woman and returned to the van. There she took a leaf out of her notebook and wrote a message in pencil. "Mingie Ramotswe," the note began. "My name is Precious Ramotswe and I run the No. 1 Ladies' Detective Agency on the Tlokweng Road. Would you like to come to see me when you are next in Gaborone? Thank you."

She wondered whether she should write more, but what more was there to write? She had issued the invitation and now all there was to do was to wait and see what happened. Some invitations, she reflected, bore fruit, while others did not. And with that in mind, she crossed the road and slipped her note under the front door of Mingie's middle-income house.

CHAPTER ELEVEN:
CHILDREN ARE ALWAYS EATING

Mma Ramotswe had left a note for Mingie Ramotswe and in turn she had been left a note by Mr. Polopetsi. It had been placed on her desk in an envelope, on which he had written, in his careful, excessively small script, For the eyes of Mma Ramotswe only. Mma Ramotswe had to strain to read the minute inscription, but smiled as she did so. Mma Makutsi was not in the office at the time, but had she been, she knew what a battle with temptation she would have had to face. To write on an envelope "for the eyes only" of somebody was surely an invitation to others to at the very least scrutinise the envelope, to hold it up to the light — in short, to do everything humanly possible to determine its contents. Had Mma Makutsi seen Mr. Polopetsi's note, it would have been as a red rag to a bull. Although she would have stopped short of steaming open the envelope, she certainly would have posed a series of probing questions in an effort to find out what the highly confidential note said. These questions would be indirect to begin with, but would gradually become more explicit, until she would eventually ask: "What has Mr. Polopetsi written in that note, Mma? Not that I am trying to pry, of course, and I would never expect you to betray a confidence, but if it's not too confidential, then it would be interesting to know what he thinks is so very secret." The question would be followed by a careless laugh, the meaning of which would be: *Mr. Polopetsi could not possibly be party to anything really confidential; he is clearly overstating matters, as he often does.*

But now there was nobody else in the office, as it was late afternoon, and so Mma Ramotswe could slit the flap of the envelope and extract the handwritten note within. Again it was in Mr. Polopetsi's small handwriting and required close examination in order to be read. It was not long — no more than two sentences — and told Mma Ramotswe that he had a very important matter to talk to her about and that this matter could not be discussed in the presence of any other person, especially of one in particular. No name was given, but Mma Ramotswe was able to assume that this person was

Mma Makutsi. Having sounded that warning, Mr. Polopetsi asked Mma Ramotswe whether she could call at his house on the way home from the office, and there, he promised, a highly sensitive matter would be revealed.

Mma Ramotswe had been to the Polopetsi house once before, on the occasion when Mr. Polopetsi's wife had held a birthday party for her husband. She had been impressed by its neatness, which is how she had imagined it would be, given Mr. Polopetsi's rather precise manner, but she had not been prepared for the range of cleaning equipment she found on her visit to the bathroom. Not only was there a whole rail of cleaning cloths, but there was a shelf groaning under the strain of cleaning fluids, disinfectants, and scouring powders. Cleanliness was a worthwhile goal, thought Mma Ramotswe, but there had to be limits to the amount of time and energy devoted to it. She belonged to the school that held that yards should be swept, stoeps and kitchen floors should be polished with that red polish appropriate for such surfaces, and that baths and sinks should from time to time be sprinkled with that sharp-smelling white powder that claimed to destroy all known household germs; but beyond that one should not worry too much about dirt and germs. Some dirt, and some germs, were inevitable, and did we not need these for our immune systems to be kept in training, ready to deal with greater dangers that might be lurking about?

When she had parked the van immediately outside his gate, Mr. Polopetsi was already at the front door. He had witnessed her arrival from the living-room window and was ready to welcome her.

"You haven't been here for a long time, Mma Ramotswe," he said. "Not since that birthday party of mine, I think."

"It was a very good party, that one," she said. "I remember it very well."

Mr. Polopetsi beamed with pleasure. "We shall have another party some day," he said. "You can never go to enough parties, Mma."

Mma Ramotswe looked dubious. "I'm not sure about that, Rra. I think one wouldn't want to go to too many. You'd get a bit tired of parties, wouldn't you, if you went to a party every night?"

Mr. Polopetsi nodded his agreement. "You're quite right, Mma Ramotswe. What I meant to say was that you can't have enough parties if you don't go to many in the first place — if you see what I mean."

She was not sure that she did, but she did

not want to prolong that aspect of the discussion. So she made a complimentary remark about the garden and waited for Mr. Polopetsi to lead her into the house.

"This way, Mma Ramotswe," he said. "We'll sit in the living room, I think."

She followed him into a scrupulously tidy room furnished with four easy chairs. The chairs were covered with transparent plastic covers, as was the low-level table at the centre of the room. Mma Ramotswe sat down, feeling the chair's plastic cover crinkling uncomfortably beneath her.

Mr. Polopetsi sat opposite her, his hands clasped together; he looked uneasy. She decided to start the conversation herself. "So, Rra," she said. "What is this important matter you wanted to raise with me?"

Mr. Polopetsi was looking fixedly at the wall, at a picture of the late Sir Seretse Khama, hanging beside a framed photograph of a proud and beaming Mr. Polopetsi holding a diploma. He looked much the same, she thought; he was one of those on whom the passage of years appeared to make little impact. She glanced again at the graduation photograph; she had no such certificates herself, but did not resent those who did have them. Had she something to display, of course, she would perhaps be a little bit more circumspect than Mma Makutsi and her ninety-seven per cent, but in the scale of human failings, moderate pride in one's achievements surely occupied a low enough place.

Mr. Polopetsi dragged his gaze away from the wall. "It's a delicate matter, Mma," he began. "I needed to talk to you in the absence of . . ."

She made it easier for him: ". . . of Mma Makutsi. But of course, Rra. I understand. Mma Makutsi sometimes has strong views and isn't afraid to express them. That can be a good attribute, as I'm sure you know, but there are times when it is better to talk more calmly."

Mr. Polopetsi made it clear that the force of Mma Makutsi's opinions was not the problem. "This affects her directly," he said. "I've learned something, Mma, that could affect Phuti Radiphuti's business." He paused, and lowered his voice. "Very badly, Mma; in fact, to the point of ruining it."

Mma Ramotswe had not expected this. "Perhaps you should start at the beginning, Mr. Polopetsi. And take your time, Rra — I am in no hurry."

She sat back as Mr. Polopetsi told his tale. "You know that we went to The Office Place to talk to the staff about Charity's firing?"

"Mma Makutsi told me you were going, Rra."

"Well, there are two sales ladies there, Mma. There used to be three, before Charity was fired by Gopolang. He's the boss."

"Yes," said Mma Ramotswe. "And then?"

"Well, I spoke to one of the ladies, Mma, and Mma Makutsi spoke to the other. As it happened, I knew the lady I spoke to — not very well, but a little bit. You see, I teach her son at the Gaborone Secondary School." He paused. "Chemistry."

She nodded. "I know that, Rra. Chemistry. So you knew this lady?"

Mr. Polopetsi drew a deep breath. "Her name is Gloria, Mma. They have a long surname that the other boys laugh at, so I've got used to not using it. I just call her son Sam, and that means he's not ridiculed."

Mma Ramotswe sighed. "Our names have a lot to answer for," she said. "Our names can decide the way our lives work out."

"You're right, Mma," said Mr. Polopetsi. "I'm glad that I'm called Polopetsi and not something ridiculous. But this lady, this Gloria, Mma, is a nice lady, but she has not had an easy life recently. Her husband is late, you see. He was struck by lightning."

Mma Ramotswe was silent. It was not as

unusual a cause of death as people might imagine it to be. In a broad, wide country with few hills, lightning could be a real danger, and each year there were people who happened to be out in the open when a sudden electrical storm brewed up.

"He worked for the railway," explained Mr. Polopetsi. "He was inspecting some track down by Kgale Siding and lightning struck the rail right next to where he was standing. Apparently he was thrown twenty feet or so. He did not stand a chance, Mma: you can't argue with lightning."

Mma Ramotswe agreed. There was a list of things you could not argue with: lightning, lions, black mambas, crocodiles . . .

"It was very sad," Mr. Polopetsi continued. "That lady has four children — three by the late railway engineer and one by a former husband who was no good. They are nice children, Mma, but you know how it is with children: they are always eating, they are always needing new clothes and new shoes. If you have children, you must have something in your pockets."

"That is very true, Rra."

"So this lady had to find a job, and she found one in The Office Place. She is a hard worker, and I think she makes enough there to keep her children. There is some kind person somewhere who helps with the school fees of that boy, Sam. And he is a hard worker, too, that boy. He is very good at remembering chemical formulae. He is a star pupil of mine, in fact."

Mma Ramotswe tried, as tactfully as she could, to nudge the story on. "So what did Gloria tell you, Rra?"

"Well, she told me, Mma, that Charity was an easy person to work with. She said that Charity had been kind to one of her daughters and has passed on some clothing she did not need. She said she was surprised when she was dismissed, but she did not really have much to say about that. She did, however, say something about Gopolang himself. She said that she did not like him very much, although she could not fault him as a boss. She said that he is a ladies' man — or thinks he is."

Mma Ramotswe shook her head. "There are so many men who think that. You are not like that, of course, Mr. Polopetsi, because you are a very polite man when it comes to ladies. But there are so many other men who have not learned yet to behave themselves."

Mr. Polopetsi said that he thought Gopolang might be one of these. "She told me that he's married but that she's seen him with another woman. She said that she went into his office one day — she thought he was away — and found him at his desk, with this woman sitting on his lap. He was very embarrassed and he told her that he was just testing the chair to see if it would take the weight of two people. He said he was concerned that some of the customers were too" — Mr. Polopetsi hesitated for a moment, but then continued — "too traditionally built for office chairs these days and there could be injuries."

Mma Ramotswe gave a snort. "Who would believe something like that, Rra?"

"Gloria didn't," said Mr. Polopetsi. "She left him to get on with his weight experiment and went back to work. But later that day, this Gopolang came to her and said that he hoped she understood never to talk to anybody about the experiment she had seen him conducting. He said that it was a valuable commercial secret and that it was most important that nobody should hear about it. Of course he meant that he didn't want his wife to hear."

"Of course he didn't," said Mma Ramotswe.

"Gloria told him that she would never talk about things she saw at work, and he appeared to be relieved. But she herself felt very unhappy because his warning had made her think that her job was at risk. She feared that he was the sort of man who might not want somebody who was working for him to know that he had ladies sitting on his lap in his office. And then, Mma, Charity lost her job and she thought that this might be because she had seen something too."

It was at this point that Mma Ramotswe stopped him. This was a possibility that she had not considered, and she needed to think about it. "Do you think it likely, Rra?" she asked.

Mr. Polopetsi scratched his head. "I don't know, Mma. If Charity knew something that he didn't want others to know, then surely he would have been worried that if he fired her she would go straight off and tell somebody."

Mma Ramotswe considered this. She thought the point was a reasonable one, but then she reminded herself that people who are ashamed of something often feel threatened by the presence of those who know their secret. It was perfectly credible, she thought, that Gopolang would feel threatened in some way by an employee who knew that he was having an affair and would want her out because of shame or embarrassment.

"We shall have to think about this," she said. "But tell me, Rra, what has this got to do with Mma Makutsi's husband?"

He raised a finger. "Ah, well, Mma Ramotswe, it is not that that has a bearing on Phuti's business. Gloria told me something else — and that is far more sensitive."

She waited.

Mr. Polopetsi now told the rest of his story, punctuating the tale with an occasional emphatic gesture. "You know that The Office Place only sells office furniture," he began. "Most of the time they sell desks and chairs, and filing cabinets, and things like that. They sell a small amount of stationery — printer paper and drawing pins and so on — but their main business is furniture for the office." He paused. "Now, Mma, if you were wanting to buy some furniture here in Gaborone, where would you go? If you wanted it for your office, then obviously The Office Place has the best selection. But" — and here a very definite gesture underlined the qualification — "but if you wanted home furniture, then you would go to the Double Comfort Furniture Store, to Phuti Radiphuti's place. They have all the best beds and dining-room tables and such things."

Mma Ramotswe agreed that they had the largest selection of such items. "And it's good furniture," she said. "It is none of this Chinese rubbish. It is good African wood."

Mr. Polopetsi nodded his head in vigorous agreement. "They buy a lot of it from a factory up in Bulawayo," he said. "They make a lot of it out of *mukwa* wood and Zambezi teak. They make some very fine chairs, I think, and big tables too."

Mma Ramotswe had heard Phuti talking about his *mukwa* chairs. He had told her that some of them had been bought for State House itself back in the days of President Mogae, and this made him particularly proud. And the American embassy, too, had bought occasional tables of the same wood and was said to be pleased with them.

Mr. Polopetsi lowered his voice again. She felt like reassuring him that there was nobody else around, but said nothing as he continued. "Now, Mma, what she said next really worried me. She said that Gopolang had told her that he had a plan to start selling house furniture as well as office stuff. Now that would be bad enough news for Phuti and Mma Makutsi, of course, because there is an unspoken agreement between the two shops that they do not cut into each other's markets. But listen, Mma, it gets worse: Gopolang has been up to see that factory in Bulawayo and is going to take all their production — *all* their production, Mma." He paused to let this sink in. "And Phuti will not be able to buy from them any longer."

Mma Ramotswe frowned. There was something in this story that did not make sense. "But why would those people up in Bulawayo sell everything to Gopolang," she asked, "when they've been dealing with Phuti all along?"

Mr. Polopetsi sat bolt upright to deliver the bombshell. "Because he's going to pay them ten per cent more," he said. "He's then going to sell the furniture at a loss for six months. He has the money to do it, apparently. And then, after six months, when Phuti's customers have all left him to come to The Office Place, he'll raise his own prices to a more economic level. But by that time, Phuti will have been put out of business."

Mma Ramotswe drew in her breath. "That is a very underhand thing to do," she said.

Mr. Polopetsi agreed. "But it will probably work."

"Why did he tell her all this?" she asked.

"Because he's putting her in charge of that

new department, and he wants her to know how everything works."

There was still something that did not quite add up. "But then why did Gloria tell you? Surely this scheme is going to work to her advantage. Why would she warn you about it?"

Mr. Polopetsi had anticipated the question. "Because she doesn't approve of that sort of thing, Mma. She is an old-fashioned lady."

He looked at her reproachfully, and Mma Ramotswe felt ashamed. Her question had made it sound as if she assumed that people would always do what was in their best interests even if it involved some underhand practice. She neither assumed that nor approved of such behaviour, and she felt she had to tell him this.

"It is not old-fashioned to believe in doing the right thing, Rra," she said. "I would never say that. It's just that it is so common now for people to think of themselves first and foremost."

He assured her he had not imagined she would approve. "And you are right, Mma," he continued. "There are many people now who just think of themselves. They don't care if what they do causes distress to other people. They just think: me, me, me."

"So this lady must be very worried, Rra," said Mma Ramotswe.

"She doesn't know what to do, Mma. She thinks that if she warns Phuti Radiphuti about this plot, then Gopolang will find out and she will lose her job. And she can't afford to do that."

"So what does she expect you to do?"

Mr. Polopetsi sighed. "She doesn't really know. She just wanted to tell somebody — to get it off her chest. She knows that I've been helping her son, and so she turned to me. She's a widow, you see, Mma, and widows may not have many people to turn to." He looked at her despairingly. "But the truth of the matter, Mma Ramotswe, is that I don't know what to do. And so now I've told you."

It seemed to Mma Ramotswe that just as Gloria might have had nobody to turn to, then the same might be said of Mr. Polopetsi.

"And I'm glad you did, Rra," she said. "Because I'm sure I'll be able to think of a way of dealing with this."

The effect of her words was instantaneous. Mr. Polopetsi smiled broadly. "Oh, that is very good, Mma. I hoped that you would say something like that. Now I need not worry any longer."

Mma Ramotswe was touched by his confidence in her ability to find a solution; she wished she were equally sure that she would do so, but she feared it was not going to be easy. At all costs they should protect Gloria from recrimination on the part of Gopolang, but they had an equal, if not greater, duty to prevent the Double Comfort Furniture Store from being damaged by this piece of commercial chicanery.

"I shall do my best, Mr. Polopetsi," she said, as she stood up to go. "That is all I can do."

Mr. Polopetsi nodded enthusiastically. "That's right, Mma Ramotswe. That's the most that any of us can do." He hesitated. "One thing, though, Mma: You won't tell Mma Makutsi, will you, that I told you rather than her about this Gopolang plan to sell house furniture? You see, I've told her about the lady in the chair — or on the lap in the chair — but I haven't told her about the other thing. I wouldn't want her to think I was holding information back from her when she's the Principal Investigating Officer."

Mma Ramotswe assured him that she would not. Then, ushered out by Mr. Polopetsi, she made her way to her waiting white van. She had rather a lot to think about for the rest of the journey home: she had the trip to Lobatse to mull over, including the thought that she might soon be meeting a new and mysterious member of the Ramotswe clan; she had the new theory on the Charity affair to consider; and then she had the disturbing news about the plot against the Double Comfort Furniture Store. And at the back of her mind, barely acknowledged but still festering away, was the information she had received from Mma Potokwane that Note Mokoti had been seen in town. All this seemed to her to be just rather too much for one woman, traditionally built though she may be, to bear with equanimity. Gloria had been able to confide in Mr. Polopetsi; Mr. Polopetsi had been able to come to her; but who did she have to turn to? Mr. J.L.B. Matekoni? That would only be natural, as a wife should always be able to turn to a husband, and vice versa, but in this case she was unwilling to tell him that Note had been seen. Note was her problem — a part of her life of which she felt curiously ashamed, and she did not want to burden him with all that. No, she would work something out, and already she was beginning to see what she must do. If you are facing a dreaded meeting, one of the best ways of dealing with it is to bring the encounter forward *on your terms.* Gain the initiative by going forth to meet the person you dread. Clovis Andersen had said something about that in *The Principles of Private Detection.* What exactly he had said escaped her, but she was sure that was the gist of it. And had he not also said something about arming yourself with support for such a difficult meeting? He had, she thought, and what better support than Mma Potokwane? If a man had been born who could stand up to Mma Potokwane in full flight, then Mma Ramotswe had yet to meet him. Together they would seek out Note and warn him off. That would be necessary, she felt, as sooner or later he would try to contact her. That is what he had done on past return trips to Gaborone, and that was what she was sure he would do again. Well, that would pre-empt that. Clovis Andersen himself had said pre-emption is often the best defence. She agreed with that, and would perhaps go even further: sometimes pre-emption was not only the best defence — it was the only one.

CHAPTER TWELVE:
WE MUST NOT
CONFUSE MEN

At tea time the following morning Charlie was looking out of the window of the No. 1 Ladies' Detective Agency when he saw an unfamiliar car draw up and park immediately next to Mma Ramotswe's white van. He watched as a woman emerged from the car and, as if engaged in a programme of exercise, slowly and carefully stretched her limbs.

"Hah!" said Charlie. "I have seen something very interesting; let me tell you what Mr. Sherlock Holmes would say about this."

From behind her desk, Mma Makutsi snorted. "Don't get ideas, Charlie. You aren't Mr. Sherlock Holmes yet."

Charlie ignored the taunt and addressed himself to Mma Ramotswe. "Would you like me to tell you what I've just seen, Mma?" he asked.

Without waiting for an answer, he continued, "I can tell that the lady who has just got out of her car outside has come from some distance away."

Mma Ramotswe looked up from the contemplation of her cup of red bush tea. She had been thinking of last night's discussion with Mr. Polopetsi and the delicate task that lay ahead of her of dealing with the threat to Phuti's business. "What lady?" she asked.

"The lady who has just parked next to your van," said Charlie. "She has got out and is doing some stretching exercises. So what does this tell us, Mma?" He waited for a few seconds before continuing, with some pride, "Why would somebody do stretching exercises, Mma? It is because she has been driving for a long time."

"Well done, Charlie," said Mma Ramotswe. "That's very observant."

Mma Makutsi, perhaps somewhat grudgingly, agreed that the deduction made sense. "That tells us something," she said. "But not much. You won't know where she's come from, for instance, will you?"

Charlie gazed out of the window again. "Lobatse," he said. "She's come from Lobatse."

Mma Ramotswe stiffened. "Lobatse?"

"You're guessing, Charlie," Mma Makutsi challenged.

"No, Mma," countered Charlie. "There is

a sticker on the back of her car. You know those stickers that say where the car was bought? Well that one is from that garage down in Lobatse — Kalahari Motors — we sometimes get their cars in here. Mr. J.L.B. Matekoni would . . ."

He did not finish. Mma Ramotswe had risen to her feet and crossed the floor to the door. If this was who she thought it might be, then she wanted to meet her outside, rather than in the office under the eyes of Mma Makutsi and Charlie.

"I think this person has come to see me," she said over her shoulder as she went out.

The woman had stopped her stretching and was looking about her when Mma Ramotswe came up to her.

Mma Ramotswe cleared her throat. "Can I help you, Mma?"

The woman turned round, and Mma Ramotswe caught her breath. She was unprepared for the shock of seeing a woman who so closely resembled her. Not only was the build the same, but the face that was looking at her with such surprise was her own.

The woman seemed to share her astonishment. "Mma?" she stuttered. "Are you Mma Ramotswe?"

Mma Ramotswe nodded. "And are you

Mma Ramotswe, Mma?"

The woman nodded. "I think we're both Mma Ramotswe."

This was followed by silence, eventually broken by Mma Ramotswe's saying, "I'm very glad you've come to see me, Mma."

Mingie Ramotswe smiled. "How could I not come and see you, Mma? I thought that you might be some distant relative, but now I see you and . . ." She stopped and made a hopeless gesture. "What can I say, Mma?"

Mma Ramotswe was equally stuck for words. She opened her mouth to speak, but no sound came. She looked into the eyes of the woman in front of her and then, from somewhere deep within her, from a place beyond her control, she began to cry.

The reaction from Mingie mirrored her own, and the two women took a final step forwards and threw their arms round each other. From within the office, a wide-eyed Charlie and an equally astonished Mma Makutsi peered through the window at the extraordinary reunion.

"That's Mma Ramotswe greeting another Mma Ramotswe," said Charlie breathlessly.

"Well, Mr. Sherlock Holmes," said Mma Makutsi. "What do you make of that?"

Charlie whistled. "I would say that Mma Ramotswe has just met her sister."

Mma Makutsi shook her head. "Mma Ramotswe doesn't have a sister."

Charlie looked at her and smiled. "She does now, Mma," he said.

They did not go back into the office, but at Mma Ramotswe's suggestion took a walk along one of the paths that led off into the scrub bush behind the garage. This was the very edge of Gaborone, and, as was often true of the immediate surrounds of an African town, there was an in-between zone where numerous paths crisscrossed one another; where cattle grazed unauthorised; where scraps of detritus from nearby roads were blown in small eddies of dust; where the sound of traffic and other human sounds were gradually drowned out by the screech of the insects that made their lives in trees and shrubs. Mma Ramotswe knew these paths because every so often, when she wanted to clear her head and get away from the office for a few minutes, she would walk out on one of them, would stand and look up at the sky, would breathe the air scented by acacia leaves and cattle dung — the smell of her native Botswana, the smell that evoked so many memories.

They did not walk fast, but ambled at the pace of those for whom the journey was less important than the opportunity to talk, and who knew that their unspoken agenda was a grave one.

Mma Ramotswe began the conversation. "I saw your photograph, Mma," she said. "That is when I first heard about you."

Mingie nodded. "That was with some other nurses?" she asked.

"Yes. Two others. And when I saw the name I was surprised, because I thought I knew all the Ramotswes and here was another one." She paused. "Where were you born, Mma?"

"Pilane," answered Mingie. "That's a place just outside Mochudi."

Mma Ramotswe caught her breath. "I know that place," she said. "I am from Mochudi, you see. That's where I was born."

"We didn't stay there long, though," said Mingie. "My mother left the country. She went over the border to a place just outside Johannesburg. She had a job there in domestic science college. She took me there with her and that is where I was raised. We were Setswana-speaking but we lived in South Africa."

"You went to school there?" asked Mma Ramotswe.

"Yes," said Mingie. "It was during the big changes. I was at school in the early days of freedom."

The as-yet-unspoken question was hanging in the air between them and could no longer be ignored.

"You mention your mother, Mma," said Mma Ramotswe. "What about your father?"

She knew that this was likely to be an awkward question. There were so many people who either did not know who their father was or had not had the chance to get to know him. It was a shameful situation, with men casually refusing to acknowledge their offspring, leaving women to assume the entire burden; it happened, but it was not something of which Mma Ramotswe was proud: her Botswana deserved better than that.

The cicadas shrilled; the sun inched its way up the sky.

It took Mingie a little while to answer. "My father, Mma? I did not know him. I never met him."

"But did your mother say anything about him, Mma?"

Mingie hesitated once more. "She did not say much, Mma. She said . . . Well, she said that he was not a good man. That was all she said."

Mma Ramotswe heard this in silence.

"My mother said that when she left Botswana she asked him to come with her, but he refused."

"He must have been working, Mma," said Mma Ramotswe.

Mingie shook her head. "No. He was not working. He could have come with us to South Africa, but he did not."

Mma Ramotswe had been looking at the ground as she spoke. It was baked hard by sun and drought, and yet it was still home to plants and creatures that could somehow cope with its dryness. She saw what she thought was a scorpion, a small, scuttling flash of brown, almost transparent under the rays of the sun. She stopped walking, standing quite still, bringing Mingie to a halt as well.

"Did your mother tell you his name?" asked Mma Ramotswe. The words came out slowly, tentatively; a question to which in her heart of hearts she knew the answer and which, in many ways, she did not want answered.

"He was called Obed," said Mingie.

Mma Ramotswe did not remember very well what happened next. She did not remember how she wrapped Mingie in an embrace, there among the acacia trees, while a hornbill, perched on a branch of one of the trees, looked down with its curious, ancient eye; she did not remember how the two of them turned back, wordlessly, both knowing exactly what their conversation had established, and overcome by the discovery. Both had too much to think about to speak, at least in those first few minutes. Then, as they approached the end of the path and saw once again the familiar building of the No. 1 Ladies' Detective Agency and Tlokweng Road Speedy Motors, they both found that they had more to say than they could easily express.

"I am very happy I have found a sister," said Mma Ramotswe. "Very happy, Mma." She was — in a way — but there was another feeling, one that she did not mention.

And for her part, Mingie said, "A new sister is a gift from God, Mma."

Mma Ramotswe looked at her and smiled. "Perhaps it's as if God has suddenly said, 'Oh, Mma, I forgot to tell you: you have a sister.' "

They both laughed. Then Mma Ramotswe, noticing a movement in the window of the agency, said, "I think you should come and meet some of my friends now, Mma. And my husband, of course."

"My new brother-in-law," said Mingie. "What is his name, Mma?"

Mma Ramotswe replied automatically, "Mr. J.L.B. Matekoni, Mma."

Mingie looked puzzled. "Doesn't he have . . ."

It was a perfectly reasonable question, but one that Mma Ramotswe did not answer. "He has always been called that, Mma — even by me. If we started calling him something different, he would be very confused."

Mingie nodded. "We must not confuse men, Mma," she said.

That evening Mma Ramotswe walked in her garden, past the mopipi tree, past the aloe plants that she had decided to think but had yet to do anything about, to the long narrow bed in which she grew her beans. These beans were struggling; they had climbed obediently enough up the strings she had provided for them, but their leaves were wilting from lack of moisture. Despite Mr. J.L.B. Matekoni's drip irrigation system, the sun had been fierce in the cloudless sky and had seemed to snatch the water back before it did much good. She would get a crop, she thought, but every bean would be fought for, wrested from an unforgiving nature.

It was a time of day when the sun had all but sunk into the Kalahari, when shadows lengthened and the glare and heat of the day was replaced by a far gentler light and a less ferocious warmth. It was a time of returning birds, of drifting wood smoke, of murmuring voices coming from somewhere nearby, beyond the scrub bush at the end of her yard, where people sometimes walked or sat or went to talk about things they needed to talk about.

She had so much to think about, and as the day had progressed, she had been unable to turn her mind to anything else. *I have a sister; I have a sister.* She played with the words, savouring the novelty of the phrase. *I have a sister.* For most, such an utterance would be unremarkable: most people in Botswana had brothers or sisters because families were large and it was nothing unusual to have several siblings. Some people had six or seven, with a wide range of ages — Charlie, for instance, had four brothers as well as two sisters; Fanwell, too, referred from time to time to brothers in Francistown and Serowe, although he never said how many there were. She had been the only child because her mother had died young, when Precious was still very small, and the tiny family — she and her father — had been left alone, joined from time to time by aunts and cousins who had rallied round.

As a child, she had been acutely conscious of her lack of brothers and sisters. While other children at school talked of the doings of their siblings, she had remained silent, pretending not to care that she had nothing to contribute; but the sense of having missed out on something was always there, and was painful. Like many children who invent an imaginary friend, she invented an elder sister, Luxury, and a younger brother called Samson. The sister's name came from an advertisement she had seen in a magazine for ladies' underwear, all lace and frills, and impossibly exotic to a seven-year-old girl living in Mochudi in those days. "Let luxury be your companion," said the advertisement, and she responded, although not in the way the advertisers imagined. Luxury was older than Precious; she was almost sixteen, an age as alluring as it was seemingly distant to a child eight years younger; she was very beautiful, of course, wore garments like those in the advertisement, and she was invited to dances by boys. But in spite of all this, she had time for her younger sister and was available for games with dolls and the toy pram with only three wheels that Obed had bought for Precious at a sale.

They would find the fourth wheel one day, he said, if they kept their eyes open.

Samson, the imaginary brother, was only five but needed no looking after. His name was chosen from exposure to the story of Samson at Sunday school, and like his biblical counterpart, Samson was unusually strong. He could lift small boulders and push cars to start them when their batteries went flat. He had once unwound a python when it had wrapped itself around one of the nurses from the hospital; the python hissed as it felt Samson wind its coils off the unfortunate nurse, but it could do nothing in the face of the small boy's superior strength.

These two imaginary siblings survived for some years and then simply faded away. One day, when she was ten, they were simply no longer there, and she was truly alone. She used to leave a small glass of drinking water on her bedroom shelf for Luxury and Samson to drink from should they feel the need; this glass was put back in the kitchen, no longer required.

She thought of this now, as she stood in her vegetable garden. There was nothing imaginary about Mingie: she had a real, flesh-and-blood sister; she was like everyone else now. And this should have given her pleasure, should have filled her with delight; yet it did not, and that was because of Mingie's age. She had not asked her when she was born; she might have done that, but she had not; she already knew. And she had not sought to confirm details because it was these details, or one in particular, that had led to her feelings of sadness in the first place.

The newspaper, as newspapers like to do, had printed the age of each of the nurses in brackets after their names. She had gone back to the cutting to check up, and there it was on the page in black and white: Mingie Ramotswe (43). Mma Ramotswe did the arithmetic. If Mingie was forty-three, then she was a year older than Precious. That in itself was neither here nor there, but it had quickly led to another conclusion, and that was the one that cut at her inside like a small and insistent knife.

She was thinking of just that when she heard a movement behind her. Turning around, she saw Mr. J.L.B. Matekoni stepping out of the back door, the door that led to the kitchen. He was carrying a mug in each hand, and that meant he had made a cup of tea. She smiled; he was a thoughtful husband: How many men made tea for women? Did Phuti Radiphuti make tea for

Mma Makutsi? Now that she came to think of it, he did: Mma Makutsi had reported that he often made tea for her in bed and then went to attend to Itumelang in order to give her the chance of a long lie-in. And Mma Potokwane's husband, did he do the same? Again she realised that he did, because Mma Potokwane had once complained that the tea he made was too weak and she had to strengthen hers discreetly so as not to hurt his feelings or discourage him. "It's most important," Mma Potokwane had said, "not to put men off from doing things. We must never laugh at their attempts to cook, Mma Ramotswe, because men can lose their confidence very quickly. My husband made a fruit cake the other day, but forgot to put the fruit in. It was very hard not to laugh, Mma, but I had to try." She had paused, while Mma Ramotswe waited for the denouement. "It was hard to eat," she finished. "It was very crumby, but I told him it was very good."

Mr. J.L.B. Matekoni handed her a mug. "This is for you, Mma Ramotswe," he said quietly. "Tea."

The mug was hot. Most men, she thought, were more sensitive than women were to hot surfaces; he was not — it was, he said, because he was mechanic, and mechanics developed a layer of grease on their hands that never went away. She had smiled at this, but did not think it was true. Perhaps it was something to do with gentleness: perhaps men who were gentle, being more like women in that respect, could pick up hot plates without feeling them. But that was another theory that was probably untrue, along with all the other theories that people held. She took a sip, and she felt calmed by it, as she always did. There was something in red bush tea that said to you *Look, don't worry;* at least, it always had that effect on her.

Mr. J.L.B. Matekoni knew what she was thinking about. He had been watching her from the kitchen window, and had seen her standing by the beans. It was always a sign of something being on a person's mind, he felt, to stand and look at beans. He had met Mingie earlier that day, when Mma Ramotswe had brought her to the garage and then into the office. She had introduced her simply as Mingie Ramotswe, her newly found sister. There had been no explanation beyond that, either to him or to Mma Makutsi and Charlie, both of whom had been agog throughout the brief meeting. After she had left, Charlie had crowed. "I told you, Mma," he said to Mma Makutsi.

"I told you — didn't I? I said that is Mma Ramotswe's sister, and you said to me: there's no sister because she hasn't got one. Those were your words, Mma. That's what you said."

He had not had the time to discuss the matter with her. When he returned from work at the garage, she was already in her garden. He wondered how she felt. He could not imagine how it would feel to discover something as important as this about your family. His own family had been uncomplicated: everybody knew one another very well and there were no secrets — at least as far as he knew. Now, thinking about it, he realised that the whole point of secrets was that you *didn't* know about them. So how could anybody, such as himself, say there were no secrets in his family? All that he could say, perhaps, was that there were no *open* secrets, and of course open secrets were not real secrets anyway. Mr. J.L.B. Matekoni frowned. That was what he did when he started to think about a matter that appeared to have no easy resolution: he frowned.

Mma Ramotswe noticed this. "You're worried about something, Rra?"

He looked at her. "It's you, Mma. You're the one I'm worried about." He paused.

"And I think I know what it's about. This sister of yours . . ."

For a few moments she said nothing. Then she replied, "It's a bit of a shock, Rra."

"Of course it is," he said. "But you do like her, don't you?"

She nodded. "She is a nice lady, Rra. She's a nurse, you know. Down at Lobatse . . ." Her voice trailed away.

He looked at her again. "There's something else, isn't there?"

She turned to look at him, and he saw the anguish in her face.

"The newspaper cutting said she was forty-three, Rra. That's what it said."

He looked puzzled. "Well, Mma, there's nothing wrong in being forty-three. I was forty-three a few years ago." His attempt at good humour did not help, and he saw that. "I'm sorry," he continued. "I don't mean to make a joke out of this."

She reached out to touch him lightly on the arm. "I know you don't," she said. "No, Rra, what's worrying me is this." There was something unusual in her voice: disappointment, he thought; even sadness. "If she is forty-three, Rra, then that means she was born a year before I was." She stared at him; he had not yet understood. "That was when my father was still married to my mother,

Rra. She was not yet late."

It dawned on him, and he looked down at the ground, embarrassed both by his slowness in realising what she had been driving at and by the conclusion itself. This meant that the late Obed Ramotswe, whom he knew she had always idolised, had been involved with another woman while he was still married to Mma Ramotswe's mother.

He cleared his throat. "Oh," he said. "I see."

"Yes," said Mma Ramotswe. "That is why I am sad, Rra. I am happy that I have a sister — of course I am — but I am also sad that she was born in this way."

"But it's not her fault," protested Mr. J.L.B. Matekoni. "How we are born has nothing to do with us."

"It's nothing to do with her," said Mma Ramotswe, her voice so low as to be almost inaudible. "It's my daddy."

He was silent; it had occurred to him what this meant.

"He was with another woman while . . ." She did not finish her sentence.

He wanted to say so much. He wanted to say to her that it did not mean much; that these things happened; that men sometimes failed in these matters and that it was not very important after all; what counted was what he was like in other respects, and there had never been the slightest doubt about that. But he did not say any of this. So he said nothing.

She shook her head, as if trying to clarify something that she could not quite believe. "Why would he do that?" she asked. "Why would he go off with another woman when he had my mother? He said he loved her. He always told me that, you know, when I was a little girl. He said that he loved my mother very much and that she was one of the best women in Botswana, and that he had never deserved her." She paused. "Now I know what he meant. He did not deserve her."

He held up a hand. "Oh no, Mma. You mustn't say that."

She looked into his eyes. "Why not, Rra? He was a hypocrite."

He winced, but she repeated the charge.

"He was a hypocrite for saying one thing and doing another. My daddy — I thought he was such a good man, and now I find that he was a hypocrite."

He tried to dissuade her from saying anything further. "You must not speak in anger, Mma. You are upset. You mustn't say things like that just because you're upset."

She took another sip of tea, and then

handed him the half-full mug. "Could you carry that back for me, Mr. J.L.B. Matekoni, please? I am going to walk about the garden for a little while, and then I'll come back and start the dinner."

"I could come with you," he offered.

"No, Rra. It would be best for me to be by myself, if you don't mind. My heart is broken, you see. It is broken."

The words took his breath away. She had never declined his company, and this rejection showed him just how deeply she must have been wounded by this discovery of her father's past. He felt powerless; no words of his, he felt, could do anything to lessen her distress, and so he left her where she was and made his way back into the house alone.

CHAPTER THIRTEEN: THE PRINCIPAL INVESTIGATING OFFICER

Mma Makutsi could tell that there was something wrong with Mma Ramotswe. As they sat in the office the next morning going through the mail, she wondered what it was that was making Mma Ramotswe seem so . . . well, there was only one word for it, she decided, and that was *sad.* And there was something quite wrong with that: Mma Ramotswe was the one person she knew who should never be sad. Mma Ramotswe being sad was like a day with no sun, a day with no birdsong at dawn, a day without tea . . . One could go on, but the essential thing was that Mma Ramotswe should not look sad.

She knew that it was nothing she had done; they had the occasional tiff, usually over something rather unimportant, but any feeling that such disagreements produced never lasted very long. That pointed to the new sister being the source of the problem.

Had they perhaps had a row? There was nobody it was easier to argue with than a member of one's family, and that must apply every bit as much to newly discovered relatives as it did to old-established ones. Indeed, in the case of a long-lost relative, the first few days of acquaintanceship might be richly productive of rows, as there would be decades of missed disagreements to make up for.

"I hope you're all right, Mma," said Mma Makutsi as she settled at her desk.

Mma Ramotswe looked up from the letter she was reading. She smiled, but Mma Makutsi thought the smile looked like a sad smile, and her concern merely deepened.

"I am perfectly well, Mma," said Mma Ramotswe. "And thank you for asking."

"I am glad about that," said Mma Makutsi. "And remember: if there is anything I can do to help, anything at all, then I am here, Mma."

Mma Ramotswe thanked her. "You are very kind, Mma, but I am fine." She paused. "What we do need to do, though, is to have a meeting about the Charity business. We need to work out where we are, and what we can do next." She noticed that Mma Makutsi stiffened at these words.

"You are, of course, the Principal Investigating Officer," Mma Ramotswe added hurriedly. "So you should be in the chair, I think."

Mma Makutsi inclined her head graciously. "That would be best," she said. "We should have a review. It is always useful to have a review." Mma Makutsi had used the word *review* before, preferring it to the simpler term *meeting*. The word *review* sat well with the term *Principal Investigating Officer*: it seemed only right and proper that a Principal Investigating Officer should attend frequent reviews and, as a result, come up with "recommendations."

"I think Mr. Polopetsi would like to be at the review too," said Mma Ramotswe. "Will he be coming in today?"

Mma Makutsi replied that he was expected in half an hour and that it would be important to include him in the review. "Sometimes Mr. Polopetsi has good ideas," she said. "Not always, of course, but sometimes."

"I shall be very interested to hear your recommendations," said Mma Ramotswe.

Mma Makutsi loved this, and offered to make tea early, so that the meeting could begin as soon as Mr. Polopetsi arrived. "This is a very complex case," she said. "There will be many different possibilities to consider."

Mr. Polopetsi arrived on time, and was immediately informed by Mma Makutsi that a review was about to begin and that all other business could wait until it had taken place. Mma Makutsi then drew her chair out from behind her desk and positioned it in the centre of the room, with Mma Ramotswe and Mr. Polopetsi on chairs ranged before her.

"Now Mma, now Rra," she began. "We must consider what we know so far about this Charity Mompoloki business."

She looked at her two colleagues. Mma Ramotswe was clearly preoccupied with something else, but was at least trying to pay attention; Mr. Polopetsi sat on the edge of his chair, as if eagerly awaiting some imminent insight.

"What are we one hundred per cent certain about?" Mma Makutsi continued. "I shall answer that myself . . . as Principal Investigating Officer. We know that Charity lost her job because a complaint had been made about her."

Mma Ramotswe now looked up. "And we know that she was inclined to be rude. Her own mother told us that. And then one of the other employees confirmed that she had indeed been rude to a customer."

Mma Makutsi made an impatient gesture. "Mma, I don't like to correct you, but even if we know that some people . . . *some* people think her rude . . ."

Mma Ramotswe gazed out of the window. "Some people includes her mother, Mma. That is significant, I think."

Mma Makutsi hesitated, but then came back with a strong response. "Mothers can be wrong, Mma. There is no law that says mothers are always right."

Mr. Polopetsi ventured an opinion. "Most mothers know what their children are like, I think."

The intervention was a mild one — as always from Mr. Polopetsi — but it bore the full force of Mma Makutsi's disagreement. "No, Rra, you cannot make sweeping generalisations like that. Mothers are the same as anybody else. They have their prejudices."

"Yes, they do," said Mma Ramotswe. "But usually those prejudices are in favour of their children. That is why it is very significant when a mother admits to a child having a fault."

Mr. Polopetsi, although wary of saying anything that might be slapped down by Mma Makutsi, felt he could add something here. "One of my students at the school is very bad at chemistry," he said. "Very bad indeed. I have to watch him like a hawk in case he blows us all up by mistake. His mother, though, thinks he is brilliant at everything, including chemistry. She wants him to become a chemical engineer, and she will not listen to me when I tell her that this is not a good idea. That is an example of a mother who is prejudiced in favour of her son."

Mma Makutsi listened to this politely enough, but now moved the discussion on. "Whatever we think about Charity's mother," she said firmly, "my instinct is that Charity herself is innocent."

Mma Ramotswe pursed her mouth. It was clear to her that loyalty to the Botswana Secretarial College was still in play here. Mma Makutsi sensed this reservation, and now sought to strengthen her hand. "We must remember," she went on, "that we have discovered a very powerful motive in this case. We know that the boss, this Mr. Gopolang, was having an affair with some lady. So, if we accept the theory that he fired Charity to give her job to his girlfriend, then we have a way of sorting this whole thing out."

Mr. Polopetsi looked puzzled. "How can we do that, Mma?"

Mma Makutsi smiled. "Mr. Polopetsi,"

she said, "imagine that you are a man . . ."

Mr. Polopetsi sat up in his seat. "I am a man, Mma."

Mma Makutsi looked embarrassed. "I'm sorry, Rra, I didn't mean to suggest you are not a man. What I meant is imagine that you are the *average* man."

Mma Ramotswe thought this rather tactless, but did not say anything. Asking Mr. Polopetsi to imagine that he was an average man implied that he was not an average man, that he was somehow unusual. But Mr. Polopetsi had not taken offence; he nodded and said, "Yes, all right: I'm an average man. What now, Mma?"

Mma Makutsi continued: "And let's say that you were doing what Gopolang did — you fired an employee in order to replace her with your girlfriend." She paused, and then, with rhetorical flourish, went on to ask, "What would you fear most of all? Let us imagine that you are still with your wife and you do not want to end up in a messy and expensive divorce — what would frighten you most?"

He answered without hesitation. "That my wife would find out."

"Precisely," said Mma Makutsi. "And that is what is happening all over the place, Rra. There are men who are shaking in their boots because they are afraid that their wives will find something out. In fact, there is probably not a man in the land who is not worried that his wife will find out something or other."

Mma Ramotswe thought this a bit extreme. She could not imagine Mr. J.L.B. Matekoni worrying about that, or Phuti Radiphuti, for that matter. But she was interested to see where Mma Makutsi's argument was going to lead.

She did not have to wait long. "So," said Mma Makutsi, "we have a big weapon in our hands, Mr. Polopetsi. Once we find out a bit more detail we can go to the wife of this Gopolang and tell her. She will soon put a stop to that nonsense if we say to her, 'Your husband is going to give his girlfriend a job.' Any wife would say, 'Not if I have anything to do with it.' "

Mma Ramotswe drew in her breath. This was a dangerous strategy, and she was not sure that it was a good idea. But she had a lot on her mind, and now that Mma Makutsi was Principal Investigating Officer it would cause a lot of upset if she intervened. So she simply said, "Interesting, Mma Makutsi. Very interesting."

This was taken as a compliment, and Mma Makutsi beamed with pleasure. "What we need to do, then, Mr. Polopetsi," she concluded, "is to confirm this girlfriend. We shall observe our friend Mr. Gopolang, and find out who is this no-good woman he's seeing. We shall then have strong evidence to lay before the wife."

"But it will take a lot of time to follow Gopolang," Mr. Polopetsi pointed out. "And the agency is not being paid for this."

Mma Makutsi shook her head. "If he's having an affair, he'll want to see her every day."

"So we follow him in the evening — when he leaves the store?"

"No," said Mma Makutsi. "Men who have affairs have them during the day. They have them at lunch time."

This view was expressed with such firmness and authority that Mma Ramotswe found herself nodding in agreement. But then she thought: How does Mma Makutsi know that?

The answer was not long in coming, and it was expressed with the same confidence. "When I was at the Botswana Secretarial College," Mma Makutsi continued, "there was a lecturer who knew all about office problems. She had made a study of them and was a big expert — maybe even a world expert on such matters. She told us that if there was an affair going on in the office, it would always be conducted at lunch time. She said that there were very few exceptions to that."

Mr. Polopetsi seemed to agree. "There were two teachers at the school who were having an affair. They met at lunch time."

Mma Ramotswe raised an eyebrow. "In the staff room?"

Mr. Polopetsi looked at her reproachfully. "No, not in the staffroom, Mma. They took to meeting one another in my chemistry storeroom. I didn't know about it until we had an incident — a chemical incident."

Both Mma Makutsi and Mma Ramotswe stared at Mr. Polopetsi.

"And?" prompted Mma Makutsi.

Mr. Polopetsi became embarrassed. "They knocked over a bottle of acid. I don't know what they were doing at the time, but they broke a bottle of hydrochloric acid. It spilled over some calcium carbonate, and well, you know what that leads to." He laughed nervously. "Oh yes, that leads to something, all right."

"We do not know, Rra," said Mma Makutsi, slightly impatiently. "What does it lead to?"

Mr. Polopetsi seemed surprised that he had to explain. "$CaCO_3$," he began, "plus

HCl gives us $CaCl_2$ plus CO_2 plus H_2O. It's simple. You get calcium chloride, water, and, of course, carbon dioxide."

"You wouldn't want to be in a storeroom with carbon dioxide bubbling away," said Mma Makutsi. "At the Botswana Secretarial College we were warned about carbon dioxide."

Mr. Polopetsi frowned. "I think that would have been carbon monoxide, Mma. That is always a danger, that gas. You cannot smell it, you see, and it can be very dangerous."

"It was carbon dioxide, Rra," said Mma Makutsi coldly. "Remember that I was there. It was carbon dioxide."

"Ah well," said Mr. Polopetsi, "be that as it may, this carbon dioxide is dangerous too. And so they had to rush out of the storeroom and it was all very embarrassing."

Mma Makutsi took control. "So, that's decided then. You and I shall observe Mr. Gopolang over the lunch hour and see where he goes — or who comes to him. Then we shall go to his wife and tell her." She paused. "Does everyone agree?"

Mma Ramotswe had strong reservations, but she did not like to voice them. Her mind was on her sister, and her father too, but it was also on Note. Her life, it seemed to her, had suddenly become immensely complicated, and these were the only things that she could think about. Charity's situation was a difficult one, but somehow her own problems seemed to overshadow everything else. And it was all very well being a professional sorter-out of other people's difficulties, but what about your own? How could you sort those out when all you could think about was your ex-husband, your new and unexpected sister, and of course your late father and how he had let you down?

It was a team of three: Charlie was at the wheel of the van, with Mr. Polopetsi and Mma Makutsi squashed in beside him. Now they sat together, somewhat uncomfortably, parked under an obliging tree not far from the entrance to The Office Place. Charlie was in an ebullient mood, excited at the prospect of being involved in some clandestine observation. He was pleased, too, that his theory as to what was happening appeared to have been accepted. "I told you this is what was happening," he said. "This is what I said was going on, remember?"

"Yes, yes, Charlie," said Mma Makutsi. "You did say something like that."

Charlie preened himself. "Well, there you are, Mma Makutsi. I'm glad you remember that." He paused. "Sometimes, it seems to me, you think I know nothing. You think that just because I'm a man, I know nothing and that women know everything."

Mma Makutsi looked pointedly out of the window. "I've never said that, Charlie." She glanced at Mr. Polopetsi. "I've never said that, have I, Rra?"

Mr. Polopetsi squirmed with embarrassment. "I haven't heard her say that, Charlie. Although that's not to say . . ."

A further glance from Mma Makutsi silenced him.

"You see," said Mma Makutsi. "You're a bit too sensitive, Charlie. If you want to make it in this life, you can't go round thinking that people are talking about you. You'll get nowhere that way, you know."

Charlie said nothing.

"And another thing," continued Mma Makutsi. "You must always remember that if you have an idea, there may be other people who have the same idea at the same time. They may have that idea but they may not say anything about it, you know. So this business of Mr. Gopolang — how do you know that I wasn't thinking the same thing?"

Charlie looked sceptical. "And were you, Mma? Were you thinking that?"

"I was thinking of many things," said Mma Makutsi enigmatically. "There were many things on my mind."

Mr. Polopetsi nodded. "I have often thought about that," he ventured. "I have often thought how strange it is that we can be thinking about one thing and then, without any warning, we find ourselves thinking about another thing."

"That is very true, Rra," said Mma Makutsi. "Sometimes we are like birds. Have you seen how birds are clearly thinking one thing and then they remember something else? They may be sitting on a tree and then suddenly they fly up and move to another tree. Or they're standing on the ground looking at something and then without any warning they fly up and go off somewhere else."

Charlie said that this was something to do with evolution. "If we are like birds," he said, "that is because we are descended from them."

Mma Makutsi gave him a sideways look. "We are not descended from birds, Charlie." She turned to Mr. Polopetsi. "We aren't descended from birds, are we, Mr. Polopetsi?"

Mr. Polopetsi gave a nervous laugh. "No, of course not. Human beings descended from apes. They are our cousins, so to speak."

Charlie whistled. "That's what you think, Mr. Polopetsi. Baboons? Not me."

Mma Makutsi looked at her watch. "It is almost one o'clock," she muttered. "He will be stopping work for his lunch."

Mr. Polopetsi looked doubtful. "That is, *if* he stops," he said. "There are many people who work irregular hours — especially if they're the boss."

Mma Makutsi replied that although that may be true, she thought that bosses who were busy having affairs would probably want their lunch-time break. "They sit there thinking about the lady they will be meeting."

Charlie chuckled. "And then, oh my goodness, they'll be busy."

The salacious note seemed to offend Mr. Polopetsi. "I don't think you should speak like that, Charlie," he said.

"I'm just talking about what's going on," said Charlie. "You cannot pretend that people don't do things like that, you know. It's going on all the time, Mr. Polopetsi."

The discussion was brought to an abrupt end by Mma Makutsi. She had seen the door of The Office Place opening. "Hush," she said. "Something is happening now."

They watched as a tall man came out of the building and stood for a few moments, as if uncertain as to what to do.

"Is that him?" whispered Charlie.

"It is," Mma Makutsi answered. "I have seen him before. He is a very tall man."

"That's why he's popular with the ladies," said Charlie. "Have you noticed that? Have you noticed how girls like men who are tall — like me?"

Mma Makutsi made a dismissive noise. "You're not very tall, Charlie. And anyway, concentrate. Your job is to drive."

"Is he going somewhere?" asked Charlie.

His question was answered by Mr. Gopolang himself, who now walked purposively towards the small car park to the side of the building. This served several nearby businesses and was almost full. He stopped at the side of a large red car, fished in his pocket for a key, and opened the driver's door.

They watched from the other side of the street as Mr. Gopolang's car nosed out onto the road. "Start the engine now, Charlie," Mma Makutsi instructed. "But don't get too close to him. Follow at a distance."

"But not too much of a distance," added Mr. Polopetsi. "There can be a lot of traffic at lunch time with people going off to their —"

Charlie completed his sentence. "Going

273

off to their lovers. Hah! All these cars full of people going off to —"

Mma Makutsi stopped him. "Pay attention to your driving, Charlie."

"All right, all right," muttered Charlie irritably. And then, after a few moments, he added, "Mind you, that man looks about fifty. What's he doing going to see a woman? How has he got the energy to do these things if he's fifty?"

Mr. Polopetsi frowned. "Fifty is not very old, Charlie. And I've known men who are eighty and above who are still interested in ladies."

Charlie whistled. "They'd better watch out, those old men. They'll have a heart attack if they carry on with —"

Mma Makutsi interrupted him again. "Don't let him get too far ahead, Charlie. Watch the road — and stop talking about these things. It's the only thing you seem able to think about."

The red car crossed the first major roundabout and headed down the road that led towards the place where fishermen sold fish caught in the dam. Good rains the previous year, breaking the drought that had reduced the dam to little more than a bed of cracked dry mud, had filled it to capacity, and more: an overflow cascading over the lip of the dam wall had revitalised streams that had long since faded from human memory, taking the water over the land, bringing a flush of luxuriant green growth, quenching the thirst of ground that had almost given up hope. Somehow fish had survived — some people said they burrowed into the mud and slept, sometimes for years, until the rains returned and they could swim once more. Others said — with greater credibility, perhaps — that fish came downstream from places where some surface water had survived the drought, and had just travelled down to the dam when the opportunity arose. For the fishermen, though, the important thing was that the fish were there again, and that they could find bream and barbel lurking in the reeds that had miraculously sprung up again where they had been before the rains had failed. Now two of them sheltered under a tree with their catch — admittedly not an impressive one, but a catch nonetheless — hung up on lines to attract passers-by.

Charlie pointed to the fishermen as they drove past. "There used to be three of those men," he said. "My uncle knew them. Now there are only two. One of them is late."

"Many people are late these days," said Mma Makutsi.

"Yes," said Charlie. "But that one is late because of a crocodile. He was fishing, and there was a crocodile watching him. It dragged him into the water."

"They are very dangerous creatures," said Mr. Polopetsi. He nodded his head sadly. "There are many things in this country that will eat you if they get the chance."

Mma Makutsi had her eyes fixed on the red car ahead, but could not let this pass. "I don't think so, Rra," she said. "Crocodiles, yes, but apart from them what creatures are there that will eat us? Lions? But that's all."

Charlie shook his head. "Leopards too, Mma. Remember there are leopards."

"They are very shy creatures," said Mma Makutsi. "You hardly ever see them. They keep away from us."

"I've known people who have been eaten by leopards," said Charlie.

Mma Makutsi challenged him. "Name one, Charlie."

"I cannot remember their names," Charlie snapped back. "But there are also pythons. A big python can easily eat a man. Not a fat lady, perhaps, but a small man will be easy for them." He glanced at Mr. Polopetsi. "Somebody like Mr. Polopetsi here. He could easily be eaten by a python." He looked thoughtful, and added, "A wild dog too, I think. He would be able to eat you, Rra. And a hyena — I think that you are small enough to be eaten by a hyena."

Mr. Polopetsi tried to smile. "I shall be very careful, Charlie, don't you worry."

Charlie was warming to his theme. "You can be as careful as you like, Rra," he continued. "But all these people who get eaten — do you think they weren't being careful? I'm sure they were. The problem is that you can only look in one direction at a time. So, if you're looking that way, then how do you know that there is not some creature coming up behind you? How do you know that, Rra? The answer is that you don't. And then the hyena or whatever it is gets you and starts to eat you and it's too late."

This was too much for Mma Makutsi. "You're frightening Mr. Polopetsi, Charlie. Stop it. Nobody's going to be eaten."

"That's what you think, Mma," retorted Charlie, slowing down to take a corner that the red car had just negotiated. "But I still think that people need to look out. Imagine being eaten! Ow! You're walking along and this lion comes up and starts to eat you. What do you think about? Do you say to yourself, 'Oh, this is very bad — I'm being eaten?' Is that what people think, Mma

Makutsi? Or do you think of all the bad things you've done and say sorry for them?"

"*If* you've done bad things, Charlie," said Mma Makutsi. "But not all of us have done that many bad things. We're not all like you, you know."

Mr. Polopetsi laughed at this, but stopped when he saw Charlie's expression.

"I'm not bad," the young man protested. "You think that I'm bad just because I have a little bit of fun."

Mma Makutsi was conciliatory. "I'm sorry, Charlie, I didn't mean that. And look, I think he's slowing down."

"That's because there is a dog crossing the road," said Mr. Polopetsi.

"That's the easiest way for a dog to become late," said Charlie. "You don't see them. Then, bang! Late dog."

The red car speeded up again. They were now getting to the Village, the part of town at the top of the Tlokweng Road. Off to their left, beyond the cemetery, was the cluster of modest houses among which Mma Makutsi had rented her room when she first worked for the No. 1 Ladies' Detective Agency. It was a more sought-after suburb than Old Naledi, which they had just passed, but none of the houses had more than two bedrooms, and many of them could have done with a lick of paint.

Mr. Gopolang's car now began to indicate a left turn, and Charlie, slowing down so as not to be too obviously following, followed suit.

"He cannot be going home," said Mr. Polopetsi. "A man like that will not be living here — not a man who owns his own business."

"Of course he's not going home, Rra," said Charlie, somewhat dismissively. "You do not go home if you're having a lunchtime affair."

"We shall see," said Mma Makutsi. "Let's not jump to conclusions." That advice she had garnered from Clovis Andersen and his *Principles of Private Detection*. Mma Makutsi had underlined the passage in red pencil: *Sometimes,* wrote the great detective, *an answer jumps out at you. Do not trust it! If an answer jumps, then you mustn't jump yourself.*

Charlie, though, was not deterred. "This is exactly the sort of place where a rich man like Gopolang will keep his girlfriend. He will be too mean to get her a better place, and so he'll choose something like this for her."

The red car was now slowing down again; a flashing indicator light told them it was about to pull in to the side of the road.

"He's stopping," said Charlie. "What do I do? I can't stop right here, it'll be too obvious."

"Drive on," said Mma Makutsi quickly. "And look the other way, Mr. Polopetsi. I will too. Then he won't see our faces if he looks at us as we go past."

She and Mr. Polopetsi gazed studiously in the other direction as Charlie drove past the now stationary red car. They need not have bothered; inside the car, Mr. Gopolang was too busy adjusting his tie and checking his appearance in the sun-visor mirror.

"What now?" asked Charlie.

"Go to the end of the road," Mma Makutsi instructed him. "Then turn round and we can drive past again once he's inside. We can park a bit further down that way — we'll get a good view from there."

Charlie did as she ordered and then started to drive back slowly the way they had come. They saw Mr. Gopolang walk up the short path that led to the front door of the house. They expected that he would go straight in, but that was not what happened. Mr. Gopolang seemed to linger on the doorstep and then, just as they were beginning to draw level with the house, the door opened and a woman came out, closing the door behind her.

For Mma Makutsi it was a jaw-dropping moment. "Violet Sephotho!" she exclaimed. And then, losing no time, she said to Charlie, "Charlie, speed up," and to Mr. Polopetsi, "Look the other way, Rra."

Had Mr. Gopolang or Violet paid any attention to the car going past, they would have spotted three astonished faces turn towards them and then rapidly look the other way. But they did not, and so, unconcerned, they made their way to Mr. Gopolang's car, deep in conversation, climbed in, and disappeared down the road in the opposite direction to the one taken by their watchers.

Mma Makutsi was breathless, her emotions in turmoil, struggling with indignation, fury, and sheer astonishment. When she spoke, her voice was cracked. "Take us straight back to the office, Charlie," she said. "I must get word of this to Mma Ramotswe without the slightest delay."

CHAPTER FOURTEEN: SHE HAD SAID HER HEART WAS BROKEN

While Mma Makutsi, Mr. Polopetsi and Charlie were in the process of making their shocking discovery, Mma Ramotswe closed the office, announcing to Mr. J.L.B. Matekoni, hard at work in the garage next door, that she was going to drive up to Mochudi for the afternoon. She spoke to him while he and Fanwell were under a car, struggling to replace a cracked oil sump. It was messy work, and when he pulled himself out from under the car she could see that his overalls were covered in the thick black oil that had dripped down from the damaged sump.

"Oh, Rra," she said. "Just look at you. I'll never manage to get those overalls clean — never."

Mr. J.L.B. Matekoni cast a cursory glance downwards. "They are very old overalls, Mma," he said. "Perhaps it is time . . ." He brushed at the dark patch, succeeding only in spreading the oil further. Now he looked at her inquisitively. "What is it, Mma Ramotswe? We are trying hard to fix this car and —"

She cut him off. "I am going to Mochudi, Mr. J.L.B. Matekoni," she said. "I have not locked the office, but I think that Mma Makutsi will be back quite soon."

"To Mochudi, Mma? What is happening up in Mochudi?"

"Nothing is happening," she said. "I'm going to think."

He knew what this meant, and he was concerned. She had said her heart was broken and he felt powerless to do anything about it. It seemed to him that she did not want to admit him into her sorrow, and he, being a mere mechanic, did not have the words to ask her to let him in on it. That was the problem, he felt: when words were handed out to the various callings by which people lived, all the words were taken by politicians and lawyers and the clever accountants, and not many were left for people like him — the mechanics and the farmers.

She saw the way he was looking at her. She wanted to say something more to him, but she could not find the words either. This sorrow that she felt was as deep as any that she had felt before, perhaps even including that numbing emptiness that had embraced her when she had lost the baby, and when she had said goodbye to her father. On those occasions she had thought that she would never again experience something so soul-wrenching, but it was dawning on her that what she felt now was every bit as much a bereavement. Something had been taken from her — something that had nourished and supported her, a light that had illuminated her whole world seemed to be flickering and dying.

They said goodbye to one another. They could not embrace, as Mr. J.L.B. Matekoni would have wanted to do, because he knew that he was covered in oil. From underneath the car, the disembodied voice of Fanwell urged him back to work. "Boss, I think we should get on with this — there's more oil." So he said, "I'm coming, Fanwell," and gave his wife a sort of wave, a motion of an oily, untouchable hand.

She drove to Mochudi by the old road, which is the road she always chose because of its familiar aspects. Normally, she would have driven slowly, because she knew each bend, each dip, and because every building, every stretch of bush — trackless and monotonous though it may have been to those who did not know it — was well known to her. Now, though, she had no desire to linger, and drove purposefully and faster than usual. The tiny white van responded as best it could, its loyal heart straining, new and threatening noises coming from the engine as she pushed it to its limits. She wondered why she wanted to get there as soon as she could. She should be dreading reaching her destination, feeling the way she did, but instead there was an urge to get there as soon as possible, even if she had no real idea what she would do when she arrived. To anybody who might be watching, it would be the same as any other visit, when people came to a family graveside and laid flowers, or stood still under the sun before they retraced their steps to the gate and to those who were waiting for them.

She was alone when she drew up and got out of the van. There had been a tree under which people would park, but something had happened to this tree — its trunk had split, its branches were now only half alive but still bore their burden of foliage, bunched up on the ground like gathered skirts. There was a black mark in the cloven wood, a searing as of a torch applied, and this confirmed what she had thought when she saw the broken tree. It was lightning, and it had chosen the tree because it was the highest object for some distance around. It had protected the graveyard itself from being struck, which meant, she found herself thinking, that it had been a sentry for those within — a sentry that had done its job. Yet, she thought, lightning could never disturb those who were in their graves; they were beyond all dangers of this world — indifferent to drought as much as to flood; safe and secure, even in the depths of night when there were creatures abroad that nobody could name or describe, but seemed to be there even though you told yourself they did not exist. You heard the breathing of these creatures sometimes, heard their footfall, sensed their presence; although they faded so quickly, like all imaginary things, when the first rays of the sun touched the land.

Just before she entered the graveyard — an enclosure bounded by a straggling cattle fence — she stopped and picked up a piece of paper that had been trapped in the twigs of a shrub. It was something that had been dropped after a burial service, and she saw that it bore the words of an old Setswana hymn. These words were familiar to her; as a girl she had sung them many times, in the small church at Mochudi to which her aunt took her on Sundays. She stared at the paper, and then rubbed it between her fingers. It had that rough, cardboardy feel of paper that has been left out in the elements, and she crunched it into a ball before slipping it into the pocket of her blouse. She heard the words of the hymn, as clearly as if there had been a congregation to sing them; then they faded and the only sound was the calling of a bird somewhere off in the bush behind her, a plea for love or food, or a warning to other birds, perhaps, that such love or food as might be had was already claimed.

She approached the grave of her mother. Like most of the graves, it was protected by a small raised structure, a traditional set of small iron posts across which a roof of fabric was sometimes stretched. This created a tent of sorts — although the wind was unmerciful and would make tatters of one's efforts, and there was no cover now. The surface of her mother's grave, marked by chips of stone within the curtilage of the posts, was open to the sky, which was better, she thought, because the touch of the sun on a grave seemed to her to be a natural and good thing. At its head was a small red-stone marker, rectangular and crumbling at the very edges, on which a few words had been carved: *Angel Ramotswe, dear wife of Obed Ramotswe, and mother of Precious.* She read the words again, and stumbled over *dear wife.* Her father must have chosen those words himself, and yet . . . She closed her eyes. Her grief was almost unbearable.

She turned and took the few steps that would take her to her father's side. There was a stone of the same sort, more recent of course and therefore less weathered. She had to force herself to look at it, because everything within her made her want to avert her eyes. She read the inscription: *Obed Ramotswe: now gathered to the Lord.* Those were her words, and she remembered why she had chosen them. It was because you gathered in cattle at the end of the day, and he had been so proud of his cattle . . . So proud; and she had been proud of him, or everything he stood for — the old ways of thinking about things and doing them; the old Botswana morality, the kindness that lay at the heart of that. And now all that was dust.

How could he have done it? How could he have gone off with another woman while her mother was still with him? Even though she knew that men could fail because they were weak, as we all were, he was not like other men — he was her daddy, her beloved daddy, and now everything that he had stood for was diminished because he must have been a deceiver, just like so many men.

She looked down at the earth. Sooner or later we all became just that — earth — and people forgot all about us. And yet we tried to keep late people alive; we tried. But we often did not succeed for very long, because the memory of them faded and we forgot how they sounded and what they said and even how they looked. She had not allowed that to happen with her daddy; she had thought of him every day, even occasionally speaking to him as if he were there at her side. She had not done that since she had found out about Mingie. It was as if somebody had finally gone away; after all these years, somebody had gone away.

She knew what she had to do. She had always believed in forgiveness, and even in her work she had applied the principle that we simply had to forgive others for what they did. This was no different; she would have to forgive him. But there was more to it than that; she knew that in forgiving him, she would be saying goodbye — finally this time — she would be saying that it was over. She would not come back here, and these graves would become like those other graves, where the people who tended them had simply gone away, or become late themselves.

She summoned up her courage, and then she spoke. It was a simple goodbye — just a few words, uttered in the Setswana language, to which late people reverted no matter how much English they spoke in their lives; because that was the language that the ancestors would understand. Then she said the words that would have to make do for her forgiveness — and she turned away and went out through the gate, her eyes filled with tears that seemed to come from the deepest place within her, from the heart itself, from the same profound wells from which love itself does spring.

By the time she got back to the office she was calmer. Mma Makutsi was at her desk, having arrived back an hour or so earlier. Mr. Polopetsi had waited for a short time in the hope of seeing Mma Ramotswe, but had been obliged to go off to teach a chemistry lesson at the Gaborone Secondary School. Nor was Charlie there: he had been sent off by Mr. J.L.B. Matekoni to collect a spare part from the motor trade wholesaler in the old industrial sites.

Mma Makutsi could barely contain herself. "Mma Ramotswe," she blurted out, "you will never guess what we have found out — never in a hundred years."

Mma Ramotswe lowered herself into the chair behind her desk. It was a well-padded and voluminous chair, but it would need replacing sooner or later, she thought, for now it squeaked whenever she moved. If a client was present, she felt that would hardly be compatible with the dignity of the agency.

"You were watching this Mr. Gopolang," she said. "So it's something to do with him? Something to do with his private life?"

"Yes," said Mma Makutsi. "That is what it is about."

"So, let me see," mused Mma Ramotswe. "You have found out who his girlfriend is?"

Mma Makutsi nodded her head excitedly. "We have, Mma. We have seen her."

Mma Ramotswe looked thoughtful. "And it's somebody known to us?"

Again, Mma Makutsi nodded. But now she simply had to reveal the name. "It's Violet Sephotho!" she exclaimed.

Mma Ramotswe raised an eyebrow. "Violet? Well, she does get around, doesn't she?"

Mma Makutsi's expression was one of complete disgust. "She's shameless, Mma. She's always been shameless, right from the

291

beginning — sitting there at the Botswana Secretarial College, painting her nails during the shorthand lectures, thinking about men. Shamelessness of a very high order, Mma."

Ninety-seven per cent shamelessness, thought Mma Ramotswe, irreverently. And then she found herself wondering how Mma Makutsi could tell when somebody was thinking about men: Did the face assume a particular, men-related look? Or did one simply assume that somebody like Violet Sephotho, who had revealed her interest in men in a hundred different ways, was more likely to be thinking about men than about shorthand, or any of the other things that might occupy the minds of those who attended classes at the Botswana Secretarial College?

"This is a very interesting development, Mma," said Mma Ramotswe. "So, do you think it means that Mr. Gopolang will be planning to give Charity's job to Violet?"

Mma Makutsi hesitated. "It must be something like that, Mma Ramotswe. It all adds up."

But Mma Ramotswe was not so sure. Violet Sephotho was an ambitious woman — and it was widely believed that she would stop at nothing to advance her career. Why would an ambitious woman be interested in selling office furniture? Surely Violet, with all her pretensions, would set her sights somewhat higher than that. Now Mma Ramotswe made that point to Mma Makutsi, who listened intently and seemed to be weighing her response.

"Unless," Mma Makutsi began, "unless the plan to replace Charity with Violet was something dreamed up by Mr. Gopolang without consulting Violet herself." She paused, giving herself time to develop the argument further. Then, when satisfied that it all made sense in her mind, she continued with conviction, "In other words, he may have been thinking about himself rather than about her — and what she might want. Yes, Mma, that seems likely, I think. I think that he might have been planning to put her into that job so that he could have an excuse to see her all day — and to have her more in his power. He would be her boss and her boyfriend too — men love that sort of thing, you know. It makes them feel even more powerful."

Mma Ramotswe considered this. It was perfectly possible, she thought, but she wondered if it made any difference from their — or Charity's — point of view. The agency's interest was in discovering whether there had been a false accusation and an unfair dismissal. That was all they needed to find out, and it seemed to her that they had now done so, or at least they had unearthed something that strengthened their case. And yet, and yet . . . Even if Mr. Gopolang had acted improperly, it was doubtful that they would be able to do anything about it, as he could simply deny that his motive in dismissing Charity had been improper. On the other hand, if Mma Ramotswe were able to confront him and tell him that she knew why he had done what he did, then that might force him to undo the dismissal. But then she asked herself: Why would he do that? The answer was that he would only act if he felt that a failure to do anything would result in the information about his affair becoming known to . . . She smiled at the thought: *to his wife.* One of the things that she had learned in her profession, and from going through life, was that there were many men who were afraid of their wives. This was a secret that men in general preferred not to be widely known, but she had seen it time and time again — confident, even boastfully strong men lived in fear of their wives, who were often the only people capable of controlling them. It started when these confident, boastfully strong men were confident, boastfully strong boys, but with forceful mothers. That set the pattern, and it continued for the rest of their lives. So if you wanted to deal with such a man, the answer was to find his mother or his wife. They were the people he would be in awe of; they were the people who could produce the desired result.

"I think we might be able to give Mr. Gopolang a bit of a fright," she said to Mma Makutsi. And then, bearing in mind that Mma Makutsi was the Principal Investigating Officer, she added, "That is, if you don't mind my getting involved, Mma."

Mma Makutsi did not mind. She had been worried about Mma Ramotswe's uncharacteristically low mood, and she was pleased that this appeared to be lifting. And the thought of having Mma Ramotswe pitted against Violet Sephotho was reassuring, as, if truth be told, Mma Makutsi, for all her ninety-seven per cent, was slightly afraid of Violet Sephotho. Not that she would admit it, of course, and not that it was *real* fear, but it was nonetheless comforting to know that Violet was facing not only Botswana's most famous detective, but one who was also traditionally built, as brave as a lioness, and capable, in extreme situations, of actually sitting on people who could not be subdued in any other way. What a delicious image, she thought: Violet Sephotho being sat upon by Mma Ramotswe; Violet would struggle and squeal, but avoirdupois would always win in such an encounter and Violet would be confounded, winded, and put to silence — a lovely prospect, but unlikely to occur, she feared. Still, one might dream, and dreams, even unlikely ones, could make you feel warm inside — if you allowed them to.

"Blackmail?" said Mr. J.L.B. Matekoni as he sat at the table that evening and waited for Mma Ramotswe to cut him a slice of fine Botswana beef. "Why should it be blackmail if you're telling the truth?"

Mma Ramotswe cut a slice off the joint on the plate before her. There were those who said that beef should be sliced as thin as possible, but she did not subscribe to that view, and neither, she knew, did Mr. J.L.B. Matekoni. He, in fact, took the opposite view, and liked his roast beef to be cut as thickly as possible, so that it resembled more than anything else a piece of steak. And he liked it to be juicy, too, red in the middle, and soft in the mouth.

"I think it's blackmail if you threaten to

tell somebody's secret unless they do something," said Mma Ramotswe. "And this is what I'd be doing if I went to see Gopolang and told him that I'd tell his wife about his affair unless he reinstated Charity."

Mr. J.L.B. Matekoni was not convinced, but he trusted Mma Ramotswe's moral sense, and if she had misgivings about a particular course of action, then there was usually a very good reason for that. "All right," he conceded. "But then why don't you go to the wife?"

"And tell her?" asked Mma Ramotswe.

He sniffed appreciatively; the smell of freshly cut beef was making his gastric juices run. "Yes, tell her. But don't tell her outright; first you should say: 'Mma, I know something that I shall tell you on one condition: that you agree to do something for me afterwards.' She will be very anxious to know, and so she will agree. Then, when you've told her, you ask her to make sure that Charity gets her job back." He paused, giving her an enquiring look to confirm that she understood. "No wife would let her husband give a job to his girlfriend. So it would suit her very well if he were forced to give the job back to a woman who is definitely not his girlfriend."

Mma Ramotswe thought about this. There

was something unpleasant, something underhand about going to a wife and informing on her husband, but then there were circumstances when one had to do something one felt uncomfortable about because it was the only way of preventing an injustice. This, she thought, might be just such a case.

"Do you really think that's what I should do?" she asked Mr. J.L.B. Matekoni.

He sniffed again. "Yes," he said. "But first, Mma, I am very keen to try this beef. Could we please have dinner and then we can talk about these big things?"

"I have already made up my mind," said Mma Ramotswe.

It was clear to her what she needed to do, and she would do it. The world could be an unjust place, and you had to get your hands dirty from time to time if you were to do anything about it. Nobody liked having dirty hands, but it was dirty hands that cleared things up. Clovis Andersen himself might have said something just like that, she thought — had it occurred to him.

CHAPTER FIFTEEN:
SOME PEOPLE SAY SHE
COULD STOP AN ELEPHANT

She went by herself. She had toyed with the idea of taking Mma Makutsi with her, and even Mr. Polopetsi, but had decided against it. This was not going to be an easy meeting, and it would be simpler, she thought, if she did not have to worry about Mma Makutsi's sometimes inappropriate interventions. As for Mr. Polopetsi, he was usually innocuous enough, and would be too timid to say anything awkward or embarrassing, but this was women's business, and the presence of a man could change the atmosphere. Women said things to one another that they would not say if a man was listening, and she imagined that the same applied to the conversation of men among themselves.

Of course, she could not be absolutely sure of what men talked about when there were no women present — she had her views about it, but she could not be certain.

She knew, though, that Fanwell and Charlie were no kind of guide. She had heard them talking in the garage; they thought they were out of earshot, but she sometimes heard parts of their conversations and had never been able to make much sense of them. If she were to try to summarise, it would be something like this: *girls, girls, football, girls, fast cars, beer, girls.* That was mostly Charlie; Fanwell would listen and make the occasional interjection, but he was more serious and spoke about other things too. He was interested in global warming and conservation and sometimes talked at length about the endangerment of Africa's elephants. But apart from these occasional insights, Mma Ramotswe had to admit that the conversation of males was a closed book.

She had found out where the Gopolangs lived. Mma Gopolang, as it happened, was friendly with a former client of the agency, a woman with whom Mma Ramotswe kept in touch and occasionally met for lunch at the President Hotel. She called on this friend and was readily given the address. "You can't go wrong," said the friend. "It's one of those new houses up at Phakalane. Its roof is the colour of the blue of the national flag. You can't miss it."

She chose her time carefully. Her friend

had told her that Mma Gopolang did not work, and that she was always in the house in the morning. "She usually goes out in the afternoon — she's on the committee of some church somewhere, but I've never found her out when I've called in before noon."

Mma Ramotswe had thanked her for the information. "But there's one further question, Mma," she said. "What sort of woman is this Mma Gopolang?"

The friend had hesitated, a smile playing about her lips. It was the look of one who wanted to say something, but who was restrained by considerations of friendship, or possibly even simple charity: there were some people, Mma Ramotswe reminded herself, who were unwilling openly to speak ill of others, and these people could be indirect in their comments.

"She is an unusual woman," said the friend.

Mma Ramotswe waited.

"But a very fine person," the friend added. "She cleaned up that church of hers. Apparently the pastor was dipping into church funds — the collection plate had been going straight into his pocket for years. Once she was elected to the committee, she began to sort it all out. The pastor was furious."

"I can just imagine it," said Mma Ramotswe.

"Yes," agreed the friend. "He preached a sermon against her. From the pulpit. He called her all sorts of things and suggested she was in league with the Devil himself. This didn't go down well with the congregation, though, and most of them walked out. Apparently the preacher resigned the next day."

Mma Ramotswe wondered what had happened to him.

"He said he was going off to do the work of the Lord elsewhere," said the friend.

They both laughed.

"If only the Lord knew," said Mma Ramotswe, shaking her head, "what is done by some of the people who claim to be working on his behalf."

The friend laughed again. "I'm sure he does," she said.

"But tell me," pressed Mma Ramotswe. "Tell me, Mma — what sort of person is she?"

The friend gazed into her teacup. Then, looking up, she said, "Very bossy, Mma. In fact, some people say — and I'm just reporting what I've heard — some people say she could stop an elephant."

Mma Ramotswe's eyes widened. "She's

that forceful, Mma?"

The friend nodded. "I'm afraid so, Mma. I don't want to be unkind, but I think that her husband is kept right there." She made a gesture with her thumb, pushing it down on the tablecloth.

"It's that bad?" asked Mma Ramotswe.

"Yes, Mma, it's that bad. Even worse, perhaps."

Mma Ramotswe thought for a moment. "So you would say that her husband is frightened of her?"

The friend replied that she would say that. "And I'd say something more: if that man ever stepped out of line, I wouldn't give much for his chances."

It was exactly what Mma Ramotswe had wanted to hear. "This is all very interesting," she said. "And who would know it? There's this Rra Gopolang, a big, tall man, and all the time he's a little boy inside — looking over his shoulder in case his wife disapproves."

"Many men are like that," said the friend. "They are little boys."

Mma Ramotswe liked men, though; she was not one of those who belittled them, as some women did. And so she observed, "Not all men, Mma. We must remember that there are many fine men."

"I suppose so," conceded the friend, perhaps a touch reluctantly. "But it's a pity, isn't it, that so many men are still hanging on to power, when there are excellent ladies waiting to run things much better than the men have been doing." She sighed. "But there we are, Mma. One day — one day maybe not too far off — we shall have women running all the governments of the world, and the United Nations, and even a woman pope."

Mma Ramotswe looked doubtful. "There is no chance of a woman pope, Mma. The men have got that job."

"I suppose so," said the friend. "But there's no reason why they should have it forever."

"It will be a very difficult battle," said Mma Ramotswe. "And it will not happen tomorrow."

Armed with this advance knowledge of Mma Gopolang, and satisfied that her strategy had at least some chance of success, Mma Ramotswe negotiated her way slowly along the streets of Phakalane, an affluent suburb on the edge of the town that had once been a farm belonging to a well-known citizen, David Magang. Her father had known him, and had spoken highly of him — one good judge of cattle recognising another — and this was in her mind as she drove past the house where his family had lived. But she did not allow the thought to linger, because she wanted to wean herself off such memories. Her father was no longer there to talk to, as he had been until only a few days ago. Things were different now — or so she told herself.

Some of the houses were very substantial — far bigger than anybody could reasonably want — but this was not so of the Gopolang house. Although it was by any standards comfortable, it was not showy in any way, and indeed seemed modest by comparison with some of the mansions on display. As her friend had predicted, it was impossible to miss, its light blue roof standing out among the predominantly red roofs of the houses around it.

She parked her van outside the perimeter fence, and then made her way up the short drive towards the front door. The garden was dry, the grass of what had once been a lawn discouraged and brittle. Although water had not been rationed since the good rains, there were many who were reluctant to waste it on their gardens, particularly on lawns, that were just wrong in this part of Africa, Mma Ramotswe thought. Planting a lawn in Botswana was like planting a cactus at the North Pole: it did not make sense. Botswana was a country of dry plains and scrub bush; of plants that had long memories of droughts and dryness, and that knew every trick for surviving in such conditions. Green lawns were easy on the eye — and comfortable underfoot — but there was just as much beauty in an acacia tree or a *mogotlho,* a camel thorn, as there was in a lush growth of kikuyu grass tamed into a lawn.

If you could judge people by their front yards — and Mma Ramotswe felt that often you could do just that — then this was a front yard with a clear message: a sensible woman lived here; not a showy woman, nor an ambitious woman, but a woman who knew what she wanted in life and was not to be trifled with.

Mma Ramotswe reached the front door and called out, as was the custom. From within the house, a voice replied quite quickly: "I am coming."

It was Mma Gopolang who answered. She was a well-shaped woman — even if not quite traditionally built — and she was wearing a neat housecoat of the sort that Mma Ramotswe immediately judged to be sensible rather than frivolous. There were many women who dressed in their best clothes in their own homes, but Mma

Ramotswe had never been able to understand why anybody should want to do that.
Such dress, she thought, indicated a wish to
go out rather than stay in; and people who
were always itching to go out wanted to do
so because they were unhappy with where
they were. The most contented people she
knew were those who stayed more or less
where they were, for much of the time, and
never ventured forth unless there was a
good reason to leave where they had been
at the beginning. Such people often wore
housecoats, and slippers too, because these
were the right clothes for people who were
not planning to go out.

Mma Gopolang's expression told Mma
Ramotswe that she was trying hard to place
her. It was a typical look of one who thought
she might have met somebody, but could
not be sure. And of course in Gaborone,
which was still a fairly intimate town, it was
always possible that you would have met
somebody, even if you had no recollection
of the meeting.

"I don't think we've met, Mma," said
Mma Ramotswe after the necessary greet-
ings had been exchanged. "I am Precious
Ramotswe. I am from the No. 1 Ladies'
Detective —"

Mma Gopolang interrupted her. "Oh, that

place; I have seen it — it's on the Tlokweng Road, isn't it?"

Mma Ramotswe nodded. "It is a detective agency, and I have been investigating something that concerns you, Mma. That is why I have come to see you."

Mma Gopolang looked surprised. "Me, Mma?"

"We could speak if you invited me in."

Mma Gopolang looked embarrassed. "I'm very sorry, Mma — please come in."

She led Mma Ramotswe into a sitting room immediately off the small entrance hall. This was furnished with large, leather-covered chairs and a somewhat cumbersome sofa. Mma Gopolang signalled for Mma Ramotswe to sit on the sofa, while she chose one of the smaller chairs.

There was a short, appraising silence before Mma Ramotswe spoke. "I shall get straight to the point, Mma," she began. "We were asked to look into the wrongful dismissal of an employee. This person — the person who was dismissed — worked in your husband's office furniture business."

The effect of this overture was immediate. Mma Gopolang, who had seemed relaxed, now sat up straight in her chair. "Oh yes?" she said, her interest clearly aroused.

Mma Ramotswe spoke cautiously. "I don't

like to raise this matter, Mma, but I feel that I have to. I believe that your husband may be a . . . a sociable man."

Mma Gopolang stared at her, and then, without any warning, guffawed loudly. "Sociable? Oh, that's very funny, Mma. All men are sociable, I think. Far too sociable for their own good." She paused. The stiffness seemed to have gone now, to be replaced by a relaxed demeanour. "If you're here to tell me that my husband is having an affair, then I have something to tell *you,* Mma: I know that he is. Men cannot hide these things."

Mma Ramotswe thought quickly. If she already knew, her job was going to be much easier. She could now move on to make her request. "I'm afraid that your husband has fired an innocent person in order to give her job to his girlfriend, and I wonder whether you would be able to persuade him to reverse that decision."

Mma Gopolang's mouth opened, and then closed. It seemed to Mma Ramotswe that she was somehow confused; perhaps further explanation was required. She could tell her about how Charity had worked in the store for years and how, even if she was inclined to lose her temper from time to time, she was a conscientious employee. She might mention the children and the fact that there was no father.

But what came next rendered all that unnecessary.

Her composure recovered, Mma Gopolang leaned forward in her chair with the air of one about to impart a confidence. "Mma Ramotswe," she said. "You've got it all wrong. Rra Gopolang — my husband — did not dismiss that lady. I did." She smiled. "That was me."

Mma Ramotswe did not understand. She tried to remember what Charity had said: she was sure there had been no mention of any involvement of Mma Gopolang in her dismissal; nor had Mma Makutsi and Mr. Polopetsi reported anything of that nature.

Mma Gopolang was now smiling. "It was very satisfactory," she said. "I heard that my husband was carrying on with another woman. At first I had no idea who it was, and then one of my friends said that it was a woman who worked for him. She said that it was a certain Charity Mompoloki. I had met this woman, of course, even though I have very little to do with my husband's business. I wasn't going to stand by, though, and let her lead my husband astray, and so I arranged for a complaint to be made about her."

"In order to get her out of the way?" asked Mma Ramotswe.

"Exactly, Mma. I arranged for a friend of mine who is a big client of the company to accuse her of being rude to him. He insisted that she be removed from her job — and my husband could not afford to lose his business." She smiled with satisfaction at the recollection. "And it worked, Mma. It worked like a charm."

Mma Ramotswe took a deep breath. "Are you sure it achieved what you intended, Mma?" she asked.

Mma Gopolang's eyes narrowed. "Am I sure? Of course I am." There was a note of defiance in her voice now. "And I was fully entitled to resort to such measures, Mma Ramotswe. That woman was stealing my husband. Are you allowed to do things like that to protect yourself from such women? I think you are, Mma — no question about it."

"But what if the person who told you that Charity was the girlfriend misunderstood the situation? What if the girlfriend is somebody else altogether?"

Mma Gopolang, who had been comfortably in her stride, now looked confused. She asked Mma Ramotswe to explain.

"What I meant," said Mma Ramotswe, "is

that your husband was not having an affair with Charity, and that your husband fired her because of what he thought was a genuine complaint. So that makes me wonder why your friend should think that Charity was your husband's girlfriend." She waited for this to sink in before she went any further. "I think I know the identity of that person — the girlfriend, that is."

"Do you, Mma Ramotswe? I would very much like to know that."

Mma Ramotswe remembered what Mr. J.L.B. Matekoni had said. "I shall tell you, but I must ask you to promise me that if I do you that favour, you will do me one in return."

Mma Gopolang was cagey. "It depends on the favour, Mma. I can't promise without knowing what you're going to ask me. Nobody would promise that sort of thing."

"I understand," said Mma Ramotswe. "It will not be a big thing and . . ." There was another very good reason why Mma Gopolang should comply with her request: she had caused the wrongful dismissal in the first place, and any decent person who did that would, in the circumstances, want to redress the wrong. ". . . and it will undo a bad situation that you yourself have brought about."

"Tell me, Mma," urged Mma Gopolang.

Mma Ramotswe spelled it out. "If I reveal what we know, will you make your husband give Charity her job back? She is innocent, Mma."

Mma Gopolang readily agreed. "Of course I will do that. *If* she is innocent . . ."

"She is," said Mma Ramotswe firmly. "Your husband is seeing a woman called Violet Sephotho."

"Of course he is," said Mma Gopolang dismissively. "But what I'm interested in is the name of his girlfriend."

"But the girlfriend is Violet," said Mma Ramotswe. "That's what I meant when I said he was seeing her."

Mma Gopolang shook her head. "No, Mma — you have it wrong again. Violet is my husband's cousin. They have known one another since they were young, although he's a bit older than she is. They see one another all the time. They are family — like brother and sister." She hesitated before continuing: "I'm not sure that she's the best influence on him, Mma, but I've never said anything."

Mma Ramotswe was silenced. A warning from Clovis Andersen was running through her head: *Never make the mistake of thinking that things are what they seem to be — often they are not.* It was very ordinary advice — maybe a little bit too simple — but this was a case where it was very obviously true.

"And there's another thing," said Mma Gopolang. "The person who told me that my husband was having an affair with Charity was Violet herself."

This revelation had a profound effect on Mma Ramotswe. Now, she thought, it all makes sense.

But then, after a few moments' reflection, she thought: Does it?

CHAPTER SIXTEEN:
ALL THE CHILDREN AND ALL
THE PEOPLE IN BOTSWANA

Mma Ramotswe had more than enough to think about and did not welcome the telephone call she received that evening from Mingie. The call came through as she was cooking dinner for the children, stirring a pot with one hand, trying to check Puso's homework with the other, and answering a question from Motholeli while performing both of these tasks. Only my feet are not doing anything, she thought; perhaps I should try to dance, just for good measure.

Mr. J.L.B. Matekoni answered the telephone. Popping his head round the door he announced that Mingie Ramotswe was on the line. "Should I tell her that you're busy?" he asked. "You look busy, I think."

Mma Ramotswe almost said yes, but something stopped her. That woman is my sister, she told herself. You are never too busy to speak to your sister. "I will come through in a minute," she said.

"Who is this new auntie?" asked Motholeli.

"She is my sister," explained Mma Ramotswe. "I have only just found her."

Puso looked up from his book. "How did you lose her, Mma?" he asked.

It was a perfectly reasonable question, thought Mma Ramotswe; but it was also one that was hard to answer when doing other things. "I'll tell you some other time," she said.

"What if I lost Motholeli?" said Puso. "How would I find her again?"

"Nobody's going to lose anybody," said Mma Ramotswe. "And I must go and speak to her now."

The telephone was in the sitting room. Mr. J.L.B. Matekoni, who had been occupying his favourite chair, reading the *Botswana Daily News,* tactfully rose to leave her to take the call alone. When Mma Ramotswe picked up the receiver, she heard Mingie sneeze at the other end. Instinctively she said, "Bless you, Mma."

"Thank you, Mma," came the reply. "There is something in the air today. Pollen, perhaps. There is a tree near here somewhere that makes me sneeze."

Mma Ramotswe said that she was sorry to hear that. Then she waited. Under her breath, inaudibly, she whispered, *Not her fault.*

"I'm phoning to invite you to my house," said Mingie. "I know it is very short notice, but will you come and eat with us down here tomorrow?"

Mma Ramotswe's heart sank. She had so much to do; correspondence had piled up in the office and there was the Charity Mompoloki matter becoming more complicated by the day. She also had to speak to somebody about the information Mr. Polopetsi had passed to her. She had to warn Phuti Radiphuti of the threat to his business without somehow jeopardising the position of the woman who had passed on the information. And there was Note Mokoti as well; she had decided to seek him out — as a precautionary measure — and yet she had done nothing about that yet. All of these things were pressing in on her and yet here was Mingie expecting her to drive down to Lobatse on a visit she did not want to make.

Mingie was her sister. That was an inescapable fact. And if you did not refuse a call from your sister, then you did not decline her invitations.

"What time should I be there?" she found herself saying.

Mingie gave her the time, and asked whether there was anything she did not eat. Those matters attended to, the conversation came to an end, and Mma Ramotswe sat down heavily on one of the sitting-room chairs, her head in her hands.

She heard Mr. J.L.B. Matekoni's voice, and looked up. He said, "What's wrong, Mma? Is there anything I can do?"

She looked at him. He was a supportive spouse and she would normally have gone straight to him in her distress, but not now. She did not want to talk about it in detail, even to him, and so she simply said, "I have to go for a meal in Lobatse and all the time my work is piling up and I don't know what to do."

He came and sat beside her. "My Precious," he said. "Your life is too stressful. You must change it somehow."

She looked at him. "How, Rra? Do something different? Should I get a job in a bank, maybe, or in a bakery? Would a regular job like that make my life any easier?"

He said that he thought it would. "You don't have to be a detective forever," he said. "There are easier jobs in life. You don't have to do it forever."

She shook her head. "No, Rra, I do. This is what I have been called to do — to help

people with the problems in their lives —
and that is exactly what I shall do."

"And who's going to help you with the
problems in *your* life?" he demanded.

She had no answer to this. In the past, it
had been her father's support that had
sustained her, that invisible bond of strength
that seemed so strong in spite of the fact
that he was not there. That had seen her
through much, but she felt that now if she
were to look for it, she would not be able to
find it.

"I shall be all right, Rra," she said. "Problems have a way of solving themselves."

She was not sure that this was true. In
fact, now that she came to think of it, it was
completely false. Problems did not solve
themselves — they required to be looked
coldly in the eye; they required time, and
that was what she now seemed to be lack-
ing. There was just too much to think about;
there was just too much to do. Where was
the time to sit quietly with a cup of red bush
tea and watch the birds in the trees? Where
was the time to take a walk along one of
those paths through the bush and listen to
the lowing of the cattle and the whistling of
the herd boys?

The following day was a Saturday and so

she did not go into the office. Mingie's invitation had been for lunch, and so she spent the earlier part of the morning taking the children shopping. Motholeli needed a new school blouse, while Puso, who was going to be learning to play cricket, needed white trousers. Those errands completed, and the children dropped off at the houses of their friends in discharge of long-standing invitations, Mma Ramotswe had an hour or so to kill before she began the drive down to Lobatse. She felt ill at ease; she would have had just enough time for a quick visit to Mma Potokwane, but she decided against that: the joy of visiting her friend lay in long talks, endless cups of tea, and several slices of fruit cake. All of that required time — and a certain languor of mood, which she felt she simply did not have at present. She was worried by this lunch at Mingie's: Would she be able to conceal her feelings of sadness sufficiently? Would this new sister of hers think that she was stand-offish, even unfriendly? She bore Mingie no ill will, but she could not help but view her as being the representative of that other, clandestine family that her father had created, and that made it difficult for her to think positively of this new relationship. She was well aware that this was wrong, but it was hard to do anything about it, especially since she still felt raw over the discovery.

The road was busy, as it often was on a Saturday. There were the ubiquitous mini-buses, overloaded and swaying, carrying Lobatse people home after a week's work in Gaborone. These overtook the tiny white van with a loud honking of their horns, the passengers crowded in upon one another, sitting on the laps of perfect strangers; some with hats, some without; the young and old, the toothed and toothless; some blaring music, others entertained only by animated conversation. These were people going home, with the hearts of those who are returning to the place they know. A few of them waved at Mma Ramotswe, smiling, gesturing in a friendly way, encouraging her van in the same terms one might use with an exhausted donkey. She waved back, and for the moment was cheered by these expressions of the spirit of her people. Because people *were* good and kind and wanted to enjoy themselves, and cared for one another; and these things, surely, outweighed the sadness of the world, all its travails and discontents.

These thoughts sustained her, but as she reached Lobatse and turned off the main road onto the road that led to Mingie's house, the feeling of disquiet returned. She particularly feared that Mingie would wish to talk about their father; normally she would have been happy to do that — for hours if needs be — but she would not be able to bring herself to do that now. And if they did not talk about him, what else did they have in common to discuss? As far as she knew, there were no mutual friends — always a fertile source of small talk — and there was a limit to how long you could converse if there was no shared past.

After she had parked the van at Mingie's front gate, she sat for a moment and collected her thoughts. She had been in trying situations before, and she had always coped. This would be the same, she told herself: all that was required of her was to smile and be civil. Surely she should be able to manage that without too much effort.

Mingie was waiting for her at the door. "You are very welcome, my sister," she said.

Mma Ramotswe took her hand. "You are kind, my sister."

"And the road? How was it?"

Mma Ramotswe smiled. "Lots of minibuses. Half of Gaborone coming down here, it seems."

"There is a football match," said Mingie. "The Township Rollers are playing the

Botswana Meat Commission side. It's an important match."

"The Rollers are very strong," said Mma Ramotswe. "Not that I know anything about it, but Puso — we have two adopted children, Mma, and he is the younger one — he is a big fan of the Rollers, and I hear a lot about them from him. The Rollers are doing this thing, the Rollers are doing that thing — it's never-ending."

Mingie laughed. "That cannot be easy for you, Mma, if you're not interested. I like football, though. You can ask me about any player, I think, and I'll be able to tell you something about him. Not all the clubs, of course, but the main ones."

Mma Ramotswe looked at her in surprise. "That is very good, Mma."

"And my friend," Mingie went on, "she is very strong when it comes to all the other African teams — the national ones, that is. So if you say to her: name one defender in the Upper Volta team, she'll say Ernest Congo."

"Ernest Congo?"

"Yes, he's a real player, I believe. I just use him as an example, you see."

Mma Ramotswe shook her head in wonderment. *Ernest Congo* . . .

"You must meet," said Mingie.

"Meet Ernest Congo?"

This was greeted with a peal of laughter. "No, Mma — my friend. I share this house, you see, with a friend. She's cooking our lunch today." She gestured to a door off the hall. "Come and meet her."

They went into the kitchen. A woman wearing an apron was drying her hands on a kitchen towel. Mingie made the introductions.

"This is Keeya," said Mingie.

They shook hands. Mma Ramotswe felt the slight damp on Keeya's hand — a damp handshake often gave rise to a desire to dry one's palm on one's clothing, but she did not do this. She looked at the other woman discreetly, and liked what she saw: Keeya had a friendly, open expression. And she liked her voice too, and the correct, well-pronounced Setswana she used in the traditional greeting. Some people mumbled; some people did not even bother to use Setswana, but greeted one another in English; Keeya, it seemed, understood.

"Lunch will be ready soon," said Keeya. "You two should go and sit on the verandah. It's shady there, and you must have a lot to talk about."

Mma Ramotswe's heart sank. "Yes," she said, trying to sound enthusiastic. "There is much to talk about."

"Keeya will call us," said Mingie as she led Mma Ramotswe from the kitchen.

"What does she do?" asked Mma Ramotswe.

"The cooking," answered Mingie.

"No, I mean, what does she do for a job?"

"She's a teacher," replied Mingie. "She teaches mathematics at a high school."

Mma Ramotswe was impressed. "Perhaps she can teach me some," she said.

Mingie laughed. "She's tried to teach me, but I'm not all that good. I can do the basic stuff, but when you get to all those symbols and signs, I'm hopeless. I just don't get it."

There were three chairs on the verandah — comfortable old wooden chairs that probably dated from Protectorate days. "The British brought chairs," Mr. J.L.B. Matekoni once said. "They took chairs with them wherever they went in the world. And they left the chairs behind when they went home."

There was a jug of water and two glasses. Mingie poured one out for Mma Ramotswe followed by one for herself. Then she sat back and folded her hands on her lap. "Who would have thought?" she said.

Mma Ramotswe gazed at the sky, half visible from under the verandah roof. "Yes," she said. "Who would have thought?"

There was silence for a while. Then Mingie said, "If you hadn't seen that article in the paper, then we would never have met."

Mma Ramotswe agreed that it had been a happy chance. "I only saw it when somebody showed it to me," she said. "I didn't see it when it first appeared."

"I thought it was a good photo of the other two ladies," said Mingie. "Not so much of me. And it got things wrong."

Mma Ramotswe frowned. "They got the names wrong?"

"No," said Mingie. "The ages. They said I was forty-three, but that was the age of one of the others. I'm younger than that."

Mma Ramotswe caught her breath. "Younger?"

"Yes," said Mingie, and she gave her age.

Whatever her self-confessed limitations when it came to mathematics, it did not take Mma Ramotswe long to do the calculation. "Oh, Mma . . . ," she stuttered. "Oh, Mma!"

Mingie looked concerned. "Are you all right, Precious?"

Mma Ramotswe sank her head in her hands. She did not want to sob; she did not want to sob, but uncontrollably and from deep within her the sobs came, loud and overwhelming. Mingie rose quickly from her chair and came to her side, putting her arms about her shoulders. "Mma, please tell me — please. What's wrong, Mma? What's wrong?"

Mma Ramotswe struggled to speak. "I thought . . . I thought that you were born while my mother was still alive. But you weren't, Mma — you were born afterwards — a good few years after she became late."

Mingie struggled to understand. "But what difference does it make . . . ?" Then she stopped. She knew now. "Your father . . . Oh, I see, Mma. I see."

But Mma Ramotswe had to get it out, and so she explained how she had thought that Mingie was the result of an affair conducted by Obed while his wife was still alive, and now she knew that it had happened afterwards, when he was perfectly free to take up with other women should he find anybody — and he clearly had: for the brief time he had before the sickness in his lungs — the result of all those years in the mines — claimed him.

Mingie listened, her arms still around Mma Ramotswe. "Of course you would have felt that, Mma," she said. "Who wouldn't?" She paused. "And there's another thing: now I know why your father wouldn't leave the country when my mother went. That was because of you."

Mma Ramotswe nodded. "And because he was getting sick by then."

Her sobs were fading now, and she was becoming aware of an extraordinary feeling that was overtaking her. This was joy. It was simple joy.

Mingie now disengaged from her embrace, but was still at her side.

"I would like to talk about our daddy," said Mma Ramotswe. "I want you to know what a fine man he was."

Mingie smiled. "I think I know already, Mma. But let's talk. Let's talk and then, when Keeya calls us, we can go and have lunch and talk some more."

Keeya served a lunch of casseroled chicken, rice, pumpkin, and green beans. This was followed by custard with a drizzling of jam, and a pot of tea. Here were small rectangular biscuits too — those odd little biscuits with animals traced out in relief on a background of hard coloured icing.

Mma Ramotswe need not have worried about the conversation, which ranged over so many subjects that she lost track of its direction. That did not matter: there was much to be said between sisters. Then, towards the end, Mingie said, "Keeya and I have lived together here for some years now, Mma. We are very happy in this house."

Mma Ramotswe reached out across the table. Keeya's hand was resting on the tablecloth, and she placed her own hand over it, gently, and with love.

"Good," said Mma Ramotswe.

That was all she needed to say, but there was something she wanted to add, and so she said, "I have two sisters now." And then she added, "That is very good."

Now she said to herself: I have a family. I have a husband, two children, and two sisters. Families come in different ways, she thought: sometimes they are given to you, but sometimes you find them yourself, unexpectedly, as you go through life. That is perhaps not all that well known, but it is still true.

The following Monday, while Mma Makutsi was preparing the tea for the first tea break, Charlie appeared in the office to say that there was a woman asking to see Mma Ramotswe and should he show her in?

"What is her name?" asked Mma Makutsi. "And, Charlie, I am the person who makes the appointments. If there is somebody who wants to see Mma Ramotswe, you must first speak to me, and then I'll speak to Mma

Ramotswe."

Charlie shrugged. "But what's the point? If all of us are in the room, then what does it matter if I speak directly to Mma Ramotswe? You'll hear what I have to say anyway."

Mma Makutsi bristled. "There are procedures, Charlie, and they must be followed. Imagine if you could just walk into State House and speak to the President directly? Imagine that. It would never work."

"But this is not State House," said Charlie. "This is the No. 1 Ladies' Detective Agency, and that is quite different, Mma Makutsi. State House runs the country, this place runs . . . well, runs nothing, really."

Mma Makutsi hissed. "That sort of talk, Charlie —"

Mma Ramotswe felt it was time to intervene. "Show this lady in, Charlie. I am happy to speak to her."

"I'd be a bit careful of her, Mma," warned Charlie. "She is a very strong lady, this one. I wouldn't like to get on the wrong side of her."

"Ah," said Mma Ramotswe. "It will be Mma Gopolang, I think."

She was right. Charlie brought Mma Gopolang into the office.

"So this is your place," the visitor said,

looking around her. "It is not very big, is it?"

Mma Ramotswe ignored the tactless remark. "This is Mma Makutsi," she said. "She is my associate director."

"Co-director," corrected Mma Makutsi.

Mma Gopolang turned to survey Mma Makutsi. "Ah," she said. "You are also Mma Radiphuti, I believe. Is that so, Mma?"

"I am," said Mma Makutsi. "Makutsi is my professional name, you see."

Mma Gopolang nodded. "I admire ladies who carry on with their careers. Otherwise men would get all the jobs, I think. They'd just wait for us to get married, and then they'd pounce on our jobs. We women must stick together, mustn't we, Mma?"

Before the wisdom of this could be commented upon, Mma Gopolang, spotting the client's chair, asked if she might sit down. Once comfortable, she launched directly into an explanation of why she was there.

"You did me a great service, Mma Ramotswe," she said. "I had made a mistake, you see, and I was able to rectify it."

Mma Ramotswe noticed that Mma Makutsi looked confused. She had not had the opportunity yet to tell her about her visit to the Gopolang house and the extraordinary facts that had come to light. She hoped that

331

she would not be offended at hearing about this from another quarter, her being the Principal Investigating Officer, after all.

"Mma Charity has her job back?" asked Mma Ramotswe.

Mma Gopolang nodded. "Yes, she is reinstated as from tomorrow. I spoke to my husband, you see. And I spoke to him about many other matters."

"I see," said Mma Ramotswe. She was imagining the meeting. She would not have liked to be in Mr. Gopolang's position.

"We talked about how this sad business had come about," continued Mma Gopolang. "We left no stone unturned. And there were certain stones, Mma — certain stones of a very suspicious nature. I discovered that his cousin, Violet, had been interfering in the business rather a lot — and I put an end to that, I can assure you."

Mma Ramotswe glanced across the room to where Mma Makutsi sat at her desk, electrified by the mention of the name Violet.

"Violet Sephotho?" interjected Mma Makutsi. "Is that the Violet you're talking about, Mma?"

Mma Gopolang turned round. "It is, Mma," she said.

"Violet is Rra Gopolang's cousin," said

Mma Ramotswe hurriedly. "I was informed of that on Friday."

Mma Makutsi gasped. "I saw her . . ."

She did not finish. "You saw her having a meeting with Mr. Gopolang," said Mma Ramotswe.

Mma Gopolang turned back to face Mma Ramotswe. "I might have told you that I was never one hundred per cent happy with Violet's influence on my husband," she said. "Now I discovered that she deliberately misled me as to the relationship between my husband and that poor innocent Charity woman. I asked myself: Why did she do this? And the answer I worked out was that she wanted Charity out of the office because she had never liked her. Ever since their days at some secretarial college."

A cry came from Mma Makutsi. "I knew it! I knew it was her! And that college, Mma, I can tell you what it was: it was the Botswana Secretarial College. And I am a graduate of that college too."

"With ninety-seven per cent," muttered Mma Ramotswe under her breath.

"Well, there you are," said Mma Gopolang. "That was the reason why she did it. And I also found out that she had put my husband up to some ridiculous deal with a furniture factory to pay far too much money for some beds and dining-room tables and such things. I put an end to that nonsense too."

Mma Ramotswe heaved a sigh of relief. She had done nothing about the threat to the Phuti Radiphuti business — and now it seemed that the competent and effective Mma Gopolang had sorted that out too.

But Mma Makutsi had been unaware of it, and she now exclaimed, "Beds? You people sell office furniture. It's my husband who sells beds — we always have."

Mma Gopolang made a placatory noise. "Don't worry, Mma. It was a very expensive deal for us and I have torn it all up. It will not happen." She paused. "I shall be playing a much more active part in the business in future — I shall see that everything is above board. And we shall not be selling house furniture."

"Good," said Mma Makutsi. "And we will not sell filing cabinets."

Mma Ramotswe now signalled to Mma Makutsi to serve tea. The main purpose of the meeting, it seemed, had been very satisfactorily settled and any remaining issues could be tied up over a cup of tea. It was a very happy outcome, she felt: Charity had her job back, Violet had been put in her place, and the threat to Phuti Radiphuti's business had been conclusively disposed of. There was, however, the question of Mr. Gopolang's affair: Was he having one with somebody else even if it was not with Violet Sephotho? This she raised — as tactfully as possible — as Mma Makutsi poured and served tea.

"Your husband, Mma," she said. "I take it that there is no evidence of his . . . his straying?"

Mma Gopolang raised her cup to her lips. "This is very good tea," she said.

Mma Ramotswe waited, wondering whether that was all they would hear.

There was more. "I think he might have been seeing some other lady," said Mma Gopolang. "But I imagine that this will not be happening any more. I made that quite clear."

"I'm sure you did, Mma," said Mma Ramotswe. "And I'm equally sure that he will not try anything like that again."

"I don't think he will," agreed Mma Gopolang. "My husband does not defy me, Mma Ramotswe. I have made that a fundamental rule of my marriage: my husband does not defy me."

"Very wise," said Mma Ramotswe. "Perhaps they should put that in the marriage ceremony. The husband should say to the reverend: 'And I promise not to defy my wife.' "

Mma Gopolang nodded her approval. "A very sound suggestion," she said. "But there is one other thing, Mma — and that is why I am here, actually."

Mma Ramotswe looked at her expectantly. "Anything we can do to help, Mma. That is why *we* are here."

Mma Gopolang took another sip of tea. "If, as I think, there was some other lady — and of course he denies it — but if, as I am sure is the case, such a lady existed, I am very keen to know her name . . . and address."

The menace, the unstated threat to the unknown woman, could not have been clearer had it been written in capital letters and then illuminated with spotlights. Mma Ramotswe waited, as did Mma Makutsi.

"So I'd like to engage your agency to find that out for me," said Mma Gopolang. "I can pay whatever fee is required."

Mma Ramotswe shifted in her seat. "But why would you want to know that, Mma? If it's over — as it sounds as if it is — then is there any point in trying to find the identity of this woman?"

"Revenge," said Mma Gopolang in an even tone. It was as if she were stating something so obvious as not to require mentioning.

"I beg your pardon, Mma?"

"I want to speak to that lady and impress upon her that what she has done has been noticed."

"And get your revenge?" said Mma Ramotswe.

"Yes, that too."

Mma Ramotswe shook her head. "I'm sorry, Mma. We cannot possibly assist you in that."

Mma Gopolang looked surprised. "Why not? Isn't that what you do?"

"No," said Mma Ramotswe. "It is not what we do — not at all. And I do not believe in revenge. We have to forgive, you see."

"I have forgiven my husband," said Mma Gopolang.

"Then you must forgive that lady too." Mma Ramotswe stared at Mma Gopolang. "You have to, Mma. You have to."

Mma Gopolang puffed up her cheeks and then expelled the air from her mouth in a complex gesture — a mixture of irritation and doubt. "Oh well," she said. "I shall say no more about it, but if there is ever any other instance of straying, then . . ."

"Then we shall be at your service," said

Mma Ramotswe firmly. "But only then."

That afternoon Mma Ramotswe drove out to see Mma Potokwane. She had plenty of time at her disposal — hours if necessary — and she was looking forward to a long session of tea and cake with her old friend. It was a warm afternoon, but not too hot, and the land, in flush after the recent rains, was looking content. Brown had become green; hard, baked surfaces had become soft; the cattle by the side of the road were plump from good grazing, no ribs on display. This was Botswana as she remembered it from her childhood, when the rains had always seemed to be so much better.

"I was hoping you would come to see me," said Mma Potokwane. "And now, here you are."

"I have been meaning to come for some time," said Mma Ramotswe, sinking into the chair she always occupied in Mma Potokwane's office. "But I have been very busy and . . ." She hesitated. "Busy — and unhappy too."

Mma Potokwane raised an eyebrow. "I've never known you to be unhappy, Mma Ramotswe."

"Well, I have been."

"Why?"

She told Mma Potokwane about the shock of her discovery — her false discovery — that Obed had been involved with another woman while still married to her mother. "I could not believe it of him," she said. "Oh, I know it's not too big a thing — that it happens a lot and that marriages recover. But I had always thought of him as . . ." She trailed off.

"As your daddy," said Mma Potokwane simply.

"Yes. He was my daddy."

Mma Potokwane waved a hand. "That's the trouble: we don't see our parents as people. Your daddy was also a man — a very good man too — but he was a man."

Mma Ramotswe thought about what Mma Potokwane had said. It was true. "You're right," she said. "But the important thing is, what I feared was true, was not true."

"Then that is very good," said Mma Potokwane.

Tea was poured, and a tin was opened. The tin contained fruit cake.

"And I have found a very good sister," said Mma Ramotswe as she took her first sip of tea.

"That lady in Lobatse?"

"Yes. She is my new sister and I am very happy with her." She paused. "And she came with another sister too. A friend of hers. She lives there too, and so I have now got two new sisters. Two, Mma! Both unexpected."

"An unexpected sister is good," said Mma Potokwane. "To have two unexpected sisters is even better."

"Twice as good," said Mma Ramotswe.

Mma Potokwane helped them both to a generous slice of fruit cake. "I have some news for you," she said. "I've seen Note Mokoti — not just seen him, but talked to him."

Mma Ramotswe had been about to take a bite of her cake. She put it back on the plate.

"But you have no need to worry," continued Mma Potokwane. "I bumped into Note in town. He told me why he was here. He's getting married."

Mma Ramotswe stared at her plate. She was not sure what she felt, nor how to react.

"And he sent a message," went on Mma Potokwane. "He said that he has met a very good lady. He met her over on that side, but she is from Gaborone originally. He came over here to talk to her people and to make arrangements. They will be getting married over in Johannesburg."

"I am happy for him," muttered Mma Ramotswe.

Mma Potokwane was watching her. "He said something else. He said that his life has changed. He said that he is a different man now that he has met this lady. He has come to understand that until now he has been very selfish. And he wants you to know that he is sorry."

Mma Ramotswe looked up. "He wants to say sorry?"

"Yes."

"Then why can't he say it to my face?"

"Because you told him last time that you never wanted to see him again. And there's something else, Mma."

"Yes?"

"It is this: sometimes it's not easy to say the things we need to say. It is not easy — maybe even impossible — because we are weak. All of us. We try to be strong, but we are weak." She paused. "If I may say so, Mma — that is well known."

Mma Ramotswe looked at her friend and smiled. "Mma Potokwane," she said, "you are always right."

"Not always, Mma Ramotswe. Sometimes, perhaps, but not always."

Mma Ramotswe fingered her plate. "Did he leave an address?"

"No, but he told me the name of his future in-laws. They live in town here."

"So I can send a wedding present there?"

Mma Potokwane nodded. "I have written it down. And let me say this, Mma: that is the right thing to do. That gives him your blessing — and that, I think, is something he really wants. I know how to tell these things, and I am sure of that. He wants your blessing."

"Then I will give it to him."

Mma Ramotswe picked up her plate again. "This is very good cake, Mma Potokwane," she said.

"There is more," said Mma Potokwane. "After you have finished that piece, there will be more."

She drove back just as the sun was beginning to sink behind the trees. The road was quiet, and she could hear the tinkling of cattle bells. It was a sound that always reminded her of her daddy because that had been his favourite sound of all. When he arrived in that other place, she knew that this is what would have greeted him: the sound of cattle bells. She stopped the van, drawing into the side of the road, under a tree. The dust behind her settled. A small breeze came up, brushed gently against the land, and then faded away. She looked up at the sky. She thought of her father, of her country, of the people she loved so much. She thought of her bean plants and the trees in her yard. She thought of Mr. J.L.B. Matekoni and Motholeli and Puso, of Mma Makutsi, of all her friends; she thought of all the children and all the people in Botswana, and of her love for all of them, which was greater than the Kalahari itself, and wider than the sky above.

afrika
afrika afrika
afrika afrika afrika
afrika afrika
afrika

ABOUT THE AUTHOR

Alexander McCall Smith is the author of the No. 1 Ladies' Detective Agency novels and of a number of other series and stand-alone books. His works have been translated into more than forty languages and have been best sellers throughout the world. He lives in Scotland.